Also by Marcy Dermansky

*The Red Car*
*Bad Marie*
*Twins*

# Very Nice

# *Very Nice*

Marcy Dermansky

Alfred A. Knopf
New York
2019

THIS IS A BORZOI BOOK PUBLISHED BY ALFRED A. KNOPF

Copyright © 2019 by Marcy Dermansky

All rights reserved. Published in the United States by Alfred A. Knopf,
a division of Penguin Random House LLC, New York,
and distributed in Canada by Random House of Canada, a division
of Penguin Random House Canada Limited, Toronto.

www.aaknopf.com

Knopf, Borzoi Books, and the colophon are registered trademarks of
Penguin Random House LLC.

Library of Congress Cataloging-in-Publication Data
Names: Dermansky, Marcy, [date].
Title: Very nice : a novel / by Marcy Dermansky.
Description: First edition. | New York : Alfred A. Knopf, 2019. |
"This is Borzoi book."
Identifiers: LCCN 2018033631 (print) | LCCN 2018035654 (ebook) |
ISBN 9780525655640 (e-book) | ISBN 9780525655633 (hardcover) |
ISBN 9781524711597 (open market)
Classification: LCC PS3604.E7545 (ebook) | LCC PS3604.E7545 V47 2019 (print)
DDC 813/.6—dc23
LC record available at https://lccn.loc.gov/2018033631

Jacket illustration by Justin Metz
Jacket design by Janet Hansen

Manufactured in the United States of America
First Edition

*To Nina*

# *One*

———◆———

# *Rachel*

I didn't think, the day I kissed my professor for the first time, that he would kiss me back. His lips were soft. He tasted like coffee. The coffee I had made for him.

"That was very nice," he said.

My professor smiled at me. Though hesitant at first, he had returned the kiss.

My professor, my creative writing teacher, had asked me to watch his dog, Princess, for the day. It was the last day of the semester. He had a standard poodle. A large dog with apricot-colored fur. I loved standard poodles. I had grown up with standard poodles. The family poodle, Posey, had just died. She was a big, white, beautiful dog. I had not gone home to say good-bye because the semester was almost over. I wished I had gone. Often, my professor took his poodle to class. He loved his dog. I understood why.

My professor lived in Brooklyn. He commuted up the Hudson River to campus. He took Metro-North. He had been sick most of the semester. A virus, he said, a flu that would not go away. He was incredibly beautiful, my professor, like his dog. Together, they were a breathtaking pair. My professor had long eyelashes, big eyes, brown skin. Silky hair. He was tall, thin, too thin. He was from Pakistan.

My professor had published a novel that had won all the big awards the year it had come out. I had tried to read his book but I couldn't. A sentence was as long as a paragraph. A paragraph was as long as a page. At a reading on campus, I asked him to sign a copy of his book. Though I had not been able to finish it, I told him that I thought it was beautiful.

"So are you, Rachel," he had said, looking up from the book. The compliment had come out of nowhere, blindsided me.

I thought he probably didn't mean it, like the way I had complimented his novel.

My professor was in my house off campus when I kissed him.

We were sitting in my kitchen. My roommates were at the library, studying for exams. My professor was drinking the good coffee I made him. His dog, Princess, was sitting at our knees and we were both petting her, our hands almost touching. He seemed agitated, my professor, agitated in a way I had never seen before.

"I couldn't get a seat on the train," he said, entering my house without even waiting for me to invite him in, Princess bounding in with him, wagging her tail. He'd accepted the cup of coffee I'd offered him, nodding as I poured in the half-and-half. "There were open seats, several, but no one would make room for me."

"Why not?" I asked.

"Because of my skin color, of course," he said, bitterly.

I stared at him.

"Because people think I am a terrorist," he said.

"You are a writer," I said. "A famous novelist."

My professor shook his head. "I had to ask the conductor to ask a woman to remove her bags. The trip takes over an hour. I was not going to stand. I had asked her, twice. I knew I should just move on, but I was tired. I am tired today. I am angry, too. This is not the first time. Normally I am used to it, but today, it was too much. I am just a person trying to go to work. I am dressed well, am I not?"

My professor was wearing faded blue jeans, a worn blue button-down shirt that looked incredibly soft. Loafers. His hair was growing long, wisps covering his ears, bangs over his eyes.

My professor had told me once that I could be a good writer if I would just let myself write. Most assignments came and went and I did not turn anything in. I wanted my work to be brilliant, which meant it was impossible for me to write anything at all. I would be getting an incomplete for the semester, in a class where everyone got 4.0s.

"That sounds horrible," I said. "She sounds like a horrible woman."

"I am sure she doesn't think of herself that way. I am sure she gives money to Planned Parenthood and votes Democrat. She doesn't even know she is racist. She is the kind of woman who says that she likes Indian food but won't eat cilantro."

I wanted to tell my professor that when I made salsa I used lots of fresh cilantro. That while I often put my knapsack on my seat, hoping that no one would sit next to me on the train, whenever it was crowded, I always made the seat available, before I was asked. I told my professor this.

"Of course, Rachel," he said. "Of course you would do that. You are a beautiful person."

He looked so sad, my professor, and this was the second time he had called me beautiful, and so I kissed him.

At first, he did not return my kiss, and then, just when I was about to pull away, he did.

"You thought it was nice?" I asked him. "Very nice? You thought it was a very nice kiss?"

Once, early in the semester, I had turned in a short story and he had deleted all of the *very*s.

"It is the nicest thing that has happened to me in a long time," my professor said.

He had crossed out all of the *really*s. All of the *just*s. There was not much story left.

"Really?" I said.

"Really." My professor took another sip of his coffee. He sighed. "If you don't mind, I would like for you to kiss me again."

"Is that okay?" I asked him.

"I don't know," he said. "Honestly, I am so fucking law-abiding. I don't even cross the street until the light changes. Right now, I just want what I want, and I would like it if you would kiss me again."

And so I did.

This time, I put my hand on the back of his head, my fingers in his hair, and I leaned in, not letting him go. I considered putting my tongue in his mouth, but decided against it. It seemed possible that at any moment my professor might change his mind.

———

Finally, my professor pulled away.

"I am going to be late for class," he said, looking down at his watch.

It was a beautiful watch. It looked like an antique. It had roman numerals, the brown leather band was soft and worn. I wanted to touch his watch, but I restrained myself. I did not want my professor to think that I was strange. I did not want him to know that I loved every single thing about him. That I loved his blue shirt. I restrained myself from touching his shirt. "I have class in ten minutes," he said.

My professor stood up. His poodle, Princess, also stood up, but he was leaving his standard poodle with me. I had been looking forward to spending the day with his dog. He had brought a rawhide bone with him for her to chew on.

"You be a good girl," he said.

I walked my professor to the door, Princess following us. I didn't want my professor to leave us. I wanted to wrap him in my arms. I wanted to protect him. I felt afraid for him. He seemed like he required protecting.

"I'm sorry," I said. "I'm really sorry."

"What are you sorry for?"

I didn't know. "For making you late," I said.

My professor shrugged. He did not disagree with me. But even then, he didn't seem in a hurry to leave. The tips of his fingers brushed my side. He had long, beautiful fingers.

"I'll bring Princess to your office at six," I said.

That was the plan we had previously agreed on. I would keep his dog for the day, walk her, feed her, play with her. Up until now, my professor used to take her to class, but there had been complaints. A student claimed to be allergic to dogs, which was ridiculous because Princess was a poodle, hypoallergenic. And then there was another student, a girl who claimed that Princess had growled at her. I didn't think it could be true. Princess was the nicest dog.

When my professor asked me how much I wanted to be paid, I had said that I didn't want any money. He'd told me he would pay me twenty dollars. My professor did not want to take advantage of my kindness. He did not want any appearance, he had said, of impropriety. That had been yesterday.


At five-thirty, half an hour early, my professor appeared at my door, his hands at his sides. It had started to rain unexpectedly and he was wet.

"Do you want to come in?" I asked him.

I took his hand and I brought him inside. Princess was resting on the living room floor. She thumped her tail, but she didn't get up. I had taken the dog out for a long walk. We had played ball. I had tired her out.

I had looked my professor up on the Internet during the day. I read his Twitter page. His job at my liberal arts college, a two-year writer's residence, was ending today. His health insurance, it also ended today. His second novel, long overdue, was not working. His advance already spent. My sad and beautiful professor had laid himself bare on Twitter. I had learned a lot.

"Would you like to have a glass of wine?" I asked him.

"You are too young," he said, shaking his head.

This, of course, was ridiculous. I had been drinking alcohol since I was fifteen years old. I also realized that there was a line my professor did not want to cross and that it did not matter that somehow we had already crossed it. I would not contradict him further.

We walked upstairs, trailed by Princess. My professor smiled when he saw my bedroom. The art posters on the wall.

My professor sat down on my bed, taking off his shoes. "She had a good day, didn't she?" he said, looking down at his dog. "Sometimes I envy her," he said. "The name, Princess, was supposed to be ironic, but somehow she has grown into it. It suits her. Do you know what I mean?"

I nodded. There was something regal about my professor's dog. She crossed her front paws when she lay down on the floor. She commanded your attention.

I sat on my bed, next to my professor. I also took off my shoes. I felt happy, even though I understood that my professor was sad. I realized that I would probably not be able to make him happy, but that I would still try.

"I am going home tomorrow," he said.

"New York?"

I thought he was going back that night. Catching the train. He shook his head.

"Pakistan."

"You are?"

"My grandmother is dying."

"Is that a good idea?" I asked him.

Things had been all wrong in America since the election. Immigrants who left were sometimes not allowed back. If you were Mexican. If you were Middle Eastern. Probably Pakistani, too. I was not sure. I wished I knew.

"She took care of me when I was a little boy," my professor said. "I have to go."

I pushed his hair behind his ears. I felt the urge to say my professor's name, but I was afraid I would mispronounce it. I had practiced during the afternoon, his first name and his last name, over and over again, it was not that difficult a name, but I didn't want to risk it. I did not want to make a mistake. My professor would not look at me, but I knew what I had to do.

For the third time that day, I kissed my professor. This time, it was not that nice. Our front teeth clattered. It hurt, even, and I jumped back. So did my professor. My professor, I realized, who had led me up the stairs, was nervous. I wanted to set him at ease. I wanted to let him know that he wasn't doing anything wrong. He wanted what he wanted. That was okay. Somehow, it was okay.

I pushed him gently down on the bed.

"This will be nice, too," I told my professor. "Very nice."

My professor did not correct me. I began to unbutton his blue shirt. It was soft, like I thought it would be.

# *Becca*


Rachel came home for her summer break with a dog, a standard poodle. I had just put down my dog. She was twelve, my sweet Posey, also a standard poodle. I thought we would have a few more years. I was not ready.

I needed a new dog. I didn't function properly without a dog, but this was too soon. Somehow, losing Posey was hitting me worse than losing Rachel's father, who was not dead. He had left me for a younger woman. He was living with her in the girlfriend's apartment in Tribeca. I would have preferred if he had died. My feelings would be less complicated. I wanted my dog back.

"Whose dog is this?" I said. "And don't say a present for me, because I will kill you."

Rachel shrugged.

Sometimes, I thought there was something wrong with my daughter. There was a flatness to her that I found unnerving. It was like she had a switch, an on-off mode. Even when she was a girl. She would want to sleep in my bed, hug me like there was no one else, and then gleefully go to another girl's house for a sleepover, and like that, I did not exist. On-off.

I knew, intellectually, that my nineteen-year-old daughter was not a sociopath. She was the way that she was, but I never knew which daughter would wake up in the morning. I had been planning to pick Rachel up later that day from the train station, but instead she arrived hours early, sweaty, pulling her suitcase and this dog on a leash. It was a gorgeous dog. Long legs, apricot-colored fur. An expensive dog.

"Rachel," I said. "Whose dog is this?"

"My writing professor's," she said. My daughter had been excited about taking his class. She had been required to submit a story to get in and was over the moon when she was accepted. "He had to leave for the summer because of a family emergency. I told him I would take care of Princess until he gets back. I know you miss Posey. I miss her, too."

Rachel was aware of me staring suspiciously at the dog, tears welling in my eyes. At least she wasn't an idiot. She also did not mention her father.

"Isn't he from Pakistan? Your professor?"

"You remember that?"

I wondered why I remembered that.

"He was striking. His author photo. Dark eyes."

"That's an inappropriate way to talk about a writer," Rachel said.

"Is it?" I asked. "Isn't that the point of an author photo?"

Rachel looked at me with that blank expression.

"You talked about him, a lot, in the beginning of the semester," I said. "I read his book."

"Did you like it?"

"It was long," I said. "I wanted to like it. Even the sentences were long."

"I know. It's supposed to be a masterpiece. I read review after review and no one complained about the sentences. I think there is something wrong with both of us."

This often happened. We did not stay mad at each other for long. I wanted to chew my daughter out about this dog and instead I was talking about her professor's overwritten novel.

"No," I said. "We appreciate short sentences. His book might just not be for us."

The poodle was panting. It was a hot day. Ninety degrees in June, too hot for June. Global warming was here. Life went on. As humans, would we learn to adapt? Here I was. Adapting. I wondered how Rachel felt about her father leaving. She had said she was no longer a child, that her feelings on the subject were inconsequential. Whereas *my* feelings had been hurt. Our perfect family had come apart and my daughter did not care. She was just like Pierre from that Maurice Sendak book. I would have fed her to a hungry lion if I could. I knelt down and petted the beautiful dog she had brought home. I scratched the poodle under her chin. It was ridiculous. Could I fall in love with a dog that quickly?

"It is going to be fine, Mom," my daughter said. "I'm going to walk her. I will feed her. It's a big house."

I heard echoes of my seven-year-old girl, begging me for a bunny. Telling me that she would feed her, that she would clean her cage. The same little girl who quickly lost interest in that same bunny, who became my responsibility, another household chore, until the bunny escaped from her cage and was cornered by Posey in the living room. That poor little bunny died of a heart attack.

"My professor was leaving and I offered to take her. He was

going to let his subletter take care of her. A stranger who works twelve-hour days."

I sighed. It didn't matter that I was not ready to have another dog in the house. I wouldn't want this wonderful dog inside, alone, in an apartment all day. I wasn't even sure if I wanted my daughter home, but here she was, standing in my yard.

"Bring her inside," I said. "Let me get her some water. She must be thirsty."

"Why don't you ask me if I am thirsty? If I am hungry?"

"You're a big girl," I said. "You can take care of yourself."

"I can't," Rachel said. "I am desperately unhappy."

I looked at my daughter. I didn't know if she was telling the truth. I didn't know if I was supposed to hug her. If that was what she wanted. I could, of course, go ahead and hug her, but there was the chance that she would just stand there, stiff as a board, and I wasn't up for that kind of rejection so early in the day. She did not look desperately unhappy.

But what if it was true? Was I supposed to take care of her all summer? She had told me last week that she was thinking about not coming home, that she would stay in her college town and find a job there, and I'd told her that would be fine. I had sort of liked the idea.

Rachel already had a job at the day camp, her third summer in a row. I'd seen the director at the farmers' market and she'd told me that she couldn't wait for the summer season to start, that my daughter was such a good counselor. The kids always loved her. I loved her.

Fuck it, I was glad that she was home.

"Let's get you both something to drink," I said.

I opened the back door and she followed me inside, bringing the dog with her. "Is her name really Princess?" I asked Rachel.

"It's supposed to be ironic."

It didn't suit this big dog, who followed us into the house, seemingly unconcerned about her change of scenery. I got out the water bowl and the food bowl, and I filled it with dry food, because I hadn't thrown away Posey's last twenty-five-pound bag, still half full. I sat at my kitchen table and I watched Princess eat and I wondered what I would call her instead. She could be Posey for right now. I did not see the harm. She was just a summer dog, after all.

I wondered about the famous writer who would leave this beautiful dog with strangers. I remembered the trip to Paris this spring I had refused to take, unwilling to leave Posey. She could barely walk up the stairs. Jonathan wanted to go anyway. He wanted to leave Posey at the kennel.

Jonathan had been looking forward to Paris, a trip he had planned for us. He accused me of loving the dog more than him. "Do you know how wrong that is?" he said.

I was unable to deny it.

And that was when he told me about Mandy. He had gone to Paris with Mandy instead. They slept in the hotel room he had reserved for us.

"That is a ridiculous name," I told him.

It was the best I had. I was never good at winning arguments. I didn't go on our romantic trip, which was a victory of sorts, to stay home with my dying dog.

And now Rachel was home, opening the refrigerator, searching for food. She took out the farmers' market strawberries, a container of plain yogurt, a bottle of seltzer. She took all of these things like she was entitled to them, and of course, she was. She was my daughter. This was her home. I was glad that she had come home. I told myself that again, as if I needed convincing.

What was I going to do otherwise?

Summers off were supposedly one of the good things about being a teacher, and yet. I wished I had made actual plans. I had not counted on my dog dying. Or my husband leaving me. He hadn't even come home to open the swimming pool. I missed the pool, swimming laps. I missed walking my dog. I missed my dog. Rachel had brought me a dog.

I took two bowls from the cabinet and scooped out the yogurt. It occurred to me that I wanted some more coffee.

"Coffee?" I asked Rachel and she nodded her head, yes. I wasn't used to her drinking coffee. I did not know what she did at college and I liked it that way. I had trouble accepting her as a grown-up. She wasn't a grown-up. Nineteen. She was borderline. She wasn't a child. Her T-shirt, I noticed, was on inside out and I found that reassuring.

"Do you know how long we have her for?"

"Six weeks, I think," Rachel said. "I'm not sure. My professor was going home to see his dying grandmother. He didn't know when he was coming back. When you go visit dying people, how do you know if they will actually die?"

I couldn't help myself. I laughed.

"What?"

"His dying grandmother."

"Do you think he's lying?"

"Yes," I said, still laughing.

Why did this story strike me as a load of shit? Maybe because of all of the lies Jonathan told me before he finally came clean about Mandy. One of them was that his mother was sick. Edith, my mother-in-law, was perfectly fine. She called on a night he'd supposedly left to see her, clearly not part of his poorly executed lie.

My husband's girlfriend worked for an airline, but she was not a flight attendant, like I'd first assumed. She was an actual pilot. I supposed that made it better.

"It sounds like a lie, sweetheart. His dying grandmother. Why not pull on the heart strings a little harder?"

"He wouldn't lie," Rachel said.

That was the moment I realized that I should worry. Who was this professor, taking advantage of my daughter? I was glad I had not bought his book. It had been a library book. I had to renew it twice. But I read the novel to the end and felt proud of myself for having done so.

"How was the class?" I asked her.

"I didn't turn in my final story," she said.

"Oh, honey. Why not?"

Rachel had always wanted to be a writer. She wrote her first short story in the second grade, eleven pages about an African elephant in the zoo who wanted a friend.

Neither of us talked while I ground the beans for the coffee and Rachel sliced the strawberries. Of course, it would be nice to have her home. Last summer, we had fallen into a nice rhythm. I had the day to myself when she was at camp. Her father was almost never home, long days at work and business trips, too. Now I wondered if he already was with Mandy, but it had been nice anyway, just me and Rachel and the dog. Sometimes she would bring her friends out to the swimming pool. I missed her when she left for college. She went off and forgot about me, returned on holidays with a suitcase full of dirty laundry.

"Why didn't you turn in a story?" I asked.

"I actually wrote it," Rachel said. "But I was afraid he wouldn't like it."

"Isn't this worse? Will you pass the class?"

"He said he would pass me in exchange for taking care of his dog."

"Huh," I said. "That doesn't sound like an ethical exchange."

"It doesn't to me, either," Rachel said. "But it's cool. It's like we have an understanding."

"Rachel," I said.

"Mom," Rachel said. "His contract ended and he isn't coming back to the college, so I guess he doesn't give a shit. It's better than getting an incomplete."

"That doesn't make it right."

"Mom," Rachel repeated. She stopped cutting strawberries. She was holding the big kitchen knife. I found it unnerving. "Don't you dare contact the school."

I hadn't said a word about contacting the school. The idea had not occurred to me, but suddenly it was beginning to make sense. Something had gone on between them. My impressionable daughter and her writing professor. You did not leave your poodle with just anybody.

"I don't want to get him in trouble. I was being kind, Mom, offering to take care of his dog. I thought you might like it. I was thinking of you."

"You weren't thinking of me," I said.

I wished it were true.

It wasn't true.

My daughter, the girl who had perfected the skill of perfect flatness, looked upset. I felt relieved. She was still in there, somewhere. I thought she might even want to tell me something. But then I saw that cloud fall over her face. Already I had blown it.

"You shouldn't pass a class if you haven't turned in the assignments," I said.

"I will let you read my story if that will make you feel better," Rachel said. "I did the work. I deserve to pass."

I still had a moral responsibility to this girl, my child, to be a role model of sorts, to comment on the things she did, to shape who she would become. I could also tell her that her T-shirt was inside out, but it seemed better not to mention it.

"It's not like you want me to fail," Rachel said. "I mean, that would be ridiculous, wouldn't it, failing creative writing? You can read my story if you want to. It's a good story. I know my opinion doesn't count, but I actually think it's really good."

"I want to read it," I said. "Why do you think he wouldn't have liked it?"

"I don't know. He liked everyone else's stories. He liked all of these terrible, terrible stories, which made me think he couldn't like mine, because it isn't terrible. I have it printed out," Rachel said. "I'll let you read it."

I poured our coffee and we drank it. We sat at the kitchen table and ate our berries and our yogurt. It felt like there was nothing left to say. I did not want to say one more wrong thing.

The dog had finished eating. From the corner of my eye, I watched her wander around the kitchen, sniffing the cupboards. She came over, putting her long snout in my lap, and I petted her soft orange poodle fur. Such a special color. A temporary dog was a terrible idea. I would not want to give her back.

"I am glad you are home, sweet pie," I said to my daughter.

And she then came to me. Rachel gently pushed Posey aside and sat on my lap, still my little girl.


Later that night, I read my daughter's short story. It was about an airline attendant. Her name was Amanda. I had to laugh out loud. There was not a side to take, that was what Jonathan and I had told her, but clearly Rachel had taken my side.

In the story, Amanda contracts a venereal disease, one she is not aware of. She meets a new man in every town. She takes each one back to her hotel and has sex with him. One of her lovers has a job in finance. He has a wife who is a teacher at an elementary school. The man comes home from his trip to Paris, guilty, and wants to make love to his wife, but she is tired. She turns him away.

At the end of the story, Amanda, the flight attendant, discovers her condition. She thinks about all of the men she had fucked, one in every town.

"What can you do?" she says to herself, downing her penicillin with a slug of vodka. "Life is a bitch."

It was a mean story. She was a good writer, my daughter, and I wished that she had turned it in.

# *Zahid*

"Now what?" Khloe asked me.

"Another shot?" I suggested.

"Aren't we drunk?"

"Not enough," I said.

Khloe got up, ordered two more shots, brought them back to our table. Of course, I was the man. It was my job to get the shots, but I was too drunk. And in this ever-changing time, gender roles did not matter. I loved hanging out with lesbians. I did not feel required to fuck them. Since my book came out, it sometimes seemed as if all women wanted to fuck me. It was exhausting. I had gotten a venereal disease. I had given it to my fiancée. She had not forgiven me. I wouldn't have told her, but because of the disease, I had to tell her the truth.

Khloe was the identical twin sister of my best friend, Kristi. My fiancée had resented Kristi, jealous of how we always talked on the phone. The twins were gorgeous, could have been models. They looked white, but not quite. They were almost six feet tall. It was hard to place the curl in their hair. Their mother was black and so that made them minorities. Kristi was always talking about race, blackness. Identity politics. Her closest friends were other writers of various minority groups. Khloe had gone into business. She had just finished her MBA. She had gotten a big job in New York and was subletting my apartment in Brooklyn for the summer. I had not figured her out. She wore short skirts and high heels but was not interested in men. She was a little bit scary, honestly.

I had come back early, but I wanted Khloe to stay because she was paying my rent. She would keep the bedroom and I could sleep on my couch. It was a quality couch. I had bought it with money from my advance. In retrospect, I should have bought a house with my book money. I could have afforded a nice one if I had been willing to leave New York. This was what Kristi told me to do. Instead I blew the money, pissed it away like water. I got a couple of nice suits, some nice pieces of furniture. I went on some very nice trips with my fiancée. We had eaten at the very best restaurants, drunk very expensive wine.

Now I was home from Pakistan, a trip my mother had insisted on, a trip she had paid for because I could not afford it on my own. "Do not continue to be the spoiled brat that you have become," she told me.

The words stung.

My grandmother had held my hand. The doctors said she was not in pain, but to me, she was the very definition of pain. Instead of saying hello, my grandmother squeezed my hand, so tightly, that tiny bony hand, and then she died. Holding my hand.

It didn't seem fair. She had laid such a burden on me. So much misplaced love. We had left Pakistan when I was twelve. I hated America at first. My parents and I lived in North Carolina, my father worked at a hospital, in a lab doing work beneath him, and we stood out, the only brown-skinned people in a small town, but eventually, I did the only thing available to me. I became American. I made friends with the other white boys. People liked me, the only Pakistani kid. I did well in school. I was polite. I listened to whatever music everyone else was listening to. I had white girlfriends. I almost always had sex with these girls, early, I was fourteen my first time, and yet these white girls never fell in love with me. Because I was Pakistani. I was practice. I knew this. I didn't love them, either.

Once a year, we visited family in Pakistan, and then it became every two years. And then, for me, three years, and then four years. I did not want to return. I did not belong. God, it was hot and it was crowded and it felt foreign. It felt awful to feel foreign in my own country. I felt grateful to be back in New York. It was just as hot, but there was also air-conditioning. Cool bars. Summer drinks.

Khloe came back to the table with the shots. I loved tequila. The salt, the lime. It tasted so good. Khloe stared at me. It occurred to me that this look was not affectionate. All night, I had sensed a growing irritation from my tenant. I should know. I was a writer. I understood people, how their minds worked. Suddenly, I did not feel so good. Jet lag, maybe. Or tequila. I looked down at my hands, placed flat on the table, and I pictured my grandmother's hand. The bones that made her knuckles, practically breaking through the skin. She was so thin. Her eyes so big.

"Will you take me home?" I asked Khloe. "I don't feel that well."

"You are a pussy," Khloe said.

This was my turn to come up with something clever to say, but instead, I draped my arm over Khloe's shoulders, we were the same height, and we left the cool, air-conditioned Brooklyn bar together and walked back to my apartment. First, I threw up on the street in front of my building. Then I threw up in the hall in front of my door. I threw up on the wood floor of my apartment, before I could make it to the bathroom.

It was cool in my apartment. We had left the air-conditioning on.

"Zahid," Khloe said. "You are a motherfucking mess."

I had nothing clever to say to that, either.

I lay down on the hardwood floor, not far from my vomit.

I woke up on the floor, a pillow under my head, a blanket covering me, the floor clean. I woke up terrified, because I could not remember who was taking care of my dog. Where was Princess? I was afraid that she was here in the apartment, under my desk, starving, and I wondered why she did not bark, why she did not come out and lick my face. Khloe was a bitch, letting me sleep on the floor, but she wouldn't let my dog starve. Would she?

"Princess? Sweetheart?"

My throat was dry. How had I forgotten about my dog? I had been back for two days and this was the first time I'd thought of her. What was wrong with me? That was what my fiancée had asked me. Two days before we were supposed to get married, I told her that she had better get tested for chlamydia. Part of me still wondered what would have happened if I had waited to tell her. We would have married. Maybe we would still be married. We could have gone to a marriage counselor. We could have kept all of the wedding presents. We would have had the ceremony and reception she had spent so long planning.

I looked under my desk. Princess was not there. Princess was not in the apartment. And then I remembered my student, the only student in the class who had not turned in her final story, the student who was in love with me. I could not remember her name. She was pretty. She had my dog. She would take good care of my dog.

# *Khloe*

It was my first summer in Brooklyn.

I thought at first that I would move to Manhattan, closer to work, but it didn't take me long to realize that Brooklyn was the place to be. My twin sister was a writer and she was the one who found me the place. Her best friend, Zahid, another writer, always with the writers, was going to be gone for the summer. My sister was clearly in love with him, but she would always deny it. She told me that he had cheated on his fiancée. That he was his own worst enemy and she would not date him for a million dollars. My sister, she protested too much. Still, it was a sublet. I would have to take care of his dog. I didn't like dogs, but it was a nice apartment in the neighborhood I wanted to live in.

Except at the last minute, Zahid decided to leave his dog with someone else for the summer. And because I did not have to take care of his dog anymore, he wanted to know if I could pay him more rent.

"Like how much more rent?" I asked him.

"Six hundred dollars," he said.

"Fuck," I said. "Fuck you. That wasn't our deal."

I cursed when I was angry. I lacked a filter, something that had gotten me in trouble on more than one occasion. I blamed it on my first babysitter, who had taught me by example, starting with *shit* and *damn* and moving up to *motherfucker*. Jane lived a few blocks away from Zahid.

I did not understand until I was thirteen, when Jane came back from college and stopped by to say hello, how hopelessly in love I was with her. I confessed my love, and she said, "Good. I was hoping you would figure it out on your own."

Good, but she didn't love me back. She was in love with a filmmaker who was making a movie in Toronto. Her girlfriend was getting famous, around less and less, and she was afraid she would not be around much longer.

"Love," my babysitter told me, "is a bitch."

"That fucking sucks," I remember telling her, thinking that she should love me instead. It was going to take time, I knew, for her to stop seeing me as a child. But I was getting older, was old enough. I had plans for her. It was why I had taken the job in New York instead of Chicago. My babysitter lived in Brooklyn. She worked in publishing. She had taken me out for drinks a couple of times already. I had met her friends, I liked them, it made me wonder why I worked in finance, but I knew the reason. Money. I wanted it. I was also in massive debt, student loans from business school, but the paychecks were rolling in, and come Christmas, I could expect a big bonus.

My colleagues were straight. Straight and male and white. Asshats, all of them, except for Danny Tang, the token Asian. Whereas I checked off two boxes. Black and female. It was not the most hospitable place. But Brooklyn was filled with lesbians. I was making good money, I was buying just about everyone drinks. I was popular among Jane's publishing friends. Sometimes, I bought my babysitter drinks, too. She was also broke. She refused to tell me what had happened with the filmmaker, but I knew that it had ended badly.

Of course, I paid Zahid the extra rent money for not taking care of his dog. I had not wanted to take care of his dog anyway. I would have had to find someone to take her out for walks in the afternoon. But that six hundred dollars a month was money I had calculated into my budget, money slated for drinks. My twin sister, Kristi, said I drank too much, but that totally wasn't true. I went to work, and after work, I wanted to unwind. I wanted to go out for a drink, and then I would find myself in a bar full of beautiful women and cold beverages served in tall glasses. There were nights when I would buy drinks for five women at a time. I loved Brooklyn. Many of these women came home with me. They were even impressed that I lived in a famous writer's apartment. I would watch my babysitter watching me, watching me go home with other women, and I knew that I was on my way.

I met Zahid for the first time at a bar near his apartment, the same bar where I bought him tequila shots when he gave me the keys to the apartment. He was leaving for Pakistan in a few days. Zahid had started to cry when he asked me for the extra money and I thought there might be something wrong with him.

Like mentally.

Later, I asked Kristi. "Duh," she said. "Zahid is a total nutjob. He needs to go on antidepressants, but he refuses."

And Zahid, he told me he was fine, but for someone with dark skin, he looked pale. Yellowy green. He was going to be spending the summer in Pakistan.

"Fun, right?" he said.

I didn't know. I had an idea about life in Pakistan, and it wasn't exactly informed. I was from the Midwest. I thought about going out for Indian food and finding out that the cooks were actually from Pakistan. I thought that Zahid could be a prince. He had delicate features. As far as men go, he was incredibly good-looking.

He came back from Pakistan in a week and a half.

A week and a half.

Motherfucker.

His grandmother had died. Apparently right away. The day after he arrived. And so Zahid changed his ticket and came home early, looking more than ever like a sad prince, an orphaned prince who had lost his castle. It was weird for me to think things like this, because I wasn't the creative one. That was Kristi. I didn't even like books. Or men, either. I had slept with two men, once in high school, and then once again in graduate school, just to know for sure. I had assumed that I was gay since I was a girl, probably because of my feelings for my babysitter. Maybe if I'd had a different babysitter, I would be a different person, a heterosexual. There is no way for me to go back in time. I wouldn't want to. ·

I also knew early on that I wanted to work in finance. I wanted to be normal. I wanted money. I liked wearing crisp suits, tailored shirts, even the shoes, the heels that made me taller than I already was. I didn't look gay, even with the short hair, because I could not take the time to straighten it. I was sexy. But it was always girls for me, even though it had been fine with both of the guys I had slept with. They had used their fingers. And probably, if I were to admit the truth to myself, they were probably also gay, using me for the very same reason I had used them.


The night Zahid came home from Pakistan, I took him back to the bar where he had taken me the night he gave me the key to his place. It wasn't my favorite bar. It was more like a dive. Not where the publishing people hung out. He seemed like he needed a drink and so I bought him several.

It seemed like the right thing to do. I was living in his apartment. I was also afraid that he would want me to leave, and that didn't work for me. I had a plan. I was spending the summer in Brooklyn, working hard and drinking hard, seducing women who didn't have the money to get out of town. I wasn't going to the Hamptons or Fire Island. I would rent my own place come fall. I was saving. As a junior analyst, I was making low six figures with a promise of a bonus at the end of the year, and then a big increase in salary if I was kept on. I would be kept on. I could feel it, understood that I had been taken on by my boss, his prodigy, not that I liked him, but that did not matter. This other analyst, a jealous prick, said it was because I was the only African American on the team with long-ass legs, but that wasn't even true. My boss appreciated my mind. I knew my shit. I fucking loved the work.

My twin sister was in Iowa, teaching where she had gone to college, getting her PhD in fiction. She was leading the most boring life I had ever heard of, but she seemed happy. We were both happy, though she said I was morally bankrupt. Not a nice thing to say, really, but I didn't tell her where to go. She had this idea that we were supposed to be closer than we were.

Zahid, the famous novelist, was a bad drunk. I had to drag him home and when we got back to the apartment he threw up everywhere. Everywhere.

"Fuuuuck," I said.

He threw up so much I was afraid that he was going to die. I could call an Uber to the hospital, but would anyone let him get into their car? Did he even have health insurance to pay the ER bill? I couldn't be sure, the guy was such a fuckup, so I cleaned the vomit off him as he turned his head and proceeded to vomit some more—not on me, I made sure of that. When he went from the toilet back to the floor in front of his couch, I cleaned up the trail he left behind.

I knew that Zahid was my sister's friend, but still, this wasn't cool.


He was still there when I got home from work.

He was drinking a beer, reading a book.

He had cleaned the apartment. It didn't matter. There he was, sitting on the couch of the apartment I paid three thousand dollars a month for. We had not talked about it last night, his coming back two months early. I had already paid him for the entire summer.

"Zahid," I said.

"Hey, Khloe." He smiled at me, a sad puppy dog smile. It was not going to work on me. "That was something last night, huh?"

"It was something."

"My head still hurts."

I was not unsympathetic.

I took off my heels. It was a tricky thing with this job I had, a black lesbian who looked white and straight. Kristi opined that I was having identity issues, but I disagreed. I liked the way I was. I figured my life outside the office was my life outside the office. I had chosen my career. I wasn't a social worker. I wasn't a poet or a PhD. My co-workers didn't like me, but they weren't supposed to. There were twelve of us, vying for six jobs. The execs loved me and that was what mattered. I was walking diversity. They all wanted to fuck me, and that wasn't a bad thing.

I took a beer from the refrigerator, realizing that, of course, Zahid was drinking one of my beers. There was also a pot cooking on the stove. I smelled something good. I opened the lid.

"I made a dal," he said. "Do you like lentils?"

I sighed. This was him trying to apologize, butter me up.

"What is your plan, Zahid?"

I couldn't help it. I could not be compassionate. Zahid was not part of my plan.

"My plan." He sighed. "I'm working on the book. I need to get a job for the fall. I have some applications out. Something always comes through. I need to write to my mother, explain why I left the way I did. I disappointed her. She does not understand my life. She still thinks I should have been a doctor."

"Dude. That's not what I meant."

"You mean about me, now. Being here?"

I nodded.

"Well, this is my apartment."

I waited.

"I realize you sublet it for the summer."

"I did," I said. "And I am paying more than I expected origi-nally."

"Because my dog isn't here."

Zahid looked worried. I felt worried. I didn't know who had the power in this conversation.

"I kind of need to stay here," Zahid said.

"But you sublet the apartment to me."

"I could sleep on the couch."

I wondered what my sister would say about this. This was not all right with me. But I tried to make it better. "And you will give me back half of my rent," I said, realizing that I did not want half of the rent. I did not want him there. Period.

Zahid laughed.

"That would make sense," he said. "But if I am sleeping on the couch, half seems like too much, don't you think?"

"Fuck, Zahid." I knew what was coming. This was why I would never be a writer. Even the editors were broke and they had benefits.

"I'm a really good cook," he said.

"Zahid," I said.

"I have nowhere to go."

"If you give me my money back," I said, "I'll find another place. I understand this is your apartment. I understand that plans can change. But this, what you are suggesting, won't work."

We stared at each other. I was not a nice person. I was not a person filled with compassion. I put myself first. If I didn't take care of myself, who would?

"Where is your dog?" I asked him.

"My dog?"

"Yes," I said. "Your dog. The one I was going to take care of until you left her with a student."

"Connecticut," Zahid said.

"Connecticut." I thought about it. "Connecticut is supposed to be beautiful."

"Then that is where I shall go," Zahid said, as if his life were a fucking fairy tale.

# *Rachel*

My mother and I had a fight about the dog.

She had started calling her Posey, for one thing, and she had the dog sleeping with her on her king-sized bed. Princess slept on my father's side.

"You can't keep her," I told my mother. "This isn't the real Posey." My mother gave me this blank, vacant gaze. "Posey is dead," I said.

"Thanks, sweetheart, thank you for reminding me," she said.

And then I felt bad.

"I just don't want you to get confused."

"Whose big idea was it to bring this dog home?" she said. "I told you it was too soon."

Clearly, it was too soon.

But I wanted to take care of the dog. My professor had left Princess with me. That had to mean something. I wanted to ask my mother, *Did that mean something?,* but then I would have to tell her what had happened between me and my professor, and she wouldn't approve. My mother was not that cool. I didn't think anyone would approve. I did not think my friends would understand. My best friend from high school, Agatha, was in California for the summer and I wasn't even sure if we were friends anymore. I understood that this kind of thing, sleeping with your professor, was considered *bad*. An abuse of power. Even if I had urged him.

"He is going to come back for her, you know," I said.

Honestly, I had this a little bit confused, too. As if he were going to come back, my professor, come back for me. But he would be coming back for his dog. I knew that I did not matter, that I was just a student, a former student, even. He didn't even like my writing, but maybe, maybe at least I had been good in bed.

Princess had absolutely no use for me anymore. She tolerated me, let me pet her. She would chase after a ball if I threw her one, but she had fallen in love with my mother. She would sit at my mother's feet and lick her face and lick her face, and my mother let her. I was jealous. It was stupid.

"This dog is a licker," my mother said, delighted.

It was disgusting.

Growing up, all of my friends thought that my mother was cool. She let us eat unhealthy snacks. She did not monitor our screen time. She would swim in the pools with us and jump on the trampolines in other people's backyards while all the other mothers watched.

I didn't know why or when it started to bother me, the way my mother was nice to my friends. My mother would talk to them and they would linger in the kitchen. One time, I saw her hugging Agatha and neither would tell me what the conversation had been about. I used to worry that my friends didn't actually like me. They liked hanging out in my house. They liked my mother. We had a swimming pool. Once, when I was much younger, eleven or twelve, I let another girl have her birthday party at my swimming pool. She invited over girls who did not like me and who wouldn't talk to me, even while they were at my house, swimming in my pool.

My mother had not opened the pool this summer.

"Your dad does it" was what she said, as if that were that. I certainly did not know how to open a swimming pool. "Can't we call someone?" I wanted to ask, but I didn't. It felt disrespectful to my mother. She was grieving somehow, even if she had no idea, and maybe this was part of it. The loss of our pool. It was sad, sitting there all covered up. And it had always been my father's job to take care of the pool, the chlorine, the shock treatment, even the vacuuming, he did it all himself, but he was living in New York, living in his girlfriend's apartment. He could have come home, at least, to open the pool. And she could have hired someone, obviously. It really wasn't fair that I couldn't go swimming because they'd broken up.

It was my mother who insisted I have dinner with my father and his new girlfriend. The pilot, my mother called her.

"You take the train," I said. "You give up your night and make polite conversation."

"But I was not invited," my mother said.

"Have you met her?" I asked.

"I have not."

And then I understood. I was going to dinner for my mother. She was not concerned that I maintain my relationship with my father. She wanted a report about my father's girlfriend. I supposed I could do that for her.

"I am insisting you go because it will be good for you."

This was such bullshit that it seemed pointless to call her on it. She had read my short story. She knew that I was on her side.

My mother put Princess on a leash and walked me to the train station. She walked to the ticket machine and paid for my tickets. I did not tell her that I had an app on my phone. I let her pay. She sat on a bench with me while we waited for the train and we both petted the dog.

Maybe we didn't have to return Princess. I could get him in so much trouble. My professor wasn't supposed to sleep with me. I was his student. Maybe, in exchange for not turning him in, we could keep this dog. Maybe this would be my gift to my mother, because it was wrong, I realized, to have brought this dog into her life.

I might have forgotten about my mother and dogs, how attached she gets. And Princess, she could also be a reminder for me. That I had had sex with my writing professor; it had not been some schoolgirl fantasy. It had happened. It was not like I could really be in love with him. It had been one night. It hadn't even been a night. It had been a few hours in the late afternoon.

I was sad when the train pulled in. I wanted to stay home with my mother and my professor's dog. I felt strangely left out. The train stopped and I got on it. I turned to wave at her, but my mother had already started walking home.


Mandy Jones was a vegan.

She wore a black tank top, skinny jeans. She had strong, muscular arms. Her blond hair fell to her shoulders. She had straight bangs. It was the kind of haircut I'd had in the third grade.

She was probably two decades younger than my mother. I knew that I wasn't supposed to like her, but I sort of did anyway. Or, I didn't dislike her. She was a pilot and that was cool. Amanda, I thought, would be a better name, like the name in my story, and I asked her if that was possibly her real name.

"Truthfully?" she said, and I said, "Sure."

I felt nervous and my father looked nervous. What truth would this pilot reveal to me?

"I was named after a Barry Manilow song. I was ashamed of this fact for a long time, but no one really remembers him anymore, so it's okay. It was my mother's favorite song."

The funny thing was that I actually knew who Barry Manilow was because my mother also loved him. I grew up listening to her sing me "Copacabana," except sometimes my mother would change the words. Instead of "Lola," she would sing:

Her name was Rachel
She was a schoolgirl
She didn't want to get out of bed to go to school.

It went on like that, my mother making up words to the Barry Manilow song while I groaned, secretly loving it. This probably didn't make sense to anyone who didn't know that song, and my father's girlfriend, Mandy, was right: Almost no one remembered Barry Manilow at this point. Which made me ponder the nature of fame. My professor was famous, but I would guess my father's pilot had never heard of him. Or my father either, who genuinely believed fiction was for women. I thought about my professor constantly, his hands on my skin. Sitting at a restaurant, across from Mandy and my father, I started to flush.

"My mother loves Barry Manilow," I told Mandy, and then I felt disloyal somehow, because it meant that my mother was old. In league with Mandy's mother. "I do, too," I said, trying to make it all right.

"Weird," Mandy said and she laughed.

She wisely tried to change the subject. Mandy wanted to know if I was heartbroken about Hillary Clinton. Because she was heartbroken about Hillary Clinton. This was eight months after the election; I figured she must be desperate to make appropriate conversation.

"Girl power, you know?" she said. "First female president. I was so sure it would happen."

How my mother would have sneered at her. Girl power. It was a line on a T-shirt, nothing more. I told Mandy I had been for Bernie Sanders. This wasn't even entirely true. I was being contrarian. I actually liked them both, which was not a popular viewpoint at my liberal arts college. I was supposed to feel passionately about a candidate, even if it was the crazy Green Party lady. It didn't even matter to me anymore, Hillary or Bernie, now that there was this god-awful new president.

"Well, we can still get along," Mandy said.

I shrugged. I didn't agree or disagree.

"I am heartbroken for the world, really," I said.

"Your daughter has depth, Jonathan," Mandy said, which was completely condescending. Which made me think that maybe I did not like her after all. Which made me feel glad. I would tell my mother that I did not like the pilot. My father was nervous. He drank two gin and tonics in half an hour.

My father had been for Hillary, too. He worked for one of those investment banks that had invested tons of money in her campaign. Paid for her to make speeches. And it was her association with bankers that helped bring her down. My father had said after she lost that it had been a bad investment. Sometimes, I wondered if his leaving my mother was related to Hillary losing.

But he didn't appear to have lost his mind.

He had just moved on.

That made me sad.

It was not until I had gone into New York and met my father's perfectly acceptable girlfriend that I realized that I was upset. There was something wrong with this woman, wanting an old guy like my father. He was handsome in that way that older men could be. Fit. He played tennis. But he was balding. He went to bed at ten. He read the *Wall Street Journal*. Clearly Mandy could have anybody. Clearly she had some daddy issues. I wondered how long they would live together in her small apartment. If she had any idea how big our house in Connecticut was. How long would he last in Tribeca? Clearly, it was not his scene.

My professor was older, but he was not that much older. He was not a father figure. It made me feel better realizing that Mandy Jones was not as perfect as she appeared. It didn't matter that she had destroyed my family. Because I was in college. I didn't need my family anymore.

———

Earlier that night, my mother had walked me to the train. Going home, my father walked me to the subway. This was my dad, the most boring dad in the universe, living in Tribeca. Otherwise, he did not seem any different.

"This meant a lot to me," he said.

I shrugged. I wondered what I would tell my mother. I could not figure out how upset she was. She had told me more than once that she missed Posey more than my father. It seemed cruel of him to have left so soon after the dog died. He should have been there to comfort her.

"There is a new associate in the firm," he said, apropos of nothing. "Black girl, new to the city, smart, sharp as a tack. Good instincts. Works hard. We're going to promote her soon. She makes me think of you."

"A black girl makes you think of me?"

That was wrong. It was incredibly sexist that he called his female employee a girl. Also, I wasn't as sharp as a tack. I was sort of slow and dreamy, something that bothered me about myself.

"No," my father said. "That didn't come out right. I'll start again. Her name is Khloe. For one thing, she doesn't really look black."

"Is she black? What are you saying?"

"She's half black, light-skinned. The new black."

My father laughed.

I didn't. I did not have that much patience for him.

"Don't you watch that show? *Orange Is the New Black*? Mandy loves it."

"You can't say hip things, Dad. It doesn't work for you. You aren't hip."

"Point taken. Anyway. It helped her get hired, her skin color. Diversity. She's also pleasing to the eye. I had some drinks tonight, sweetheart. I shouldn't say these things. It's not PC. I am so sick of PC. Look, anyway, that is not the point, Rachel. I brought Khloe up because this is her first big job out of grad school and she is kicking ass. It pleases me, watching her run circles around her co-workers. It makes me wonder what you will be like in a couple of years."

"You want me to go into finance?" I said. "I don't see it."

"Don't rule anything out, honey."

Though he had explained it to me, so many times, I still did not understand what, exactly, my father did. It was like when I was a kid, watching the U.S. Open on TV and I never knew what any of those ads were about, the investment firms and the life insurance. I'd recently had a revelation, an unpleasant one, straight from Bernie Sanders himself, that I might be the daughter of a genuine scumbag. The one percent. That I was guilty by association. By the simple fact of my birth. My privilege. The swimming pool. Even if my father seemed nice and gave money to liberal causes. And he was nice to me. He gave money to me, too. I was not so sure about the company he worked for. I knew that I could Google it. That all of the answers were on my phone. I did not want to know. I knew I was not going to like whatever I found out.

"Maybe I will be a pilot," I told my dad.

"You could do that," he said. "I'm sure Amanda could give you some tips."

Obviously, I was full of shit. I would not become a pilot. It was understood about me; I did not have focus. I did not know what I was interested in. I had floundered all through high school. I was not Ivy League material. I was still floundering in college, but I had made it through my sophomore year, had even done well in every class except creative writing. Which was, of course, ironic. I had always been a good babysitter. Kids loved me.

"Or I could teach pre-K," I said.

This conversation we were having was my least favorite and I was not sure how we had gotten there. Every conversation with my father ended this way.

My father sighed. "Whatever you do, honey, don't be a teacher."

My mother, of course, was a teacher. He had never respected her job, had made jokes about how little money she made. It hadn't mattered for her, because she had married well, but this was not the way things worked anymore. She also had a kid come into her classroom with a gun. She had talked the boy down, she had been a national hero even, appeared on the *Today* show. Schools, my father had said, are not safe.

My mother had scoffed at this.

"Let's keep all the children home then," she had said. "How about that?"

It had been a stupid fight; it had occurred when they came to my college to tell me about their separation, but it reminded me how much my parents had been fighting. Or not talking at all.

"Seriously, honey."

My father wanted me to promise him then and there that I would not teach. But maybe I would; maybe I would teach little kids. I liked my kids at day camp. I always had. This made me think about my professor, too, his tweets about money, about how broke he was, how he had spent most of his salary on train fare. My professor was a writer, really, not a teacher. He wasn't even a good teacher. He had been so critical of everything I turned in. My mother, at least, liked my short story. She did not pick at it at a sentence level; she said it was wonderful.

I realized how pathetic that was, this inner dialogue I was having. I probably didn't want to teach pre-K anyway. I just wanted to upset my father. We had reached the subway, a small thing for which I was grateful.

"Do you need money?" he asked me.

I did not need money, not in any real sense of the word, but I also saw that this was the way it was going to go.

"Sure," I said.

My father pressed a wad of cash into my hand.

On the train home, in my own row, on my way back to Connecticut, I counted the bills. Ten bills. Two hundred dollars. It used to be my dad would just give me a couple of twenties. This was too much. The money made me feel dirty somehow. Was it supposed to buy my love? Somehow, my father didn't know that I loved him no matter what. He was my father. Parents could be so stupid. It was staggering.

I would give the money away. I would keep sixty, the amount I was due, to pay for my time, for my Friday night, and I would donate the rest. I didn't know where. I would check Twitter. My writing professor was always tweeting about organizations that needed money. I took out my phone. Right away, I found an article about a man who had been deported, a Mexican who had been living in Texas for thirty-two years. He had been pulled over by the police because he had not come to a full stop at a stop sign and now he was being sent home. He had four kids. There was a link in the story to his GoFundMe campaign. I clicked on the link. I donated $140 to his family.

Did that make me a better person? I didn't think so. I was not a good person. I prayed that my professor would safely come back from Pakistan, and then I laughed at myself, praying. I was Jewish. Now, with the rise of anti-Semitism, that made me into the new minority. Even I could be discriminated against. I could be the victim of a hate crime. Did that make me a better person? I didn't think so. I could start going to temple, then it would be real, but who was I fooling? I wouldn't do that. I thought of my professor's blue shirt. How soft it had been.

"You," he had said. "Are very nice."

I was such an idiot.

This was nothing new.

# *Becca*

I tried to think about the divorce in simple terms. I wanted the house. I loved my house and my flowers and the yard. I loved the pool, which was outdoors but still part of the house, accessible from a door in the living room, looking down onto the lawn, the swing set we put up for Rachel, which she had not used in so many years. I loved the front porch and I loved all of the art on the walls. I loved the amethysts and the gemstones on the bookshelves. I loved the books. I loved the green soaps in the downstairs bathroom, which matched the tiles on the floor. I loved my plates and my cups. The way the vase filled with flowers looked on the kitchen table. The house was me and it was mine.

I wanted some cash from Jonathan, too, money that some people would say I did not need, because I had a job. Still, it was money I deserved. Jonathan thought of life as a series of bonuses, and I felt like I deserved a bonus for lasting twenty-five years. Twenty-five years.

He owed me.

Son of a bitch.

That was what I thought, the phrase that went through my head when I didn't think I was thinking about it. He owed me. Fucking hell. I did not want to be angry. I did not want to be hurt. Earlier this year, Theo Thornton, a former student, had come into my classroom and pulled out a gun, and that, I'd thought, was supposed to change everything. I was supposed to have a new perspective, light, clarity. I pretended not to care, but if I let myself feel anything, if only for a moment, I was furious with my cheating husband. He never even said good-bye to Posey.

I had talked the student down.

I had been lucky, of course. It could have gone either way.

So I wasn't going to worry about dust on the picture frames. I was going to accept life as it came at me, for better or worse. At some point, the money would bring me pleasure, and I wanted it. It helped, according to my lawyer, that I had been wronged. It helped that my husband was currently living in Tribeca with his pilot. Jonathan wanted out, fast, and so he could afford this divorce. Money would help ease the pain. There was that trip to Paris we didn't take. I could take it now. I could go to art museums and not worry about being rushed.

But some nights, awake at three in the morning, I would think: I am a failure. Jonathan was my husband, he was my family, and he no longer wanted to be my family. And then, then I would remember how bored I had been. Bored and bitter and how I had stopped doing his laundry on a regular basis, which seemed wrong even to me, cruel, petty, considering the hours he worked, not having clean socks for him in the morning. And then I realized that maybe, maybe I had stopped washing his clothes because they had a new smell to them.

Had they smelled like sex? He was having sex with another person. How long had it been? And then, then I would reach for the dog on my bed and I would cry.

It wasn't my dog, this Princess, she was such a beautiful poodle, I had to stop calling her Posey, but it made me feel better and so what harm was there in that.

I felt happy now that Rachel was home. I had thought I might resent her presence, but I didn't. I genuinely liked my almost-adult Rachel. She was interesting, she was moody, she would read the books I took out of the library before I could read them. She was good at her job and she was responsible, and I took credit for that. I was glad that she'd brought me the dog.

I had been allowing myself to fall into a lazy kind of depression—left by my husband, dog dead—and then Rachel came home with her laundry and this constant need to be fed, the minute she walked in the door, and I got to mother her and I liked mothering. I always had.

I had dedicated years and years to the mothering of Rachel and she might be in college, but I wasn't done yet. I packed Rachel a lunch for camp every day, just as if she were still in elementary school: a turkey sandwich and a Tupperware container filled with watermelon balls. One day, searching for something sweet, I found only Baker's chocolate and so I made brownies. I packed them for Rachel's dessert. She ate them, I assumed, but she never mentioned them to me, as if she took it for granted that there would be homemade brownies in her lunch box. Of course, I ate them, too. I made good brownies.

When Rachel was at camp, I took the dog on walks. My town was charming. I could get into the car and Posey and

I would be at the Sound in less than five minutes. We would walk to the main square and go to my favorite café. The people who worked there would always bring me water for her. Everyone commented on my new dog.

"She is a good dog," I said, not confirming or denying her place in my life.

Of course, if I were to get a new dog, I would get a puppy. There is nothing better than soft poodle puppy fur. The idea is to get a puppy, to bond with your poodle from a young age, but I'd felt a bond with this apricot poodle right away. It seemed as if she had been waiting for me.

I was sitting outside at my café, drinking an iced coffee, Posey at my feet, waiting for Rachel's day camp to let out. She was not eight, of course, she could find her way home, but Rachel seemed to like it when I picked her up. Her friend Agatha had not come home for the summer. The friends who had come home she claimed not to like anymore. This came as a surprise to me. Mollie and Bryn. They were very nice girls, all of them. I used to buy them pizza, drive them to the mall. I expected Rachel to moan and complain, but she didn't. She had perfected, instead, the unhappy "don't bother me" look. She wanted an audience for her misery and there I was.

I had my sketch pad open, I was going to draw this summer, I was going to paint, and in fact, I had begun a sketch of Posey when I noticed a young man, a dark-skinned man wearing a long-sleeved shirt and linen shorts, stepping out of a silver car. Clearly he was not from here. It was a sad truth, the lack of diversity in our town, but there it was. You had to be married to a banker to afford a house here. That limited the population. The Armstrongs were African American; Donna and David were both lawyers. Of course, there were always exceptions. The silver car pulled away from the curb, and this young man simply stood there, arms at his sides.

He reached into his pockets, retrieved a pair of sunglasses, and put them on. He proceeded to make a full circle, not leaving his spot on the sidewalk, and then he scratched his head. He looked rumpled, hungover even. His hair hung in his eyes.

"Oh, Posey," I said.

This, of course, had to be Rachel's writing professor. It could be no one else. I recognized him from his author photo. He would want his dog back. It hadn't even been two weeks. Rachel had said we would have her for the summer.

I felt a panic. I stood up, sat down. Posey stood up, too, but I told her to sit. She hadn't seen him yet. I could pretend not to have recognized my daughter's professor. I could walk with Posey in the opposite direction, fast, and hope he did not see us. My daughter's professor did not know me, but he would know his dog.

The man obviously didn't know where Rachel lived or he would have taken the car directly to our house. I tried to imagine what he was thinking. It was a small town. He could talk to some people here on the square and he would find my daughter, just like that. He was not too far off. He had been here for all of a minute and I had found him.

It was bad luck on my part. The idea of not greeting him was appealing. The man was obviously a mess. And he was attractive, enormously so. There was something lovely and lonely about him and suddenly I understood my daughter's melancholy. Her writing professor.

Anyone but him, I thought.

I could feel other people's eyes on this man.

Suddenly, I felt afraid for him. He seemed so ill at ease—there was a way he reached into his pocket, as if he was going to pull out a pack of gum and someone was going to think it was a gun. I was afraid someone would call the police. Like the two old biddies on the park bench across the street who had obviously noticed him and were whispering. Small-town America. Motherfuck.

"Zahid," I called out. I was not going to cross the street. I would not make it that easy for him. The least he could do was come to me. "Zahid Azzam."

What a funny name it was. Like a comic book character.

He looked at me, confused.

"Yes, you." I gestured for him to come over. I wondered if he thought that there was another Zahid in this nearly all white town. Maybe I looked dangerous to him. I had been doing a lot of yoga over the years.

Zahid crossed the street, and only then did he notice his dog beneath the table, her front legs crossed.

"Princess," he said, delighted. "Baby."

He knelt down and petted his dog. He put his face in her poodle hair. Oh gosh, this man was a mess. His eyes were bloodshot. His blue shirt was dirty. He was carrying a leather backpack that looked expensive. He was wearing loafers in the middle of summer. Without socks, at least. I wondered if that was uncomfortable. Posey licked him. Again, I was struck by the unfairness of it all. I felt tears well in my eyes.

"I don't know you," Zahid said. "Do I?"

"No," I said with a fast smile. "You don't."

Zahid waited. I could make it easy. I could introduce myself, explain how I'd come into the possession of his poodle. I could ask him to join me.

"My name is Becca," I said.

Zahid's face was blank. It made me wonder about him, as a writer. He should have been able to make the connection all on his own.

"I am Rachel's mother."

"Oh." Zahid laughed, and for a moment he was still at a loss. "Of course. Rachel. Rachel would have a mother." I nodded. Depending on his relationship with my daughter, this could be problematic for him. "You look too young to be her mother."

I would take it. That was one of the ironies about being left for a younger woman. I had come into a style of my own around the time I turned fifty. My arms were toned. I liked all of my clothes, expensive and well made, simple. I had thrown out everything I didn't wear.

"I could be her older sister," I said.

"Yes, exactly." Zahid smiled at me. He was still kneeling down, still petting his dog. "Or a cousin, maybe. Her favorite cousin. You are so pretty," he said, thoughtlessly, maybe because I was older and so my prettiness was a surprise to him.

"I am Becca," I said again.

I did not want to be known to this man as somebody's mother. I did not want to disappear. I was fifty-four. My life was not over. I held out my hand and Zahid took it. He had soft hands. Long fingers.

"Zahid," he said. "But you already know that."

His brow was sweaty. It was late afternoon in early July. I should get him something to drink, but that would be something a mother would do. He could figure it out himself, the fact that he was thirsty. We were at an establishment that sold beverages.

Zahid sat down at my table.

"I can't believe how easy it was to find you," he said.

"I found you."

"Yes," he said. "That's true."

"Did you come for your dog?"

"Well." Zahid paused, and I felt hopeful. He did not know what he had come for. I did not want to let Posey go, and maybe that meant I would have to keep Zahid, too. Two grown-up children for the summer. My own sleepaway camp. That would be fine. I had already begun to clean out Jonathan's office. It could make a nice bedroom. My mind was going too fast. I had drunk all of that iced coffee, had also had a pot of hot coffee in the morning. But it wasn't the coffee. I just wanted to blame my thoughts on the caffeine. I did not want to give up my poodle; it did not seem fair.

Not fair, not fair, I kept thinking. Not fair.

"Yes," Zahid said. "I wanted to see how my girl was doing."

I breathed out air. He had said nothing about taking her home. It was going to be fine.

"Oh, Posey is having a great summer."

"Posey?" Zahid asked.

"Oh," I said, laughing to cover up my mistake. "It's my pet name for her. Is that okay?"

"Sure," he laughed. "That's okay."

Maybe it wasn't okay, but what was he going to say?

"I take her for long walks on the Sound." I felt like there was something else I should say. "She sleeps on my bed," I added, and then realized that of course I should not have said that.

Was this the first time I had talked to a man since Jonathan left me? Was Zahid Azzam even a man? More like a grown-up boy. A Peter Pan. An asshole. An artist. Again, my brain, it had to slow down. Slow down, slow down. My left leg, I realized, was shaking.

"I think Posey is having a better summer than I am," Zahid said.

"She is having a great summer," I said.

I looked at my daughter's professor, the sheen of sweat on his brow, and I caved. This mothering instinct of mine. Maybe it was because I was a teacher. Maybe it was just because I was a human being. "Would you like something to drink? A lemonade. An iced coffee. I'm waiting for Rachel, actually. Is she expecting you?"

I knew she wasn't expecting him. Or I hoped that she wasn't expecting him. I hoped that she wouldn't keep something like that from me.

"No," Zahid said. "She isn't expecting me. I am just back from Pakistan and, well, the trip, it was a lot, and I wanted to see my dog. I didn't want to wait, to go through the proper chains of communication. I just got on a train and then I took an Uber, which I didn't need to, the drive was so short, and here I am."

"And I found you."

"You found me," Zahid said.

Zahid Azzam was a writer. He seemed to understand that this was not any old tossed-off phrase. This was meaningful. We looked into each other's eyes. He had dark brown eyes. My eyes were blue. He had beautiful eyes. Perhaps he thought my eyes were beautiful, too.

Was I kidding myself? Had I become delusional? Was I in

the land of make-believe? How had I dressed this morning? A sundress, my favorite sundress, a dress I wore three times a week. I had gone swimming in the Sound before coming to the café. Had I showered after? Was there still salt water in my hair? I forced myself to remember.

I had showered. I was clean. Sun-kissed, even. I had brushed mascara onto my lashes for my walk into town. I had read somewhere that this was a good thing to do, all the makeup you ever needed. And moisturizer with a strong SPF.

I had found him.

# *Zahid*

I had not had much experience in the suburbs. My writer friends were uniformly disdainful of American suburbs. I had been told repeatedly that they were not places for dark-skinned people. That the owners of big houses were hypocrites. That the food was bad. That the great American suburb was a place where one could die of loneliness. My student, Rachel Klein, lived in a gorgeous house.

Her house was like a dream, really. The outside made it look like a barn. The interior could have been in a magazine. High ceilings, wooden beams running through the center, blond wood floors, tall green plants, a perfect ceramic vase on the kitchen table filled with wildflowers, small blue glass bottles on the windowsill. Wicker porch furniture. A hammock in the yard. A yard, a very big yard. A swimming pool, strangely still covered, the only odd spot in a perfect picture. If I'd saved all of the money I had made on my novel, if I saved all the money I would ever make until the day I died, I would never be able to afford a house like this.

And yet somehow, here I was.

Connecticut.

The absent father was a banker. He was a fool, obviously, for leaving these two women. I had had sex with the girl. My student. This was something I should not have done, I did not want to think about it, but it had also led me here, to this house. Artists' colonies—and I had been to many—had nothing on this house. I made a sudden promise to God that if I was allowed to stay, I would write again: No more excuses. While I had not packed a change of clothes, I had brought my laptop with me.

To Connecticut.

The air felt clean and light. I could smell the sea. On the walk back from town with Rachel and her mother, I saw two baby rabbits on the road.

"Look at the little rabbits!" I exclaimed.

Becca laughed. Rachel smiled shyly at me, then looked away. She pulled her hair out of its ponytail and then she hid her face behind her hair. I was afraid that she was going to misunderstand, that she was going to think that somehow I was there for her. I had made it clear, I hoped, that I was there to check on my dog. Still, I returned Rachel's smile. I did not want to be rude, either. I didn't want to appear as if I was acting strangely. I had seen two old women on the square, looking at me, whispering. I had smiled at them, too.

Rachel's mother, Becca, I liked the name Becca, seemed to like me. She grilled chicken for dinner, cooked on an impressive gas grill out back. She made a salad with cucumbers and tomatoes and fresh mozzarella. Good lettuce. We had corn that had been picked from a farm down the road. It was such delicious corn. It was a meal that could be photographed for a magazine, served outside on beautiful plates. Becca made it seem effortless.

I drank white wine with the meal, even though I had told myself earlier that day, hungover as I had ever been, that I wouldn't drink for a good long time. The wine was too good to refuse.

But conversation proved difficult. And because it was difficult, I felt reluctant to try. I felt it would be safer to keep quiet. I didn't know, really, how Rachel felt about me. What her mother knew. Becca had told me during dinner that she had read Rachel's story, the one she hadn't turned in, and I'd noticed that Rachel kicked her mother underneath the table.

"Ow," Becca said. "That hurt."

There was something about Becca that had appealed to me from the moment I saw her. This was the kind of woman I needed in my life. A beautiful woman with a big, beautiful house. A woman who would walk my dog, who would not want children, who would not expect me to produce another masterpiece. A woman who had been let down by another man. She would not have unrealistic expectations. I could hear Kristi, hissing in my ear, telling me to get off my lazy ass. To get over the self-pity. To get over myself. To find a woman I could treat as an equal. Some feminist nonsense babble. Sometimes, I fucking hated Kristi, always talking into my ear.

I realized they were both looking at me, mother and daughter. The conversation, it seemed, suddenly required that I participate.

"Look," I said. "A firefly."

Fireflies are magic. I smiled. It was a real smile. I felt genuine delight, gazing at this firefly, knowing that I wasn't likely to find one in Brooklyn. It was also a smile that, I knew from experience, could be considered charming. I did not want to upset either of these women. Women, who, as a gender, were so easy to upset. So unforgiving, so much of the time. I was not sure where I was going to sleep that night. When I had boarded a train to Connecticut earlier that day, I hadn't thought that far ahead. Khloe had asked me about my dog and I had taken off, a chicken without a head, to find my dog. Now I had found her.

I couldn't take her back to Brooklyn. Khloe had made that clear. And I could not afford to bounce Khloe from my apartment. I would have to start making calls. Or post something on Facebook. Someone would put us up. There was always someone. I figured I must have a friend on social media with a spare room, friends with country houses. Friends who had left the city and moved to scenic towns on the Hudson. I thought of Aimee, who had an empty beach house in Asbury Park. Professor friends in Cambridge who were always traveling.

And yet, I had never anticipated this house. I had never fallen in love with a house before. The bathroom on the first floor had small green soaps in a crystal bowl, soaps that matched the tiles, small square green tiles. I was a straight man, I was not supposed to care about these things, and yet I did. I had always loved beautiful things.

After an animated greeting, Princess, renamed Posey, barely registered my presence. At dinner, she lay beneath Becca's feet. She had clearly fallen in love with Becca, and I could understand why.

"My dog Posey died in May," Becca told me, watching me watch her with my dog. "She was also a standard poodle.

Somehow, I feel like your dog knows this and she wants to comfort me. What a good girl she is."

I loved Princess, even if I did not always seem like the best dog owner. Owning a dog was a bigger commitment than I had anticipated. I had gotten Princess after my fiancée left me. It was an impulsive decision. I must have known, when I left her with my student, a girl who wore such ratty clothes that somehow I knew she was rich, what a good thing I was doing for my dog.

Look at the yard this dog had. The walks she was taken on. Look at Becca. I felt pleased that I could do something good for her, too, by letting her take care of my dog.

I could be selfish, but I was not a bad person. I worried that my mother thought that I was a bad person, but I had made it in time, I had been with my grandmother when she died.

"I am so sorry your grandmother died," Rachel said.

Like a snap of the fingers, I was back in that room where my Amma died. In her small house, the ceiling fan clicking overhead, making an all-too-insufficient breeze. My grandmother had squeezed my hand so tight that it hurt, and when she let go, she was gone. It was like my mother said: The old woman had waited for me. She had waited for me to die. And what if I had not gone home? Maybe she would still be alive, waiting for me.

"We cannot live forever," I said to Rachel, repeating what my mother had said to me, speaking in my professor voice. I annoyed even myself, imagining the way I sounded. And this idea, that we all had to die, it was not a comfort. I really did think Amma would live forever. No one had ever loved me as uncritically as she had. Amma was not the littlest bit surprised when my book received so much acclaim. "You are a bright star," she had said. She had thought I would train to be a doctor, like so many of the other men in my family. Except I could not pass organic chemistry. I also did not try hard. Writing had come easy to me. And now, that was hard, too.

"But you are glad you went?" Rachel asked. "To Pakistan? Was it good to go home?"

This girl, she wanted something from me with these questions. I did not know what. Maybe for me to stop looking at her mother. I thought I had only stolen one look and that was when Rachel had gone to the refrigerator to get more seltzer. What did Rachel think right now? Did she understand I had come for my dog? I *had* come for my dog. Did she think I wanted her? Rachel Klein was pretty, sure, but I did not want her. She'd been wearing a camp T-shirt and a pair of cutoff shorts when she arrived at the café. She looked like she could be in high school. I felt shame. I had taken candy from the candy jar and I could not put it back.

"It did not feel good to go home," I told her. "I can't say why. I was supposed to stay much longer, another month, but I changed my ticket. Home, Pakistan—it isn't my home anymore. North Carolina is not my home. Brooklyn is fine, but I have a subletter living in my apartment. Which makes me think I don't have a home. I don't know where I belong."

I wondered how much wine I had drunk to be speaking so honestly. Only two glasses. I realized I needed to eat. I cut into my chicken. It was perfectly grilled.

"Is this tarragon?" I asked Becca, and she nodded, pleased, I think. "It is very good," I said.

"This is how I grill my chicken," she said. "Salt, pepper, tarragon and lemon juice."

I'd had no idea that complimenting Becca on her chicken would please her so much. She was holding her wine glass, smiling, as if I could not see her. This mother, beautiful and charming, was not helping the situation. If Becca knew what I had done to her daughter, I would no longer be welcome. I had to be careful not to flirt.

I had not meant any harm. I had not meant anything at all. It had seemed, at the time, as if I was being given a gift. A kindness. I was in need of kindness.

Anyway, what did it mean? Rachel was of the younger generation. A millennial was what they were called. She was hip, she was educated. She was the master of her own body. Girls her age hooked up all the time. Every day. She was in college. She had a summer job. She had this house to come home to. She was fine.

And was I really to blame?

She had kissed me. Not once, not twice. She had unbuttoned my shirt. She had been wet when I entered her.

I wished I had not remembered that.

# *Khloe*

My babysitter was fifteen minutes late. She brought a friend, a younger woman, blond, wearing cat's-eye glasses and a long-sleeved blouse, even though it was ninety degrees.

Jane handed me flowers and a bottle of wine.

I had not told her she could bring a friend.

"Wait," Jane said. "I thought this was a dinner party."

I shook my head.

"Dinner," I said. "I invited you over for dinner."

"Oh gosh," Jane said. "I guess this is awkward then."

The blond friend blushed. She looked aristocratic, like she was from a wealthy family. She was not my type. She had a nose that was thin, straight, sharp. A perfect nose. Maybe it was a plastic surgery nose. She was thin. Her hair was long and shiny. This was who Gwyneth Paltrow aspired to be. Jane was Jane, short and sturdy, mousy brown hair. Maybe it was strange that I was still fixated on her. There were so many good-looking women in Brooklyn. Jane was my type.

"It is awkward," I said. I did not feel the need to smooth things over. "I invited you over for dinner. I may not have enough food."

"Can we come in?" Jane asked. "Make up your mind. We can leave, if you want. Say the word."

"Fuck," I said. "What the hell? Of course. Come in."

"That was not convincing," Jane said.

"Do you want us to take off our shoes?" the blond asked me, still standing in the hallway. It was the weirdest question. Did I look fucking German? Take off your shoes?

"No," I said. "I don't want you to take off your shoes. I would have had to vacuum the floors. Who are you? I don't even know your name. What is your name?"

"Winnie?" the blonde said.

It seemed that I scared her.

"What kind of name is Winnie?" I asked.

"It's short for Winifred," Winnie said. "It's a family name."

"Of course," I said. "No one in my family is a Khloe. My mom thought it was pretty. And fancy-sounding."

"We will leave if you are going to be rude," Jane said.

I sighed.

"Come in already," I said. Winnie looked like she wanted to bolt. Jane was just pissed. I had never been much of a host. "You can keep on your shoes. What do you want to drink? I have beer. I could mix drinks. We could start off with the wine you brought."

"Let's do that," Jane said. She was, at least, used to me. I led them into Zahid's apartment. "It smells good in here. What is that wonderful smell?"

I shook my head. I hadn't cooked anything. It still smelled like the lentils Zahid had cooked the day before. I had eaten them for breakfast and then heated them again when I got back from work, crazy hungry because I had worked through lunch.

Anyway, I was not planning on serving day-old dal. I had bought a ton of food at the gourmet store: a baguette and cheese, fancy salami, olives, quinoa salad, grilled vegetables, marinated artichokes. Expensive and easy. I did not cook. Kristi, of course, cooked. My perfect sister. Fuck her. She had started making jambalaya, dishes with okra, going on about our African American heritage, a grandmother we could not remember from Louisiana.

Jane walked over to the pot and took off the lid.

"Ahh," she said.

"Zahid made the lentils," I said.

Jane actually gasped.

"So is he back? I heard a rumor," Jane said. "I thought he was in Pakistan."

Fucking Zahid Azzam.

That was why Jane had texted me.

I took the bottle of wine, it was a rosé, it felt like everyone was ordering rosé this summer, and I opened it. I found two wine glasses. I was not a wine drinker. There were too many kinds to contemplate, it was too expensive, too ridiculous. Wine. Even this bottle of wine made me angry. Rosé. I needed to get control of the anger in me; it rose so quickly that I felt the need to spit. I swallowed it back down. Jane looked much too excited. This was the first time she had been here. Her eyes darted all over the apartment, scanning the living room, the closet door, the bedroom, there was a glass door that opened up to a teeny tiny yard. Maybe she thought Zahid was magically outside, smoking a cigarette. I had gotten rid of him, fast as I could.

Jane wanted to see the apartment where Zahid Azzam lived. She couldn't believe that I was subletting his apartment. Her publisher had published his first book and was waiting on his second—as if he were the next Salman Rushdie. Maybe Jane thought she would be able to get information out of me. Dinner was a ploy on her part, a way to get her inside.

Jane could keep on fooling herself, because I had no doubt that Jane actually had feelings for me. She was having trouble realizing it. She had placed me into the wrong category. To her, I was still a kid. The girl she had tucked in. Those had been sweet bedtime kisses, lingering. But I knew how I felt, even when I was seven.

And Jane understood.

That was why she brought Winnie.

So, maybe, I would seduce Winnie instead. Why not? She was hot. It would make Jane jealous. It might make her take me seriously. I wouldn't mind being with a girl like Winifred. In fact, I sort of liked the idea. I could hear what Kristi would say: *You are not a nice person, Khloe.*

I didn't know if it was a twin thing, Kristi always talking to me, though she said that that wasn't true for her. I didn't necessarily believe her.

It was a relief that my sister had turned out straight. We had been in competition our whole life, for grades, making sports teams, the attention of our parents, but not—thank fucking God—for lovers. There was nothing alike about us except for the fact that we looked alike, though not as much anymore since I cut my hair. We were also both good at tennis and I beat her at tennis, almost every fucking time. I loved my twin sister but she was a judgmental bitch.

That was something Zahid had said, too, when he first talked to me about subletting his apartment.

"Your sister," he said, "is more judgmental than anyone I know."

But we kept on calling her. Both of us.

I realized that I had already begun to drink the glass of wine I had poured for Winnie. I got another wine glass. I didn't pour Jane her wine. She had pissed me off.

Anyway, I was glad to be drinking what Winnie drank, even if it was a fucking rosé. It tasted like fucking fruit punch. All the guys at work, they would wet their pants for Winnie. Danny Tang, the only guy on the team I could remotely deal with, said none of the guys knew what to do with me. My co-workers were all pricks, literally, but it didn't matter. I was kicking ass at my job.

"I like this wine," I told Winnie.

I don't know why I had thought that tonight would be the night for me and Jane. Why did I think that? I had thought that. I had spent so much money on all that stupid prepared food.

"It's good, isn't it?" Winnie said.

I could tell that my gaze was making her nervous.

"Zahid is in Connecticut," I said. "Checking in on his dog." I poured Jane her wine after all. I was not going to be a total ass. "Let's go sit at the table," I said.

There was a nice round table in Zahid's kitchen. It was a nice apartment. It made sense that he couldn't afford it. I had all the food spread out. Plates. Napkins. A bowl for the olive pits. Classy. I did not understand the necessity of hosting people when there were so many good restaurants. But Jane had wanted to come over and so I'd bought this food. I was angry. I was more angry than the situation warranted. Fuck Jane Aronson, fuck her with a broomstick. That was what I thought. I took another slug of wine and brought the bottle over to the table.

"I am going to serve the lentils, too," I said. "Just for you, Jane. They're from a recipe his grandmother used to make."

I had no idea if this was true. I figured I would give them what they wanted. Winnie's eyes actually lit up. Kristi had told me Zahid was famous in the literary world but I had never heard of him. I also realized this did not actually mean anything.

"Winnie works with me," Jane said.

"I'm a publicist," Winnie said, drinking her wine.

"Are you two a thing?" I asked.

Winnie blushed again.

Jane sighed.

I was sure she already regretted coming over. Fair enough. She had totally fucked up. She shouldn't have brought Winnie. It was like a chess match between us. The question was how long I would be interested in playing. It was not like I would wait forever.

"We work together," Jane said.

"You could still be a thing," I commented.

"We are sort of a thing," Winnie said, shyly. "Only no one knows about us."

"Winnie also has a boyfriend," Jane said.

"Not a boyfriend," Winnie said.

"Someone you have sex with?" I said.

Winnie turned pink. It was adorable.

She would be easy to seduce.

Ridiculously easy. I was like no one else she had been with

before. I felt tired all of a sudden. I had left for work at seven a.m., got home at seven-thirty p.m., bought the food, cracked open a beer to drink with Zahid's lentils, drank another waiting for Jane. Now it was almost nine o'clock. I had work tomorrow.

"This is a very nice apartment," Jane said.

"Fine," I said. "Look at whatever you want, Jane. You can go through his drawers, for all I care."

"Are you serious?" Winnie said.

They wanted to go through his drawers. Read his letters. Maybe they would find a journal. Jesus fucking Christ.

"It's not unethical," I said. "This is my apartment for the next two months. If Zahid Azzam had anything to hide, hopefully he hid it. I seriously doubt you are going to find a drawer with a finished manuscript in it."

"Is he writing?" Jane asked.

I sighed. How the fuck would I know that? I was his tenant. I was sure he didn't have any idea that I was in love with an editor who worked at his publishing house. That his apartment would be open to this kind of scrutiny. But at that moment, I felt less in love with Jane. *You are blowing it,* that is what I wanted to tell Jane, who maybe thought she could bask in my adoration indefinitely.

Winnie did not seem to be aware of any tension in the room. She ate the food that I had bought for Jane. "This is all so delicious," she said. "I really like this cheese."

Winnie, in fact, ate all of the goat cheese.

"Seriously, tell us the scoop, Khloe," Jane said, which told me that she was as stupid as her little friend. She did not know how to read a room. She didn't know how close I was to smashing my empty wine glass. She refilled my wine glass. "Zahid made these lentils. Which, as you said, means he is back from Pakistan. This is big. He has been so erratic lately, we were afraid he wouldn't come back. He has stopped responding to our e-mails. Friendly e-mails. Supportive e-mails."

"He's back," I said. "I bought him shots. Tequila."

"Khloe," Jane said.

"What? I am not his babysitter," I said. "I am his tenant."

"When is he coming back from Connecticut?" Jane asked.

I stared at her. It was as if he owed her money.

"I don't know," I said. "He doesn't keep me informed of his schedule. I am not sure I would tell you anyway."

"Is he coming back here anytime soon?"

"Jane," Winnie said. "Ease off."

"But he has to come back," Jane said. She was not easing off.

"I have this place rented through August," I said. "So I would guess September. I'm apartment hunting, if you hear of anything."

"All right," Winnie said. "What neighborhood are you interested in?"

"He's not coming back before then?" Jane asked.

"Of course not," I said. "I am renting the apartment. He actually wanted to stay here. He wanted me to keep paying rent while he slept on the couch."

"And you told him no?" Jane asked.

The distress on her face was real.

"Don't you care about literature?"

It was such an odd question. "I actually don't give a shit about literature," I said. "I work in finance. Sometimes, I guess, I need a good book to take to the beach, but then again, honestly, I don't end up reading it."

"Zahid's editor took a job at another publishing house,"

Winnie explained to me. "She can't take Zahid with her, and so Zahid is officially now one of Jane's writers. It's a big honor. It's a really big deal."

"No one else wanted him," Jane said. "This could be the end of my career. If he doesn't produce."

"So we have come to the truth," I said. "This is a work dinner."

Jane shook her head. "You know that isn't true, Khloe. We have been meaning to get together."

Jane grimaced. Maybe she knew that it had come out all wrong. I didn't want her to think I was pining for her, even if I was pining for her. I had been pining and pining for her. And now this. I could feel something shifting. I had followed her to Brooklyn, I had found an apartment blocks away from where she lived, but it turned out, I genuinely liked it here. This was where I belonged. I was surprised by the tears in my eyes. I blinked them away.

Winnie smiled at me, concern in her eyes.

She seemed to understand that something had happened.

Winnie had a girlfriend. She had a boyfriend. Why not add another person to the mix?

"You are nice," I told Winnie.

"Thank you," Winnie said.

I poured the rest of the bottle of wine into her glass. No more for Jane. I looked at her and shrugged. I did not think I would be taking her out for drinks anymore.

"Anyway," I said. "I am sad to report that your author is a motherfucking mess. The other night, he had way too much to drink and he puked all over this apartment. He has no money. I wouldn't expect much from him. I wouldn't be surprised if it was a fast downward trajectory."

"How would you know?" Jane asked.

"I am telling you what I have witnessed. That is why you came here," I said. "To find out what I know. Obviously, I know more than you do."

Winnie looked worried. She was one of those types who could not bear conflict. Kristi was like that. She was always trying to make everything better.

"Do you know how Jane and I met?" I asked Winnie.

She didn't. Jane shifted in her seat. I did not think I was drunk. Two glasses of wine. Two beers. That was a regular day after work.

"Jane was my babysitter," I said.

"Seriously?"

"In Minnesota. I was five years old when she started taking care of me."

"She never told me that," Winnie said. "That is adorable. And now you are all grown up."

"Hard to believe," Jane said.

"No, it's not," I said. "Everyone grows up at some point."

What was the point? I wanted that out there. I was mad, again. Jane had said that they were seeing each other. Winnie was too pretty. I realized I was in competition with Winnie. I was confused. I was a little bit drunk after all. I had found a love poem Zahid had written in a drawer on the bedside table, a poem torn in two. I had taped it together. Kristi had said it was probably to the fiancée who dumped him. I wondered if Jane would want to read that. That would probably put me right back in her favor.

Winnie wanted ice cream.

There was a gelato place nearby.

I was grateful.

It got us out of Zahid's apartment. We walked down the block, a cool breeze in the air. Jane was holding Winnie's hand. I could not bear to have Jane angry at me. This was what Jane still did not understand about me, what I was realizing about myself. I could play the long game. It would never work with Winnie. Winnie was a kid. She was experimenting. I took Winnie's other hand and that made her grin, just like a little kid. She swung both of her arms, as if we were her parents, and we lifted her up into the air. Jane and I smiled at each other, and in that moment, I understood that everything was still possible. It was magic.

# *Rachel*

My professor accepted a bottom sheet and a comforter. Zahid Azzam. He was in my house. I could say his name out loud. He was going to sleep in my father's office. I had never seen this coming. We could sleep with each other again. I felt like my skin was on fire. I kept looking at him, looking away.

He was wearing the same blue shirt.

My mother has already begun to clear the room out. She had told me that maybe it was going to be her new painting studio. She already had a painting studio, a beautiful room on the first floor that looked out onto the lawn, but she said my father's office got better light.

Really, she just wanted to take over his room. She wanted to let my father know that he was not welcome to come back. My mother had told me that she was fine about his leaving. I had found out via e-mail, which seemed cowardly, on both of their parts, but it had been easier for me, too. Then they came to the college to take me out for brunch, and I wished that they hadn't. They fought the entire time.

Anyway, I was not sure she was fine.

I did not think she would want my professor sleeping in our house if she was fine. I did not think she would want my writing professor sleeping in our house if she knew what had happened between us. But she didn't suspect anything. If anything, she probably thought I was still a virgin. That night at dinner, she had looked at me affectionately, as if I were still a child. She had told my professor what a good writer I was, probably aware of how mortifying that was. Why would she do that to me? I had the perverse desire to tell her everything. I had a strange feeling that my mother was flirting with him. Worse, I felt like he was flirting with her. He was being charitable, obviously, but I wanted to warn him. My mother was vulnerable. She could misunderstand. We were all lobbying for the affection of Princess.

It was weird.

My mother won the contest over the dog. Once the food was brought to the table, the dog attached herself to my mother's legs. We had only had Princess for about two weeks but I had this strange feeling we might end up keeping her. I actually felt bad for my professor. All year long, I had watched him with his dog. Walking her on campus. Going to office hours, Princess asleep on the couch where students were supposed to sit. I had not meant to steal his dog.

I was glad I had stolen his dog.

I had not meant to sleep with him.

I had no idea what I was doing.

Now it was almost eleven, and they had both been drinking. My mother would not let me drink, which was ridiculous. By the end of dinner, I had become annoyed by their conversation. He had mysteriously become one of the adults, one of my mother's friends, and I was fidgety and started looking at my phone, which was something my mother hated, but I would not leave the table, because I would not leave them alone. I stared at his long fingers, holding the stem of his wine glass, and I blushed. I had kissed those fingers. They had cupped the back of my ass, gone inside me. I wondered how and when I could get him alone again. My professor said something about taking the train home.

"You will do no such thing," my mother said.

I watched this happen. Suddenly, I became vigilant, wondering where she would put him. My father's study actually made the most sense, with a couch that turned into a bed. Could I sneak into his room? Would he sneak into mine? I had no idea what would happen tonight. The next day. I would have to wake up early and go to camp. It was a job, but still: Go to camp. I hated the way it sounded. Like I was a little kid.

Would he be gone when I got back?

Back to New York, taking Princess with him?

Maybe he would stay.

His hair had gotten longer.

It had been only two weeks since the last time I saw him. All through dinner, he almost compulsively pushed the hair out of his eyes. I could imagine my mother giving him a haircut. I had a flashback of her cutting my bangs when I was a child. Having me sit on the kitchen table and getting out her sharp scissors, trimming my bangs. It never came out right, always a little bit crooked, choppy, somehow uneven, wrong, until I finally revolted, refused to ever let her cut my hair again, and I had not had bangs since then.

My mother gave Zahid a pair of my father's pajama bottoms

and a plain white T-shirt to sleep in. I found this reassuring. She was behaving like a mother, like the elementary school teacher that she was, and that was how my professor would see her. I did not want my life to become a Lifetime movie.

My professor. My lover. Zahid Azzam. Sleeping in my house. I would start calling him by his name. I had assumed it was all over, but maybe it wasn't. He was sleeping down the hall. He liked me, I knew that he did, he had to, even if he had shown no signs over dinner. Of course he hadn't. We were with my mother.

He wanted what he wanted and what he wanted was me.

I could not sleep, tossing and turning, waiting for a knock on my door.


He was still asleep when I woke up for camp the next day. Zahid. I hesitated in front of his closed door. Maybe he had been waiting for me to come into his room. That must have been it. I had made the first move before. We had a pattern. A history, even. Now I felt awkward, going downstairs in my clothes. A red camp T-shirt. Shorts. Sandals. Could I make that sexy somehow? I couldn't. The shorts were short, but still.

I didn't wear sexy clothes, anyway. That wasn't me. I was relieved that it was just my mother in the kitchen. There was a fresh pot of coffee. She had cut me a grapefruit.

"Do you want avocado toast?" she asked, kissing me on top of my head.

Of course, I wanted avocado toast.

It was good coffee. This was nothing new. This was not for Zahid. Everything was nice in my mother's house. She bought expensive coffee beans, ground them herself. My mother served me my breakfast. She liked to joke that she was the best restaurant in town.

"Best restaurant in town," she said now.

I groaned.

"So what do you think?" she asked.

"Of what?" I said. I knew what she was asking me. "You mean the strange man upstairs?"

My mother sat down with her coffee. She laughed. She seemed pleased about the man upstairs. My mother. I had no idea what was really going on inside her head.

"How do you feel about him staying here?" she asked.

"Do you mean for more than one night?"

"I do."

I nodded, pretending to consider the idea. I had already resigned myself to having the most boring summer in the history of summers. Now my writing professor was here. In my house. I thought about Zahid, sleeping down the hall, his hairless chest. Maybe, fingers crossed, soon he would be sleeping with me again, back in my bed. I could not really believe it.

"Are you serious?"

Luckily, my mother was in motion again. She did not notice anything. She was refilling Princess's water bowl. The toast popped and she was mashing avocado and then smoothing them onto the bread.

"The truth is," she said, "I am not ready to let go of this poodle."

"I'm sorry, Mom," I said.

"Yeah." My mother sighed. "It was too soon."

I looked at Princess, drinking from Posey's old water bowl.

If I were my writing professor, I would get my dog away from my mother as fast as I could.

"You heard him. He has a subletter staying in his apartment," my mother said. "I don't think he has anywhere to go."

"So?" I said.

It was so strange. My mother lobbying for Zahid to stay. I knew from Twitter that his life was a mess. It would be stupid for so many reasons to get mixed up in his problems. This was completely obvious to me. But, of course, I wanted him to stay. He had told me that I was beautiful. When I was naked, he had said it again. Beautiful. Me. My mother wanted him to stay. I would go to him, sneak quietly under the covers.

"I'm just surprised," I said.

"Honestly," my mother said, "so am I."

She handed me a plate with two pieces of perfect avocado toast and then took one for herself.

"Hey," I said.

"Hey what?" my mother said. "Half of this is for me."

"The tip is going down," I said.

"Ha," she said.

I had one friend at college whose parents made her pay for her own groceries. She paid for groceries and tuition and housing. She was on financial aid, worked two jobs and was always studying. I understood that I was lucky.

"You really want him to stay?" I said.

It felt important to act as if I did not care.

"Let's just see how it goes," she said. "Day by day. He might also say no. It's just an idea."

I nodded.

It was more than a little bit surreal. I remembered them

at dinner. They had been talking about a French movie I had never seen. They had talked on and on about New Wave cinema while I checked Instagram on my phone. My writing professor might be staying with us. Zahid Azzam. I blushed again. The thought popped into my mind that my mother and I were in competition. It was a ridiculous idea. She was a million years old. She could have the dog.

# *Becca*

Zahid was grateful.

He kept on thanking me.

Thanking me for every little thing, as if any minute I would kick him out. He was incredibly polite. He put all of his cups into the dishwasher. He had been at the house for a couple of days when he asked me if I might like for him to open the swimming pool.

"You know how to do that?"

"Lifeguard," he said. "Pool man. It's my sideline. Every writer needs a sideline."

"I thought it was teaching," I said.

"That, too."

I laughed. It was pleasant in the house, when Rachel was away at camp. Zahid borrowed the car, shopped for chemicals in the next town over. I had given him money for chlorine, shock, whatever he needed. He opened the swimming pool.

"Amazing," Rachel said, when she came home from day camp. The water was blue and sparkling. I watched, curious, when she showed up at the pool wearing a tiny bikini. Rachel was not the type to wear a bikini. Within minutes, she had covered herself with a T-shirt.

Zahid had set up his laptop computer on Jonathan's desk. He was writing. Downstairs, I painted. We would take breaks. At lunch, he would tell me how many words he had written. The numbers did not mean anything to me, but I understood the significance of what he was sharing with me. I would show him what I had painted. We would take Posey on long walks, down on the Sound. We would eat turkey sandwiches together. "This is my very favorite lunch," he said. "Thank you."

It was as if I had made him something fancy.

He seemed nothing like the man in the author photo, the oh-so-serious man in a suit who had written such an inscrutable award-winning novel. I had not particularly liked it, struggling to get through, but now I wanted to read it again.

I drove to a neighboring town where there was a bookstore. His book was not in stock. This seemed like a sad thing. I ordered a copy. On impulse, I went into the J.Crew next door. I bought him a bathing suit. It was on sale.

"Thank you," Zahid said when I gave it to him. "Thank you so much."

It was selfish, really. I found it discomfiting to see him in Jonathan's bathing suit. Zahid had gone back to New York and returned with a small suitcase, but he seemed to wear the same clothes over and over again.

"This is so incredibly generous," he said, gazing at his new bathing suit. Somehow, the comment hit me the wrong way.

"It was twenty-two dollars on sale," I said. "You can pay me back if you want."

Zahid went upstairs. He returned with a twenty-dollar bill and eight quarters.

I laughed.

I also took the money.

It was fine. All of it. The bathing suit, the companionship, the distraction he provided over the summer. He was almost as good as his dog, and that was saying a lot. I was attracted to my daughter's writing professor, but I didn't see what was the harm of it. My husband had left me. My daughter was too young for him, though she clearly had a crush. He was a beautiful man. He had slender fingers, eyelashes too long for a man. He had long limbs, dark eyes. I had been married for such a long time.

I found that I was thinking about him, all the time. Christ, I had bought him a bathing suit. He went into the bathroom and he put it on.

He looked good. The suit was dark purple. Trunks. They really had been on sale.

"Got to get my money's worth," he said.

It was a terrible joke.

"Terrible joke," he said.

Which was weird, this man speaking my thoughts out loud, only with a slight English accent.

"Join me at the pool?" he asked.

I nodded. I would join him at the pool. I went upstairs to change into my new bathing suit. I had bought one for myself as well. It was also purple. A bikini. Boy shorts and a midriff top that covered most of my stomach but left my belly button exposed. We matched. It was a little bit ridiculous. I had bought one for Rachel, too. A one-piece.

---

At the pool, Zahid thanked me again.

"For what?" I said.

"For letting me stay here."

I did not respond. If he thanked me one more time, I would have to ask him to leave. Instead, I dove into the water. I looked good in my new suit. I was glad about this. Posey started to bark. I swam the entire length of the pool. Underwater, I could still hear Posey barking. She was worried about me. I touched the wall and swam back. *Bark, bark, bark, bark.*

I swam the length of the pool three times in a row without taking a breath. I swam until I was completely out of air. I had been on a swim team, once upon a time. Zahid was looking at me when I emerged for air. He whistled. I wanted to thank him, but I refrained.

# *Jonathan*

I woke up with the chills. I was sweating. For the first time since I'd left my wife, I wished that I were home. Becca would take my temperature. Becca would put a cold washcloth on my forehead. She might not go so far as to make me chicken soup, but she would certainly go to my favorite deli in town and buy my favorite chicken soup. If anything, I missed my butcher. I missed my gas grill. I missed my swimming pool. I missed being taken care of. What was the saying? It was too late to teach a dog new tricks.

I thought I would be an exception to this rule.

Mandy had flown to Houston the night before. From there, she would go on to Los Angeles and then Hawaii. She was going to spend a couple of days in Hawaii and then take the trip back in reverse.

"A pilot's life," she said.

It was a nice one. I missed Mandy when she was gone. It was so wonderful, wanting a woman, counting the days until she got back. There was absolutely nothing wrong with Rebecca. She was a beautiful woman. She took yoga classes and took care of the house. But she had been practically invisible to me for years. She talked to me about book reviews in *The New York Times* or her day at the elementary school and my eyes glazed over. It was right after I had left that the boy came into her classroom with the gun. Becca shrugged it off, but I should have been there for her.

She had been terrific on television. She looked good, she was articulate. "I got lucky," she said, but clearly that wasn't true. She was good in a crisis. She had poise.

"I am fine," she said, not bothering to hide her irritation when I called. She did not want to go to dinner. She did not want to see me. It was painful. I had to remind myself that I had left her.

I had already made my choice. Mandy was fun. Mandy adored me. She had those bangs. Those perky breasts. The uniform. My fever had to be high. I had a horrible headache. I could not find any ibuprofen. I downed two Motrin instead.

I texted Mandy. I asked her if she had a thermometer. I wanted her to know, I supposed, that I was not feeling well.

As a rule, I did not get sick. I played tennis. I swam laps. I was, as my best friend and personal physician told me, vigorously healthy. I would not be sick today.

I got out of bed and lost my balance. I was dizzy. I was definitely sick. I made it to the bathroom and I sat down on the toilet to take a piss. This was not me. Something felt wrong, disturbingly. I had a red sore on my dick.

"Mandy," I bellowed, my voice carrying into the empty loft. "What the fuck?"

———

I had some things to take care of at the office, an allocations report to turn in, a deal almost ready to close. I called Khloe. I asked her if she could take care of these things for me.

"Um, Jonathan," she said. "You know that I am not your administrative assistant?"

I almost hung up the phone. I was giving this girl a shot and she wanted to piss it away with college feminism. Things had certainly changed at the office. It was this brave new world, where you had to be careful about every little thing that you did or said. Blink at a pretty intern and it was sexual harassment. My own daughter thought I was racist because I'd told her Khloe was black. What the hell? I had a sore on my penis. A sore on my penis.

"No, you idiot." The insult slipped out. I had a fever. I did not have time to be polite. I was her boss, for Christ's sake. "I know you are not my admin, I have a very good one, thank you very much. You are my best junior analyst and I am entrusting you with some important tasks. You want me to ask Baxter, say the word. I will hang up right now."

That shut her up.

I told her what needed to get done. I hung up before she could thank me.

Women, I thought contemptuously.


I called a car to take me to Connecticut.

My doctor would see me. I had been seeing him for twenty years. Michael was also my closest and perhaps only friend. I was not much for having friends.

———

Mandy returned my text.

Poor sweetie. Get a therm at Duane Reade. XOXOXOXO
Feel better! No reception. Will call from Cali. ☺👍☺☺

Therm. Cali. I hated her insipid abbreviations. Emojis. What
was I doing with this woman? Was it that I could walk to my
office from her apartment? I marveled at her proximity to
my office. Why did I get such a kick out of that? I had always
liked my commute. The quiet on the train. I would stare out
the window and look at the landscape passing by.

Michael took my temperature. It was 101. Not too high, but
definitely a fever. "You are not dying," he said with a laugh.

And then I told him about the sore on my penis. He took a
swab test, which was uncomfortable, to say the least.

I wondered if my tennis partner would be able to treat me
without judgment. Becca and I had shared so many enjoyable
dinners at his home, Michael and Trudy, and I had gone and
ruined all that. His son, Aaron, was the same age as Rachel.
He was close by, studying at Yale. I used to have this fantasy
Aaron would marry Rachel. They had gone on a date once, but
apparently it had not gone well. I could not get details from
my daughter. For now, the wedding was on hold. I had not
given up hope.

"Diagnosis?" I asked Michael.

"I'll need to get this back from the lab to confirm, but what
it is, I can tell you right now."

It was going to be herpes or prostate cancer. Left and right,
all around me, men my age were getting prostate cancer. I was

too old to get a venereal disease. I was a married man. Except I wasn't married. I wasn't divorced yet, either. I was a married man. "Please don't tell me I have cancer."

Michael laughed. "Nope, nothing that bad. You're not going to like it, but it's nothing. A classic case of good old herpes. I'll prescribe you some antivirals, give you some literature to read. You'll feel better in a couple of days. You might have future outbreaks, and then, you know, you have to refrain from sexual activity. This might be a one-and-only case. You absolutely must not have sex during an outbreak, but I don't need to tell you that."

"Herpes," I said. I couldn't say that I felt good about this.

"What can I tell you?" he said. "You old dog. You'll have to tell Rebecca, you know that?"

"I left Rebecca," I said. "You didn't know."

I had wondered what the local gossip was. It didn't seem like Rebecca would smear my name, but I had never thought that I would leave her.

Michael sighed. "I had heard something to that effect, but I had hoped it wasn't true."

"True story," I said.

"For the woman who did this to you," Michael asked.

"Indeed."

"I'm sorry to hear that."

"So am I."


I had my driver take me to the Sound. I wasn't in any condition to be out in the world, but I wanted to look at the water. I just wanted to sit on the bench in the parking lot, looking out at the sand and the water. I wanted to breathe in the salty air and feel sorry for myself.

Instead, there was my wife. She was walking a dog, a standard poodle I had never seen before, and she was with a man, a man I had never seen before, either, an Indian man, significantly younger, with ridiculous hair. My wife said something and the man leaned back and laughed.

# *Zahid*

"Don't even think about it," Kristi said.

Of course, I was thinking about it.

"I will kill you," Kristi said. "I will get on an airplane and then drive to the front door and kill you. You shouldn't be in that house to begin with."

"Can you imagine the fallout?" I asked with a laugh.

"When the daughter you slept with finds out you are sleeping with her mother?"

"Correction. I am not sleeping with her," I said. "Nothing like that. I just like her. That is not a crime."

I had this strange compulsion to tell Kristi Taylor everything and then regretted it, immediately. Nothing ever happened in Kristi's life. She was writing, always writing, but she lived in a completely imaginary world. Nothing was from her experience, because she never went out. Yet she had written a novel, published by an indie press, about a little girl and her babysitter, molestation and regret and had even managed to throw September 11 in there, and while not many people had read it, she'd won a major literary prize. She had also been put on a list, writers under thirty-five to watch out for. Like me, she had been anointed.

We would have been a perfect literary couple, we would have been gorgeous together, and I had let her know, years ago, after my breakup, that I could be interested, but Kristi said I was full of shit. She said she pitied any woman who got involved with me. She had actually written to my fiancée to tell her she had done the right thing in breaking it off with me. I should have ended our friendship then, but I didn't. I couldn't. I was more than interested. I was a little bit in love, but was smart enough, at least, not to let her know.

Last year, Kristi had left New York and gone back to school for a degree she did not need. She said it was too distracting and too expensive to be a writer in New York, that she was always going to an event, shopping for clothes to wear to events, going out for drinks. Her dissertation, she said, would be her next novel. She would not tell me what it was about. I was afraid that she was writing about me. According to her twin sister, Kristi's first novel had been about her. I had had no idea. The girl in the book was a twin whose sister had died.

There was something horrible about **that.**

I had vowed to stop calling her, giving her new material, but Kristi was always happy to hear from me. Every time I called, she answered the phone, saying my name with unmistakable delight. It was intoxicating. Somehow, Kristi never got tired of me.

"I can write here," I told her now. Kristi, for a change, had called me. "For the first time in a long time."

"In some rich white woman's house in Connecticut?" she said.

"Yes," I said. "Exactly."

"How long do you think this situation can last?"

"Obviously, it can't. I am writing against the clock. I think that helps. All the pressure."

It did. I woke up, I told her, and I started writing like I was on fire. It had been six days in a row. It felt like I was on speed. In fact, I was on speed, though only for the last couple of days. I had found some diet pills, pills prescribed eighteen years ago, all the way in the back of a drawer in the bathroom. There weren't many left, but clearly they still had kick. I worried what would happen when I ran out—there were only eight more. Obviously, I would be fine when I ran out. You could not get addicted on just a handful of pills. For now, they gave me the jolt that I needed. A good old-fashioned jump start. I had begun something new, that was what mattered, and I could keep going when I was out of pills. I had written my first novel flying on cocaine. I was not a cocaine addict, either. It was another skill I had, recreational drug use.

"Can you let me talk?" Kristi said.

"Of course," I said. "I always let you talk."

I wondered if that was true. Sometimes, my mind would wander when Kristi told me about the details of her life. What I liked was that she was such a good listener.

"The reason I called," Kristi said, "was not to hear about your love life."

It had been a surprise, Kristi calling me. I had felt good about that, a little bit triumphant.

"I don't have a love life," I said. "It's just a tiny crush. It's nothing."

I had told Kristi about Princess and Becca and our walk on

the beach, about throwing the tennis ball, the breeze in the late afternoon, how sometimes we even picked Rachel up from day camp, how pleasant it all was. Kristi had turned it into something tawdry. I was glad I hadn't told her about my purple bathing trunks. I'd been surprised when Becca had taken my money. Even the quarters.

"The reason I called," Kristi repeated, "is because a position is opening up in the fall. A one-year visiting writer. One of the professors here is pregnant and she just got put on bed rest. They need to hire someone fast."

"Seriously?"

"They're looking to fill their diversity slot," Kristi said.

"They always are."

"I already told them about you. They seem keen."

"Starting this fall?"

"This fall."

"They are interested in me?"

It always happened. Whenever the bottom dropped out, something new came along. It was enough to almost make me believe. My mother, of course, would love for me to believe, but this was not what she meant. Religion was not meant to be self-serving. She had given up on certain things a long time ago, and that was a relief. I just did not want her to give up on me.

"Honestly, the job is yours. E-mail me your CV and your teaching-philosophy statement. I can proofread it for you if you need me to. It's fantastic you are working on a new book. Write a few lines about that. They will love that. I think they might want to fly you out for an interview in the next couple of days."

"I have to interview?"

"Zahid," Kristi said. "It's a great job. I can think of six other writers off the top of my head who would take it. You might have to do a little tap dance, okay?"

This pissed me off for some reason. Kristi thought I didn't work. I had just spent two years at that overrated liberal arts school on the Hudson. I'd taught a class at the New School. Had written book reviews for *The New York Times* and the *L.A. Times*. I worked hard. The things that came to me, I deserved them. I had earned them. I had written a great book, an important book.

"You sister is a bitch," I said. I wondered why I was switching the subject. It felt necessary, somehow, to get that out there, even if it wasn't entirely fair. Honestly, I understood how Khloe felt. She had paid for my apartment. Why would she want me on her couch? I had liked her up until then.

"I know. I know she is." Kristi sighed. "I think Khloe was born without a heart. Or I got her heart and she got a piece of my brain, the part that can do math."

"The part that handles finances."

"That part."

"I don't think she will ever let me back into my apartment. She scares me."

"Perfect," Kristi said. "She can keep your sublet when you come to Iowa. We will have the best time, Zahid. I can't wait. It is so milk-toast white here. It is so boring. I need you."

I felt sad. Iowa. I would have to go there and put my teaching face back on. Kristi loved her students. I was bored by them. They tried so hard, they had so little talent, they wanted so much praise. I had only had one good student during my last semester. It was Rachel. I had put some edits on her work, and she'd shut down completely. She did not submit her final story, like the child that she was. And what did I do? I fucked her. I had not meant to. I had never considered her that way; she was my student. It was just that day, something was off in me, the semester was over and I slipped. I knew that it was wrong. She was just so pretty. So pretty and so very willing. She had made it so easy.

And now, now I preferred her mother. A grown woman with a big house. There was something wrong with me. I would go to Iowa. It made me sad to know that I would have to leave Connecticut one day soon. To me, this place was like paradise.

I would be leaving paradise.

Paradise Lost.

Now, that was a famous book. I had to go to Iowa. Just the thought of it made me want to cry.

# *Becca*

We started swimming laps in the afternoon. After Zahid wrote. After I painted. After lunch. Most of the time, I made us turkey sandwiches with avocado. The pool looked better than it ever had. The water sparkled, rays of light rippling across the sparkling blue water. We swam for half an hour. I swam without stopping, crawl, breaststroke, backstroke, the occasional butterfly to show off. Zahid took a lot of breaks. Zahid was thin but not muscular. He did not have any kind of regular exercise in his life. I gave him a hard time about that.

"How do you stay so thin?"

"Smoking," he said.

Fortunately, Zahid was not a regular smoker. I had only seen him smoke a few times, usually after getting off the phone.

"Sometimes I forget to eat," Zahid said.

That made more sense to me. Not forgetting to eat, because I never forgot to eat, but that Zahid did. Zahid Azzam was absentminded. He would come out to the pool and realize that he hadn't changed into his bathing suit. Then he would go back inside. He would forget his goggles. He would go inside to get his goggles and check his e-mail and come back outside to swim and realize that, yes, he had forgotten once again to bring his goggles. He would come back out with a book to read instead. I would tell him we had to do laps first.

I did not feel comfortable having him watch me swim laps. It was better to also have him in the pool. The pool was such a gift. And now, I had rediscovered swimming, as if it was brand-new.

I had been a yoga person during the rest of the year, but I had gotten burned out. Too much stretching, tranquillity, peace of mind. Several classes a week. Hot yoga, regular yoga. I had perfected my handstand. It was easy enough to do.

I was on autopilot when it came to teaching. It was not that I was a bad teacher, but I had been doing it for so long that I had five different years' worth of lesson plans to rotate, and I would throw in a new book, of course, or make the kids do a project on current events when it occurred to me. I had my third graders free-writing about the election. The girls had wanted a woman president. I educated the pink-cheeked boys who said they were happy about Trump. I had to set them straight, as carefully as possible, to avoid confrontations with parents. Children, for the most part, are good. They repeat back what is taught to them, and I was grateful for the chance to reprogram young minds.

I was not a bad teacher. I was a good one, but not a great one. It was a small school, a small town, easy kids, except for the Republicans, their entitled offspring. There was nothing to remark about until the Theo Thornton incident.

"All in a day's work," I had joked on the *Today* show.

I wonder that I'd had the presence of mind to make a joke.

It was live TV. But I wasn't a hero, whatever that was. No one had died. No one had even gotten hurt. It was real, of course. Theo Thornton threatened to kill me and my classroom full of third graders. I had all of my kids hide in the supply closet while I talked him down, a very large gun pointing at me the entire time, but he wanted to be talked down. He lay the gun on a desk. He said that he was sorry.

I ended up hugging the boy. I did not want to let him go. He was never going to be all right. Theo had been a terrible student, unable to concentrate, always interrupting me, hitting other kids, kissing the girls and literally making them cry. He was terrible at math and reading and spelling and basically every subject. I was the one who had figured out that he was dyslexic, got him into a special education program. Obviously, he had only gotten worse in the years out of my classroom. Had turned into a public menace. A potential killer of children. Still, that day, when he put down the gun, I hugged him and held him tight. The police had to break us apart.

I wasn't surprised when his parents sent the boy away, a boarding school for troubled children in New Hampshire, and I found that I increased my yoga dramatically after that. I started taking four classes a week. Five. Six. Yoga was like a drug. Empty your mind, improve your body. It is amazing how strong you can become in just a couple of months. Sometimes, demons would sneak in during relaxation: a memory of Posey lying at my feet, the joy I felt, scratching her beneath her chin; Theo telling me that only killing people would make him happy; Jonathan calmly explaining to me that everything was my fault. All I had to do was go to Paris. How hard was that? An entire yoga class would be ruined by the thoughts in my head. Still, I went to yoga. As if it were my job.

Then, this June, the school year over, the manager at my yoga studio asked me if I wanted to teach a class for elders during the summer.

For elders.

I politely declined.

I pretended to have forgotten something and left. I did not even take a class that day.

Something in me snapped.

My obsession with yoga. I was fifty-four. I could do a terrific handstand. I looked great, better than I ever had. I was certainly not an elder. I did not need dark thoughts let out when I wanted my mind to be empty and clean. I did not renew my monthly pass. I stopped going, cold turkey. I got e-mails and then phone calls, asking what had happened, begging me to come back. I could be petty.

It was the only yoga studio in our town. I could drive to the next town, ten minutes away. Instead, I found a young and pretty yoga teacher on the Internet. She was the first person who came up on my Google search. She was popular. Her name was Adriene, and I gathered from her videos that she lived in Austin, Texas. She had had a small part in a Richard Linklater movie. I liked her. She made a pot joke by mistake while doing a crow pose and laughed at herself. I did *Yoga with Adriene* every day, and then Zahid opened the pool and we started swimming.

"I want you to teach me how to do one of those flip turns," he said on the fourth day of our private swim club. We were wearing our purple J.Crew bathing suits. I was the faster swimmer. After the humiliation of the yoga studio, the humiliation of Jonathan leaving me for a much younger woman, after the loss of my dog, the best dog I had ever had, it seemed like this was what I needed. I needed a younger man. I needed this even more than another poodle.

I showed Zahid how to flip over right before reaching the end of the pool. "And then you kick off the wall with your legs," I said. "It's easy."

Zahid flipped too soon, every time, too far away from the edge to push off. He had trouble with the flip turn, but he had a slow, lovely stroke. It was as if he were gliding through the water. There was no splash when his arms cut through the surface. The water remained still.

I demonstrated for him, four flip turns at the edge of the pool, and he stood in the water, watching.

"It's genius," he said. "What a body can do."

It was unnerving, having him watch me like that.

It was funny to think of my daughter, off at work. She came home from camp and told me stories about her day, paint on her clothes, a girl in her group who attached herself to Rachel's leg every day, pretending to be mud. I had heard that Theo Thornton's younger sister, Amelia, was going to this day camp, a first grader, but I did not say anything to my daughter about it. I felt bad for the little girl, born into a family like that. I had seen her at school, she was a cutie, she wore her hair in braids, and I did not see why she should be treated different at day camp. I was glad my daughter would be kind to her.

Rachel got up, got dressed and went to work, while Zahid and I spent all this time together. She didn't ask what we did during the day, but she did not know what to make of us at dinner. She tried flirting with Zahid, but he was never anything but appropriate. She came to the table once wearing a tiny tank that exposed her belly button, red lipstick and dangling earrings, and we pretended not to notice. She had begun to leave the table before we were done.

"You don't have to help her with the dishes," she had said to Zahid. "Let's go for a walk. A swim. Do you want to?"

Zahid did not want to. He stayed and he helped.

Rachel became bratty before my eyes.

It was painful.

I also understood her heartbreak.

She stopped watching TV in the living room. She watched shows on her laptop in her room instead, door closed, headphones on. Rachel didn't like my friendship with her writing professor and she did not like how his dog was attached to me.

I didn't like it that Rachel was unhappy, of course. I wished that she were having a better summer, I wished her friends could have been home, I wished she had a boyfriend, a boy her age, young and uncomplicated, and yet, I was not unhappy. For her sake, I pretended to enjoy Zahid's company less than I truly did. I even thought about telling him to sometimes have his dinners somewhere else, but then, I never did. I did not want to. I had gotten used to his gratitude, to his attention, to his company. One night, he cooked us dinner, the best lentils I had ever had, and a cucumber raita. I was impressed. For some reason, I was surprised to discover him competent at basic things: cooking a meal or balancing the pH of the swimming pool.

I felt that if we tried, I could teach him the flip turn, but part of me was glad that his progress was slow.

"Swim," I told Zahid.

I let myself touch his back when it was time for him to flip. That was all that it took. That touch. Something clicked.

Zahid was positioned at the right place in the pool. His legs touched the back wall and he glided over. I was pleased. I was a teacher, a good teacher. I could have taught a wonderful yoga class. I knew that. He stopped swimming after the flip, turning to me for praise. We were inches away from each other.

"That was easy," he said, with a big happy smile. "All my life, I thought I wasn't capable of a flip turn."

"And it's easy."

We were both grinning.

It was easy, in the pool, to put my hands on his waist. A Tuesday afternoon.

"Try it again," I said, turning him back to the edge of the pool.

He tried it again. He did a perfect flip turn.

I grinned at Zahid. He grinned back at me. Easy. We were in a beautiful swimming pool on a beautiful summer day. Not a cloud in the sky. We were wearing matching purple bathing suits; we were beautiful. I wiped a drop of water from his cheek. I pushed the wet hair off his eyes. He pushed his goggles up onto the top of his head. He had such beautiful brown eyes, such long lashes. His features were distinct, sculpted, as if he should have been a woman.

"You did a beautiful flip turn, Zahid," I said.

I had noticed that my daughter was unable to say his name. My heart was beating fast. I was so incredibly happy that he had done a flip turn. My hand was still on his face, touching his hair, and so I kissed him. Easy. Zahid returned my kiss. A kiss. It had been so very easy.

"Is this a good idea?" he asked.

It was not the best question.

What he was saying was: This is a bad idea. But it wasn't. There were so many bad ideas: Rolling back government protection for the environment, deporting hardworking immigrants who had lived in this country for years and years. A boy bringing a gun into my classroom was a bad idea. Driving without insurance was a bad idea. Not turning in your short story for a writing class was a bad idea. Thinking about my daughter when kissing her handsome writing professor, that was a bad idea. Kissing Zahid, that was a good idea.

"It is a very good idea," I said.

That was all that he needed. He needed permission. We kissed again. I pressed my body against his. Years of yoga, all in preparation for this moment. For the purple bathing suit that fit me so well. For the erection pressed against my leg.

Human relationships are complicated. Human relations are messy. I remembered, as long ago as it had been, that sex could be messy. Not just the act itself, but the emotions attached to it, the confusion, the obsession. I had had an affair, only once, five years into my marriage, with a married gym teacher, of all people. Jonathan never knew about it, but I was wrecked when it ended. The gym teacher had ended it. I had decided that adultery was not for me and that had been it. I had been careful with my emotions. I had given all my love to Rachel and my poodle. To my house. I did not want to be careful anymore.

I was lucky. I did not have to go on the Internet, create a dating profile like friends had told me to. I did not need an app. I simply had to take what was given to me. Zahid Azzam.

We kissed in the pool for what seemed like a very long time, too long, until my lips got tired, until I became almost bored. He was nervous, my daughter's professor. He had his hands in my hair. My hands on his waist. I slipped a hand under his bathing suit, touched him. That worked. It didn't have to be good, the sex, but we had to have it. I had started this and could not back out now. I knew that I didn't want to do it in the swimming pool. I had never liked having sex standing up. Or in water. I took Zahid's hand. I pointed to the deck. The pool chairs.

We climbed the steps at the shallow end of the pool.

Zahid looked afraid.

"Are you afraid?" I asked him.

"No," he said. "Of course not."

He looked almost terrified.

I touched him again. I wouldn't let him bolt; it would be too hard to move on from there. Too awkward. It would ruin our turkey sandwiches. Our walks along the beach. I would not let everything be ruined. This was simple. It was good. I wanted him, more than anything else. I took off my bikini shorts.

"Should we go inside?" he said.

I shook my head. The pool was in the back of the house. It was private. This could not wait. Anything could go wrong.

"Next time," I said.

Zahid nodded. He was following my lead. I had my hand back on his cock and he seemed powerless to think. I had forgotten about this, how easy it was, to be with a man, any man. They were almost incapable of saying no. I had been with so many in college. I wished I had been with older men, when I was young, when they might have had time to teach me something.

I lay back on the lounge chair. I took off my bikini top. It was the early afternoon, broad daylight. Years of yoga, I told myself.

"Come here," I said.

Zahid took off his bathing suit and lay down on top of me. I guided him inside me. It was shocking, really. I felt his penis slide in, and there was a moment of resistance, like when I first put in an earring after months of not wearing earrings. I could feel him breaking through.

"Oh," I said.

"Oh," Zahid repeated.

I kept my hands on Zahid's ass and he started to move inside me. I moved with him. In the house, I could hear Posey barking. I could hear the *blip blip blip* of the swimming pool. Zahid's lips were on my breast. His hands were on my body. We were moving, together. His skin tasted like chlorine.

# Two

# *Rachel*

One of my kids showed up at day camp half an hour late, in tears. She ran right into my arms. She was wearing mismatched shoes and her hair was loose instead of her trademark braids.

"What's wrong, little bean?" I asked her.

Amelia told me that everyone was fighting at her house. Her mother, her father, her older brother, home for a visit. Screaming at each other in the morning. "My brother said fuck you to my parents," she said. "And my dad said, Right back at you, fuckface."

"He said that?" I asked, surprised.

Amelia nodded.

"That's a lot of cursing."

Amelia nodded. Amelia's other older brother was at boarding school. He was the kid who brought a gun into my mother's classroom, and in Connecticut, especially after Sandy Hook, this was not okay. The director of the camp had taken me aside before the kids arrived on the first day and talked to me about Amelia. She had asked me not to say anything to her about her brother.

"Why would I do that?" I asked.

It seemed like such an idiotic request. Like, duh. Did I not have any sensitivity to human feelings? Why would I go out of my way to upset a little girl. Anyway, I liked Amelia, even if she was a little bit clingy. Literally clinging to my leg, playing mud in between activities. It seemed nice that there was someone in the world entirely enamored with me. Unlike Zahid, who I caught looking at me, sometimes, but would never acknowledge it. We had never looked at each other, once, at the same time, simultaneously, this entire summer.

Amelia had snot dripping down her face. I did not have a tissue. I used the bottom of her T-shirt. I wondered what my mother would say to this crying little girl. I wondered if my mother had been good at talking me down when I was a kid. She must have been, though I don't ever remember having big emotions, until now, with Zahid in my house, so close and yet somehow, inscrutably, so far away. I could not understand it. Maybe it was because my mother never went out. Every night, she stayed home, cooking her perfect dinners. Did she not have friends to see, I asked her, a movie to go to? Did she not want to go out? My mother smiled at me stupidly, as if she did not understand the question. Go out? I had the urge to smack the strange smile off her face. What I was feeling, at home, was close to fury. It was uncomfortable.

I gave Amelia a hug. I kissed her on top of the head. She was so much younger than her brothers. Probably she had been a surprise baby, a mistake.

"I'm an only child," I told her. "It's quiet at my house in the morning. No one calls anyone fuckface."

This made Amelia laugh.

I realized that I could get in trouble if I was overheard cursing, even if I was just repeating what she'd heard at home. Maybe I was not supposed to hug Amelia, either. Jesus. There were so many rules. I had spaced out during orientation, but I knew there were a lot of them. More than the years before. Probably it was only the male counselors who couldn't hug the girls.

"You should come to our house for dinner," Amelia said.

"Okay," I told her.

"Tonight," she said.

"Sure," I said. I had not actually meant it.

"Tonight," Amelia repeated.

I hated having dinner at home. It had become a freak show. My mother was performing for Zahid, wearing her Eileen Fisher sundresses, her hair loose. I swear, one night, she was actually wearing perfume. My mother never wore perfume. My mother smiled too much and drank wine and cooked those ridiculous meals, salads with farro and pine nuts and grapefruit. I wanted to inform my mother that my writing professor was not interested in her. That she was old. Only for some reason, inexplicable to me, Zahid seemed to urge her on. It was painful to watch. He had been at our house for more than two weeks already.

I did not understand why he was not interested in me.

I was still waiting for him. I left the light on, music playing. I walked down the hall to the bathroom in my nightshirt. I left the door open, sometimes, in the afternoon, changing out of my camp clothes. I was leaving signals, but they were too subtle.

Back at college, I had kissed him.

I had undressed him.

I did not know why I was so scared now. Make a move, I kept telling myself. Make a move. But something held me back. Zahid, probably. The way he did not look at me. Sometimes, I told myself, he acted as if he was not interested in me because he *was* interested me. And this somehow made sense. He was fighting his attraction to me, because it would make life uncomfortable for him. My mother wouldn't let him stay in the house if we started up again, and I did not want Zahid to leave. I could wait. If he could wait. And this made me feel a little bit better.

We were both uncomfortable.

He was working on his book, my professor. Clearly, he was letting my mother feed him. He did not have a wife. She had bought him a bathing suit, for Christ's sake. I would not get in the way of his new book. I was not that selfish.

I was a good person. Caring. Amelia, for instance, stopped crying when I told her I would come over for dinner. I was curious anyway. The famous fucked-up family. I had heard that they were insanely wealthy, even by Connecticut standards. I had seen her father driving around town in a gold Lamborghini. My father loathed him.

Just like that, Amelia flipped a switch. It was unnerving. It seemed unlikely that there could be two sociopaths in one family, but suddenly I was worried. Where had her brother gotten a gun? From the house where I would be going to dinner.

"Do you like corn?" Amelia asked me. She latched on to my leg. This habit had begun to get annoying.

"Sure," I said. "Who doesn't?"

"And lobster?" she said. "Do you like lobster?"

Sometimes, it felt ridiculous to me, how rich everyone was in our little town. Except for the people who weren't. The Mexicans who worked at the deli and the supermarket, for instance. I wondered where they lived. There had to be a magic bus that came in the morning and brought them all in and took them home at night.

"I love lobster," I said.

"Me, too," she said. "It's my favorite food."

"You're serious," I said.

"It is. It's my favorite food," Amelia repeated. She was seven. It made sense, actually. I remembered eating artichokes when I was her age. My mother was so proud of me. She told people that I was precocious. We used to eat Brie and M&M's on New Year's Eve.

Amelia was still holding on to my leg.

"No, I mean, for dinner," I said. "Are we having lobster tonight?"

"Of course. Lobster Friday. All summer. My mother says lobsters bring people together. That it is impossible to be mad when you are eating a lobster. It's too messy. She doesn't trust people who don't eat lobster."

"That makes sense," I said, though it made no sense at all.

"So you are coming? You said you can come. You are going to come, right? You promised. You can't take it back."

Was I going to go to dinner at Amelia Thornton's house? Home of the kid who'd waved a gun at the little kids in my mother's classroom. Later, he told the police that my mother was his favorite teacher. That was why he picked her classroom.

"Another reason not to be popular," my mother said.

Probably no one would ever accept a dinner invitation to their house. The Thorntons were tainted. On top of everything else, they were Republicans. They gave money to the GOP. The father had had his picture taken with Trump at some event, standing next to the man, smiling.

"What was everyone fighting about?" I asked Amelia.

"Oh," she said. "Well, Theo can't stay at his school for the last two weeks of summer, and my mother doesn't want him to come home. And my brother Ian made her cry. He told her it was time for Botox."

"Ow," I said.

"What is Botox?" Amelia asked.

I shrugged.

"My mom called Ian fuckface, too. For talking that way to her."

"Well, fuck," I said. "She might have a point."

I had told my mother Amelia was in my group this year and my mother had taken a moment.

"Check her backpack for a gun," she had said.

She was kidding, but she also wasn't.

"Let's text my mom right now. Tell her to get you a lobster," Amelia said. I had cell phone numbers for all of the parents. "Tell her I invited you."

"It can wait," I said.

I had really said I was going there for dinner. Even my father would be distressed. He had argued with Richard Thornton about local development at a town hall meeting. Apparently, the meeting had erupted into a screaming match.

"Text her," Amelia said, pulling on my arm, while still attached to my leg.

She would not let it alone.

"Get off me and I'll text her," I said.

Amelia got off me. She watched me send the text, informing her mother that Amelia had invited me for dinner.

"Wonderful," her mother wrote back, right away. "Do you eat lobster?"

We were having lobster.

That was fine.

I also loved lobster.

My father used to take me and my mother out to this restaurant on the bay, and I would get broiled lobster, with spaghetti as my side. My parents would get baked potatoes. Remembering this made me miss my father. Strange. Because I thought that I didn't care one way or another that he had left us.

Amelia seemed totally fine after I agreed to come to her house for dinner. Probably they fought all the time at their house. I would be going to dinner at a house full of crazy people. It would be a break from the insanity at my home, another night of not touching my professor, aching with desire and pretending that I was fine. Amelia had a normal day at camp. I watched her during her swim lesson, learning to do the crawl.

"I am swimming, I am swimming," she cried.

I snuck up next to her during arts and crafts and squeezed her skinny leg.

"Look what I am making," she said.

She was making me a bracelet with wooden beads that spelled out my name.

"I love you, Rachel," Amelia said.

"That's so nice," I said.

I didn't say it back. I was very aware of the fact. Probably Amelia was, too.

I wished that it was my professor who loved me and then I wished that I had not wished it.


Amelia lived in one of those modern glass houses right on the water. It would be a good house to film a movie in. You could shoot from outside looking in. This would also be a dangerous house to fight in; it was as if the glass walls were begging a body to be thrown through. I realized right away that I should not have accepted the invitation. I understood that I had not told my mother where I was going because she would have told me not to go.

The table was already set. There was a tall silver pot on the stove, the water boiling. Amelia's parents had this glassy-eyed look to them. Drunk, that's what they were. They were drinking wine, but I saw empty martini glasses on the counter. Theo was still away at "school." The older brother was there, drinking a beer. Amelia had not prepared me for him. He was good-looking in a way that was unnerving. Ice blond, blue-eyed, muscled. A hard jaw. He was wearing boating shoes. It was like Richie Rich grown up. I did not talk to boys who looked like this. They did not talk to me.

"This is Ian," Amelia said. "And Amy and Richard. My mom and dad."

Not Jews, my mother would have said, about all of them, in a way that was judgmental, though I am sure that was not what she had been thinking when the other son brought a gun to her classroom. I had talked to my mother on the phone that night and she had laughed it off.

"You could have died," I said, and she agreed.

"It was fifty-fifty," she said. "I have always been lucky."

Maybe Theo Thornton was lucky, too, getting out. I certainly did not feel lucky to be in this house. The older brother, Ian, looked me over, head to toe. He looked right at my tits. He nodded as if to say they would do. My tits were small. For the most part, I was glad about this. I didn't have to wear a bra. He poured me a glass of wine.

"So you're the camp counselor," he said.

"Rachel," I said.

"Welcome to lobster night," he said.

Amelia was wearing a lobster bib. The scene was stranger than what was happening at my house, which seemed pretty fucking strange to me. The stress of having Zahid sleeping down the hall, lying in a bed, in his boxer shorts, not wanting me, was starting to be too much. I looked at the wine Ian poured me and I took a big gulp. I wanted to return to a normal world. To summers where my father grilled hamburgers and my mother made salads. When they loved each other.

My father left while I was in my second semester of sophomore year, but his leaving didn't seem real to me as I was already gone. I could not remember them ever yelling at each other. They had seemed like parents who would be married forever.

Amelia's father peered at me as I drank from my glass of wine. At home, my mother would not let me drink, but his son had given me this glass of wine.

"Your last name is Klein," Richard Thornton said.

I nodded.

"Your mother is the teacher," he said. "You look like her. I saw the resemblance the second you walked in the door. She is a good woman. Your father is a fool."

"Who?" Amelia said.

"We sent her flowers," Amelia's mother told me. "Did she like the flowers?"

"I don't know," I said. "I was at college. I'm home for the summer."

Ian refilled my wine glass without my asking. I was grateful.

"What are you talking about?" Amelia said.

"My mother used to be Theo's teacher," I told Amelia. "In two years, she might be your teacher."

"I think about it every day," Amelia's mother said. "What if he had killed one of them? What if he had killed your mother? Or himself?"

I did not know what to say. It seemed like this subject would be something that was not brought up at dinnertime.

"We're so glad you are here," Richard said. It was as if I was an honored guest. I chewed on a strand of loose hair and then noticed Ian, still looking at me. "I haven't seen your father in some time," Richard added. "I think the last time, I beat him at tennis. I owe him a rematch."

I had never heard such a thing. I could not imagine my father even agreeing to play tennis with a man he did not like.

"Your father doesn't like me much, as I recall."

"I don't know," I said. I was a very bad liar. "You don't seem to like him, either."

Amelia's father laughed. "Good thing your mother didn't know that."

"What?" I honestly could not understand what he was getting at. His son had brought a gun, probably his gun, to school. Was he making jokes?

"What would our lives be?" Amelia's mother said. She was having trouble sitting on the bar stool in their perfect kitchen. She slipped off. She was crazy drunk. "We would be ruined," she said, her arms waving. "That's for sure. How can you come back from such a thing?"

"Amy," Richard said.

"We would not be allowed back into the tennis club, that is for sure."

"You hate the tennis club," Richard said.

"I am just making a point."

"Children could have been killed," Richard said. "Don't talk about the tennis club. What will our guest think?"

"I don't think anything," I said. I wondered immediately if that could possibly be true. This was too much, too over the top. I did not know what to think. I glanced up at Amelia's brother, the handsome one. He raised his bottle of beer, as if to say cheers. Was he drunk, too? I wished I could tell. I looked away from him. I had never been so attracted and repulsed at the same time.

"You have to stop drinking so much," Amelia's father said to his wife. "Listen to you. Forget about the tennis club. Keep on drinking like this and I won't be able to take you anywhere."

"You stop drinking," she came back at him, without missing a beat. "You motherfucking hypocrite."

I winced. This felt ugly and inappropriate. We should not have been here to witness them. Amelia's parents should have known this. Basic parenting. I felt bad for Amelia. This was what she lived with. It was lobster Friday but there was nothing festive about it. This had to be one sad house to grow up in. There was nothing welcoming about it. They didn't even have a dog. I would have asked if there was another lobster bib, just for Amelia's sake and then I remembered Ian.

"Amelia," Amelia's father said. "Take your friend outside. We are going to eat outside. The water's finally boiling. I'm going to cook the lobsters and we will eat."

"You mean kill them," Amelia's mother said. "Poor helpless lobsters."

I saw then that the lobsters were still alive, climbing on top of each other in a large plastic bag. Of course, I knew this was how you had to cook a lobster, but I had only eaten them in restaurants. I waited outside, with Amelia and Ian, for dinner to be served.

We sat at a picnic table, overlooking the water. The sun was setting by the time the meal was ready. It was breathtaking, the sky red and orange and a little bit of purple, and all of this beauty was wasted. The wine was cold and delicious. The corn was overcooked. Somehow, I didn't even taste the lobster. I barely ate any, in fact, because Ian was watching me and lobsters are hard to eat, messy, and Ian was gorgeous and he had not stopped looking at me. I did not like the way he was staring at me, as if he was waiting for me to drip butter on my face or down my breasts even. It was not a kind gaze.

I had never enjoyed a lobster less.

Amelia ate hers. "Yummy," she said, cracking open all of the joints, sucking the meat out of the legs. I was glad to see her happy. I felt bad for her, growing up in this house with so many hard edges. It made me miss my mother, who never turned mean when she got drunk. When I was a kid, it used to be fun when she drank too much. She would come home late from a party, tipsy, and find me still awake. She would let me watch TV in between her and Dad on their big bed and tell me all about their night.

When the meal was over, Ian offered to take me home and I said no.

"Are you sure?" he asked.

"I'm sure," I said.

I wasn't.

I looked at Ian again and my face turned hot, but I stuck with my answer. I would be safer alone. I walked.

# *Becca*


He was going away for the weekend.

I was only half paying attention to the details. A friend named Kristi, an interview for a job. The University of Iowa. He was leaving. He had only been here a few weeks. It was almost August. It had not been that long ago that I had heard this speech before. *Becca, I am leaving you.*

I hoped the shock didn't show on my face. He was leaving. It was unfair how he told me, right after we made love, outside, again, at the pool, when I was at my most vulnerable, when I was feeling nothing but pleasure, when I had left myself wide open. I was naked, literally and metaphorically. I knew that this was sex, nothing more, purely chemical, but at that moment I thought that I might love him. More than his beautiful poodle, that's how far gone I was. I loved him. I hugged my knees to my chest.

"A job interview, Becca," Zahid said. "For the fall. That's all it is."

My expression must have been blank.

"I feel the same way," he said. "I need to make some money."

A job. He was leaving for a job and not for a Kristi. I had not begun to think about what would happen next. After the summer. Rachel would go back to college. I would start teaching again. I could not spend my days at the pool, having sex in the bright sunshine. Everything would have to change. What we were doing felt too good. It couldn't possibly be real.

"How long are you going for?"

I just didn't know how to be cool about it. I had been calm and collected when Jonathan told me he was leaving, even though I hadn't seen it coming, had no idea he was having an affair. Now I started to shake. Was I cold? The sun was hot on my skin, but I felt ice-cold all over.

"I don't want to go, Becca," he said.

Zahid sat at the opposite end of the pool chair. He put his hands on my knees. My chin was already resting on my knees. He lifted my head, forcing me to look at him. "Believe me. It is the last thing I want to do."

His voice was so earnest I suddenly wanted to laugh. What was this? Shakespeare. Who was dying? The man had to get a job. It was not like I was going to support him for the rest of his life.

"How long are you going for?" I asked.

"Two nights," he said.

"Two nights." I actually laughed. That was not very long. Look what a fool I had made of myself over two short days. But then, would he come back? How could I be sure?

"And then I will come straight back," Zahid said, answering my question as if I had spoken it out loud. "I will come straight back to you, Rebecca."

I could be wrong, but it felt as if we had skipped over all

the traditional steps. We did not go on dates. We had not once before talked about what was happening. To talk about it would ruin everything. But what it seemed like, to me, was simple. Stupid. Laughable even. We were in love.

"You will?"

"I promise," he said. "I will come straight back."

The words were ridiculous, but they were also what I wanted to hear. I let go of my knees. I climbed on top of Zahid and we were doing it again, again, again, again. God, I loved this, this secret and magical world of sex. Zahid had his hands on my waist, and I was moving, slow and then fast and faster.

# *Zahid*

I was the last person off the airplane.

I had fallen asleep and when I woke up, the other passengers were all unbuckling their seat belts, collecting their belongings from the overhead compartments, exiting the plane. I watched in a stupor. I had had one drink, only one, but it was early in the day on an empty stomach. Iowa City. The middle of fucking America. What the fuck was I doing? I could still taste Becca on my fingers.

"Are you all right, sir?" a flight attendant asked me, and I was grateful that she'd called me sir. Since 9/11, every time that I got on an airplane, I understood that I was a potential terrorist. I always made sure to shave, wear good clothes. The drink had been a mistake.

I rubbed my eyes.

I got my bag from the overhead compartment. I had packed a suit for the interview, my shiny shoes. It was like tap dancing. I had been dancing since the book came out and Kristi would agree, though to us it meant two different things. She called me a party boy. "Be a writer," she'd said recently. "For a goddamned change." It was a fucking slap in the face. And now, now that I was writing, she was dragging me away from it, wanted me to get a job.

I thought an ugly word about her.

I wished that I hadn't. I loved Kristi.

At least, for the first time in a long time, I no longer wanted to sleep with her. That was over, finally. I walked slowly through the empty airplane. The entire crew was standing at the exit, even the pilot. It was a woman, a small and pretty woman with straight blond hair. She had bangs like a schoolgirl. I looked at the wings pinned on her chest.

"Thank you for flying with us," she said, with that perky voice that came when anyone from a corporation ever thanked you for patronizing their business. It was incredibly patronizing.

"You are welcome, Mandy," I said.

It was an unusual name. The name of a 1970s cheerleader. It suited her. This Mandy, the pilot, looked annoyed at me. I had taken a liberty saying her name, but she was wearing a name tag, after all. She, of course, did not know that I was an award-winning writer. She thought I was a dark-skinned alcoholic, preventing her from getting off her airplane and getting on with her day. But somehow, I was not willing to get off the airplane.

"It was a smooth flight," I said. "Your gentle flying rocked me to sleep like a baby."

"Oh, no," she said, laughing. "You did not just say that."

I shrugged.

"Have a nice stay in Iowa City," she said.

Okay, so she obviously was not flirting with me. Was I

flirting with the blond pilot? I was. I felt like a shit then. For being a man. Walking around with my swinging penis. Probably this pilot went through this bullshit every day, dealing with men who refused to treat her with respect. I did not want to get off the plane. I wanted it to turn around and fly back.

This morning, I had kissed Becca's eyelids. I had gently fingered her in the kitchen. Rachel was already out of the house. Day camp, fortunately, started early. I wanted to pretend that nothing had ever happened between me and the girl, Becca's daughter, but sometimes I saw her looking at me, almost ready to pounce, and I knew she held too many cards. I knew that she was trouble. I had to get out of her house; I wanted desperately to stay in that house, forever and ever. I got off the plane, one step at a time. I could feel daggers from the pilot's eyes, shooting into my back. I had not charmed her.

Kristi wasn't even waiting for me at the gate. I turned on my phone and I found a text saying I should get an Uber. I was fucking pissed. An Uber. She had dragged me here and didn't have the decency to pick me up.

"Do they even have Ubers in Iowa City?" I texted her.

The population of the airport was doughy and unnervingly blond, beefy white guys wearing baseball caps. This was not for me. Where was my VIP treatment? Where was the car waiting for me, an adoring undergraduate at the wheel to take me to campus?

This, of course, was Kristi, putting me in my place.

"Fuck you," she wrote back. "And see you soon. Xoxoxo."

———

My Uber driver turned out to be a grad student in the English department. It wasn't a campus car, of course; I was still going to have to pay for it. It was shameful, how fucking broke I was, and Kristi knew this. The ride from the airport cost me thirty-two dollars. I would have to leave a tip. Kristi should have picked me up. I could not understand it.

"I can't believe it's you," my driver said.

She started to blush. She had a crush. They always had a crush. It had stopped being flattering. I could not get myself into any more trouble than I was already in. Fortunately, the student was not my type. She had short hair. A nose ring. Tattoos. For all I knew she was gay. Bisexual. Gender-fluid. I never knew anymore.

"I saw your name on my phone, and I swear I started to speed. I am lucky I didn't get a ticket. I already have points on my license and holy fuck I need this job. I'm going to your reading tonight. I am so fucking psyched Zahid Azzam is in the back of my car. You made my year. Seriously."

It was a clean car, but nothing special. An old Honda. It was no town car. I did not merit such treatment. I used to be treated like a star, but obviously I was no Salman Rushdie.

"A reading?" I asked her.

As far as I was aware, I had not agreed to that. I was interviewing for a job that, according to Kristi, was already mine. I would teach a class tomorrow, go out for lunch with the head of the department. Now they wanted me to read. Didn't I have to fucking agree to that? Probably I fucking had. I had only half listened to Kristi, trusting that she would take care of the details. Well, fuck. Fine. I would read to them. I had packed my suit. I had my new pages.

"Yeah," she said. "Didn't you know?"

"I must have forgotten."

"Everyone is going," she said. "Well, a lot of people aren't on campus for the summer, but everyone who is here."

"How old are you?" I asked her, curious, comparing her to Rachel.

"Twenty-six," she said.

I shook my head. Fuck, Rachel was young.

"How old are you?" she asked.

I was thirty-six.

"That's a good number," my driver said.

"Why?"

"I don't know. There is a nice quality to it. Six times six. Twelve times three. Four times nine."

"I thought you were a writer."

My driver laughed. "Next year, thirty-seven, is a prime number, so watch out. That's unlucky."

"Huh," I said. I wondered if I was required to talk anymore. I closed my eyes and my driver seemed to get the hint.

Earlier this summer, in Pakistan, my mother had asked me when I was going to get married. When I was going to start having babies. She no longer cared if I married a Muslim woman. She was past religion. She was almost as American as I was. She bought her clothes at the Gap and Old Navy. She just wanted grandkids. She said that it was long past time to be over my broken engagement.

Often, when I thought of my fiancée, my mind flashed to all of the presents we had to return. So many good, expensive things. I had kept a Le Creuset pot when I found out how much it would cost to put it in the mail. I am a man but I had always wanted that big orange pot. I was the one who'd put it on the registry.

I had thought I would miss her, my beautiful and talented fiancée, but I did not miss her. I missed the life. But as far as babies went, there I was lucky, at least, to be a man. I did not have to worry about my eggs going bad. Becca, of course, would not be having any more babies. My mother would not like that.

"Oh, Mom."

I realized I might have said it out loud. I did not want to have any babies.

My driver laughed.

Yes, I had said it out loud.

I had to put my dancing shoes on.

Why was I such a fucking mess? I needed a few more weeks in Connecticut. All that equanimity. All that good health. Fresh air and good food. Good sex. I was swimming laps every day. I could swim a length of the pool underwater without taking a breath. I could do a flip turn. I had made significant improvements. I was not ready for this next step. I did not want to have a job. I was a writer, for Christ's sake.

Here I was.

Iowa City.

Was this where my life was leading me?

Was I a little bit self-pitying? Could I bear to hear Kristi mock me to my face? I was tempted to ask my driver to take me back to the airport. She would do it, of course. She would have a story to tell tonight at the local bar where the grad students hung out.

"You're here," my driver said. "This is Professor Taylor's house. Are you okay?"

It was like the plane, again, déjà vu. All of these women, rushing me along, wanting things. Do this. Do that. Why did I not have any male friends? And there was Kristi, stepping out of a small white house. Her hair was wet, long and dark, a single braid soaking the shirt above her breast. Kristi Taylor. It had been too long. Why had I thought I could live without her?

"Zahid," she said with a grin.

I got out of the car and she ran to me, wrapped me in her arms.

"It's been too long," she said.

I kissed her hair.

One day, someday, Kristi was going to regret letting me go.

# *Khloe*

The phone was ringing and ringing.

"What?" Jane groaned, sitting up, looking for her cell phone. It was my phone. My fucking sister, Kristi, trying to ruin my life. I answered, but didn't say a word. I kissed Jane lightly on the lips and she returned my kiss.

"Shhh," I said. "You are still asleep. Go back to sleep."

I took the phone into the kitchen.

"Khloe, is that you? Are you there, Khloe? Khloe?"

"What, Kristi?" I said. I didn't have to take the call, I realized. But it was too late now. "What do you want at ten in the morning?"

I wished that our parents had given us different names. Names that did not have that ridiculous alliteration. Khloe and Kristi. It was a twin thing, something done to us by my idiot parents, a tradition inflicted upon twins since time began. Kristi had always complained that I had the better name. She was right. I did have the much better name, even if it was constantly spelled wrong. My mother randomly liked the *K*'s, as if the unusual spelling would make us that much more special.

Jane was asleep in my bed. There was nothing Kristi could do that would spoil that.

"It's nine in the morning in Iowa."

"Of course it is," I said. "What do you want?"

"What do you mean, what do you want?"

"I mean you are calling me, so you must want something."

"Can't I just want to talk to you?"

"Yes, you might want to talk to me, but you probably also have a reason."

"I don't have to have a reason," Kristi said.

"But you probably do."

Sometimes, I got a kick out of being obnoxious. I did it at work, too. I liked to mess with the heads of the other analysts. The news had been overflowing with sexual harassment stories, and it was working out for me. Everyone was being extra careful. On their best behavior. No one grabbed my ass anymore and I was going to get promoted soon, I could feel it in my bones. This meant more money. More money to spend on Jane. I would take her on vacations. She had complained, more than once, about how low her salary was. But I was getting ahead of myself.

"Can I tell you something good?" I said to Kristi. "Something really good."

"Yes, of course," Kristi said. "Tell me."

"But what about what you want to tell me?"

"It's not important," Kristi said. "I don't have anything to tell you."

"Yes, you do," I said.

"Well, okay, I do, but you go first."

"You called me," I said.

"Khloe."

"Kristi."

I laughed. I was so fucking happy, that's what I was realizing. Jane had actually listened to me, it was a small thing, but she'd gone back to sleep. We had had a lot to drink last night. And thank God for alcohol. I wanted to scream from the rooftops. I really did. I was grinning. I pressed the phone between my ear and shoulder and I made coffee. I was a talented person. I had skills: finance, lovemaking, making coffee.

"Guess who is sleeping in my bed right now?"

"Ooh," Kristi said. "This has to be someone good. I know. I know. Keri Russell. Is it Keri Russell?"

"No," I said, laughing. "But that's a good guess."

Keri Russell lived in Brooklyn, reportedly in the same neighborhood as Zahid's apartment, and I had had a crush on her since *Felicity*. She was hot in *The Americans*, with her straight hair and martial arts skills, but she was completely unattainable, remarried with kids.

"Better," I said. "It's Jane."

"Jane, the babysitter?" Kristi said.

"Yes."

"Seriously?"

"Seriously."

"Oh my God, Khloe." I could actually hear Kristi clapping her hands. "I am so happy for you."

I nodded. I was biting my lip. I shouldn't have told Kristi. It was too soon. It was last night. I put on a short dress and met Winifred at a literary party in Chelsea, and went home with Jane instead, the true target of my affection. There was good music playing at the party. There was dancing. There were unlimited mojitos.

The jealousy plan had worked better than I could have

anticipated. Jane and I had taken the subway back to Brooklyn together, fingers entwined, not looking at each other. Knowing. Knowing what we were going to do. We had left Winnie in tears, shouting at us, "I am not even gay. I don't care. I am not gay." And I think a gay writer might have thrown his drink at her. It was an amazing party. At literary parties, I had discovered, everyone got good and drunk.

I had thought Jane would change her mind, every step of the way, on the subway, when I was fumbling for the key to the apartment, taking off Jane's dress, kneeling in front of her, pulling down her underwear. I knew just what I wanted to do, I had imagined it for so long, and she didn't stop me. And now, she was asleep in my bed. It occurred to me that I should have a hangover, but I didn't. I felt great.

I sat down on the floor, watching the coffee percolate.

"How?" Kristi said.

"I was flirting with this girl she was with. She got jealous. That's what did it."

"You are so bad, Khloe," Kristi said.

"I know."

"I can't believe it," Kristi said.

"I know."

For a while, we didn't say anything.

Seriously, I had achieved one of my life goals. It was a little bit scary. Where did I go from there? I had slept with my baby-sitter, something I had dreamed about for years and years. I wanted it to be more, of course. This was not a drunken hookup. This was real. I was in love.

I looked at the closed bedroom door, reassured. Jane couldn't sneak by me, make a fast exit unnoticed.

I had not expected this. I had genuinely planned on going

home with Winnie. I was curious, actually, about her apartment. Her life. She did not seem real to me, too perfect to be true. I wished I could have been born into family money.

"This is epic," Kristi said. "Epic."

"You are not allowed to write about this."

"Awww."

"I am serious, little sister."

I had told Kristi about the first time I slept with a woman and she put it in a short story and then, later, in the novel that had made her almost famous. The character in her novel had been molested by her babysitter, something I had never told Kristi about. There was no way she could have known. The girl's twin sister had died of some random illness not long after birth, as if somehow that made it okay. Kristi could not be trusted. I made this mistake over and over.

"It is so romantic," Kristi said. "You have had a crush on her forever."

"It is romantic," I said, with a long sigh. I guess I had wanted to tell someone in order to believe that it was true.

Part of me was also afraid that it wasn't even flirting with Winnie that had precipitated this enormous event. It was Zahid Azzam. It was that I was living in his apartment. I was afraid that my babysitter thought she was somehow getting closer to her writer by being with me. She had had sex, for instance, in Zahid Azzam's bed. That sounded weird, but Jane wasn't weird. She was ambitious. I could totally believe that Jane had ulterior motives. That was something Jane and I had in common. We were both ambitious. She could try to use me, but I couldn't help her in the Zahid Azzam department. I had fed her some day-old lentils. Her orgasms were real.

"Why did you sigh?" Kristi said.

"I don't know," I said. "I guess I am worried. It's brand-new. I shouldn't have told you."

"No, no," Kristi said. "It's good. Of course you should have told me. Who else would you tell? Who else would understand?"

It was true. No one else would understand. I stared at the closed door.

"Why did you call?"

"Actually, it's sort of connected," Kristi said. "Maybe."

"What?"

"Well, it's about Zahid."

Normally I would have no interest in Zahid Azzam. But whatever I found out now, Jane would want to know. Jane might not have slept with me if I did not live in his apartment. How was I supposed to know?

"Okay. Tell me."

"Well, Zahid is here, now."

"In Iowa?"

"Yeah," Kristi said. "He came for an interview. He gave a reading yesterday. He read new stuff. It was terrific. They are going to offer him the job. Isn't that amazing?"

"Is it?"

Wasn't Jane anticipating him back to New York in September? The summer was going by so quickly. It was already August. I had spent June and July working. I was going to call a real-estate agent. I had been saving money. I could rent a nice two-bedroom. Jane could move in. She could bring her books. Her cat.

The coffee was ready. I got up and poured myself a cup, poured half-and-half into my coffee.

"What this means," Kristi said, "is that you can stay in Zahid's apartment, probably for another year if you want it."

I nodded. I could stay in Zahid Azzam's apartment and fuck his editor, my babysitter. I had to stop thinking of her that way. We were equals now. I was a grown-up. I made more money than she did. I wore better clothes. Her underwear was a disgraceful mess. Mismatched, cotton, a hole in the crotch. I closed my eyes. I took my first sip of coffee. It was good. I loved good coffee.

"What about his dog?" I asked.

"His dog?" Kristi asked. "The dog is with this rich woman in Connecticut. Wow, now that I think about it, this job is better than I thought. I have to get Zahid away from her."

"Why?"

Zahid had gone to Connecticut to check on his dog and he'd never come back. I had thought he would be trouble, the situation with his apartment, his need to sleep somewhere, but he wasn't. He had stopped in once during the day while I was at work and packed some of his clothes. The apartment was mine.

Connecticut, he'd written in a note, is like a dream.

"Why?" Kristi said. "He does not need to be mixed up with some rich white woman with nothing better to do. She is cooking Zahid salmon."

"That sounds awful."

"She is giving him expensive wine. Letting him swim in her pool."

"Really awful."

The situation actually made sense to me. The man clearly needed someone to take care of him. Kristi was not a caretaker.

I could attest to that. Sometimes, she might take a person on as a project, but she would grow frustrated when the person she set out to help did not cooperate. She would get angry then.

It was funny that she objected to the woman being white. This was a new thing for Kristi, always emphasizing her blackness. Publishing essays about being a black person mistaken for white. Only hanging around with people of color. People of color who might as well have been white: Ivy League, good jobs, people who ate arugula.

"The woman is still married, Khloe. She is going to ruin him. I'm afraid that they are fucking."

"Maybe he will ruin her."

"He already fucked the daughter," Kristi said.

"Jesus." I did not know that. "What an asshole."

"I know. And somehow, we are still friends. I am trying to save him from himself."

I drank more coffee. I wondered what would happen when Jane woke up again, this time for real. Hopefully she would not be too hungover. We would drink the coffee. We could make love again. She would probably want to go to brunch. Jane loved all of that Brooklyn yuppie bullshit. Poached eggs. Sautéed brussels sprouts. I would take her to brunch. We could order mimosas. Hair of the dog. She could read *The New York Times*.

I thought about Zahid in Connecticut, the note he had written to me. "You might have trouble getting him back," I said. "I don't think he wants to teach. Maybe he shouldn't. You always complain that teaching drains all of your energy. Takes away from the writing."

"All writers teach." Kristi was annoyed with me now. Invariably, with every phone call, one of us got on the other's nerves. "And complain. It's what we do."

I could hear Jane getting up, the creak of the floorboards. I had to get off this phone call.

"I can keep his apartment?" I said. "Is that what you are saying?"

"Well, he has to take the job first," Kristi said.

"Or he can stay in Connecticut," I said. "I can still keep the apartment. It's all good."

"No," Kristi said. "No way."

"You sound jealous, little sister."

Kristi was ten minutes younger than me.

"That is ridiculous," Kristi said.

Kristi sounded completely jealous. Whereas I didn't care what Zahid Azzam did. Honestly. It was ridiculous to think that Jane was suddenly attracted to me because of my summer sublet. You did not have sex with a woman to get into an apartment. Jane had been denying her feelings for me. Now she knew better. I had proven to her that I was no child, once and for all. This was a stupid conversation. I would get my own apartment. I made the money. It was too early to be talking to my sister. I should be back in bed, waking Jane up with sweet kisses.

"I have to go," I said.

"I am not jealous," Kristi said.

"No," I said. "Of course you aren't."

"I'm not."

"That's what I just said." I took another sip of coffee. "Look, I really have to go."

"She is really there?" Kristi giggled. "Jane. Your heart's desire."

I nodded.

"Go," Kristi said. "Call me later. Tell me details."

"As if."

The problem was, I might.


Jane was awake, already dressed even, looking inside Zahid's closet. I was disappointed. I did not see how I could get her to take her clothes back off. Morning sex was out. Damn, Kristi. It was like she had a sixth sense, like she knew something good was happening in my life and she had to mess it up.

Of course, this situation was not unfixable. I did not need to panic. We would go to brunch and then come back, make love. That could work. What else could we do? Go to Coney Island. Jane, I was sure, would want to go to Coney Island. She could take a canvas bag full of books. We could make out on the beach, go to Nathan's, ride the Ferris wheel. A perfect day. We would have a perfect day.

"I made coffee."

"Great," Jane said. "I need to get going soon."

I closed my eyes. Again I reminded myself that I was not going to panic. Jane knew that I loved her, and so, she would not treat me shabbily. She was better than that. The day was not lost. She would not look at me and say, *This was a mistake.* I had heard that speech too many times before. Jenny Meyers at tennis camp. My academic adviser at college. The married headhunter who tried to recruit me for another investment firm. Women who denied their homosexuality. Women who denied me because I did not look homosexual. A black woman who said I was not black enough. I had laughed at that one. She had been serious, too. I had been rejected for too many reasons, big and small.

"I'll get you coffee," I said. "One second."

I went into the kitchen. It was good coffee, and that would slow her down. And I had good granola I could give Jane for breakfast if she claimed she did not have time for brunch. I could make this work. I was not going to panic. I was not going to panic.

"He has so many pairs of shoes," Jane said.

I walked over to Zahid's closet. I looked at Zahid's shoes. I handed her the mug of coffee.

She drank from it.

"This is good," she said.

I nodded.

I touched Jane's cheek.

I was going to slow this morning down.

I turned her face to me and I kissed her. Slowly. I put my hands on her waist. It was a good kiss. I was a good kisser.

"Khloe," she said.

Of course, Jane was not one to allow herself to be happy. She thought life should be twisted and complicated like a literary novel. She thought that I was a drunken mistake, but we had not been that drunk. The alcohol had simply allowed her to give in to the inevitable.

"Don't," I said. "Whatever you are going to say, just don't say it, okay?"

Jane nodded.

I was right. I knew Jane too well and had for so long. She was going to say it was a mistake when of course it wasn't a mistake. She was going to mess everything up.

"You don't have to say anything at all. Seriously. Just don't say anything."

We were standing there, in front of Zahid's open closet. The asshole hadn't cleared it out for me. I had a lot of clothes, but I'd managed to make room. Jane was going to give me that "it was a mistake" speech but I had cut her off.

"Look at all of those linen shirts," Jane said.

Zahid had six blue linen shirts. It was like a uniform. The dressed-down writer. The more I knew about Zahid Azzam, the less I liked him. His student. I wished I did not know about that.

"He's in Iowa," I told Jane. "Interviewing for a teaching position."

Jane looked at me. I had her attention again. I was useful to her. I decided at that moment that I would stay in his apartment. I would suffer indignities beneath me. For now. I would play it casual. I was not done with Jane and she was not done with me.

"That was my sister on the phone."

"How is Kristi?" Jane asked.

Jane had babysat for Kristi, too, of course. She had actually helped Kristi find her agent.

"She said that Zahid interviewed for a job there," I said, grateful that I had something to hold her attention. "They are going to give it to him."

Jane bit her lip. "He needs to be writing," she told me.

"Maybe he needs the money."

"After the advance he got?"

I shrugged.

"Wasn't that a long time ago?"

"It's a lot of shoes," Jane said.

There were six pairs of Italian leather loafers on the floor of his closet. Four pairs of white Converse high-tops. He had probably spent his advance long ago.

"I have a lot of work to do today," she said. "Shit. I really drank too much last night."

Still, she had not said it was a mistake. She had not made a beeline for the door. Sunlight streamed in through the window. All I wanted was for us to spend the day together, but I would take the morning. The afternoon.

I tucked a strand of loose hair behind her ear.

# Rachel

Ian Thornton came to get Amelia at the end of day camp.

The pickup line was all stay-at-home mothers and nannies in expensive cars. But Ian had walked. He was wearing his boating shoes. A white T-shirt and a pair of swim trunks. I blushed, looking at him. His hair was so blond. His eyes that icy blue. It occurred to me that maybe he had come to see me.

"You!" he said, surprise in his voice, and I understood that of course I was wrong. He had come to pick up his little sister.

"We're going swimming," he said. "You should come with us."

"Oh," I said.

Did he or didn't he? Like me. It was not as if I could ask him.

"Rachel is coming!" Amelia screamed, jumping up and down. "Rachel is coming!"

Ian stared at me, making it clear that we were both aware of the alternate meaning that could be applied to that sentence. I wanted to disappear. Amelia grabbed my hand.

"Hooray," she said. "For Rachel."

It was unnerving, how attached this little girl was to me. It was not mutual. I liked her fine, but not more than the other kids in my group. In fact, she seemed a little strange. She liked me too much, for one thing, and now, after having been to her home, I understood. She was a witness to grown-up behavior she should not have to see. But she seemed happy now, with me and her brother.

And so, like an idiot, I went.

I changed into my bathing suit and left the day camp with them, to go swimming out on the Sound.

"Rachel is coming. Rachel is coming," Ian said, as we walked to the beach.

"Stop it," I said.

We were out in the water, at the small public beach in town, having what I thought was a good time, when Ian held my head under the water. It was a perfect day. Hot sun, clear sky, late in the afternoon. Ian, Amelia and I were the only people on the beach. The lifeguard was mysteriously absent. Held underwater, I started to count, not sure of what to do, not wanting to panic, not wanting to assume that I was, in fact, being drowned.

One Mississippi, two Mississippi, all the way up to sixteen, underwater, caught in Ian's firm grip, his fingers holding on to my scalp, and then, right before I would have started to kick and flail, he let go.

I came up for air.

I was not completely out of breath. I was not close to actually drowning. It wasn't *scary* scary. I had never smoked, my lung capacity was good. But it seemed that Ian fake-drowning me could only be considered a bad thing. Maybe not as bad as his brother holding a gun to my mother, but not good all the same. When I came up for air, he started to laugh.

"Scared ya," he said.

Amelia laughed, too.

And then, it was weird, I started laughing, too.


I texted my dad. *How R U?*

My mother was driving me crazy. Zahid was still ignoring me. It turned out I actually missed my father. Did he know what was going on in his house?

*A little lonely,* he wrote back. I was glad that he had started texting. *I miss you, kiddo. Don't use abbreviations. Please. OK?*

Lonely. Miss you.

My poor dad. It was not what I was supposed to hear from my father. Who was always upbeat. Who was in control of his universe. Who played tennis and racquetball and went running. Who made tons of money. Wore expensive suits. Even now, in his new life, he had seemed good to me. Happy with Mandy, his blond pilot. She seemed smart enough. She seemed nice. She was not completely inappropriate. She was too young, but that was what men did. They had sex with younger women.

I thought about Zahid, how he might think that I was too young. I wasn't. I was old enough. I had blown it somehow. He had moved into my house and I had played it too cool. I thought it was obvious, how much I wanted him. Sometimes, I could not breathe in his presence. I could not formulate a coherent sentence, while my mother went on and on. I wanted to go back in time. Why hadn't I slipped into his room that first night? Or even the night after? I had had so many chances. Day after day, I'd blown it. Every day, it got harder.

Mandy, at least, looked at my dad with affection. It was weird, but it was almost nice. My mother could be cold. Indifferent.

Why was my dad lonely? Maybe it wasn't going so well with his pilot after all. Why wasn't I surprised? Why was it that I didn't respect my parents for making changes in their lives? Why was Zahid in my house and we still hadn't gotten it on? I knew that he liked me. We had fucked. Of course, he liked me. He was just afraid. That was all. On the Fourth of July, we had all gone to see the fireworks, and it was surreal. I watched my mother, afraid she would say something dumb, but she barely said anything at all. We went home early, my mother worried about Princess, alone and possibly afraid, and it was a relief. It was weird, the three of us out in the world; it was as if I were their kid or something.

My father and I made plans to meet for dinner. I would take the train into the city straight from day camp. I would pick him up at his office. I brought a change of clothes with me.

I thought about texting my mom to let her know my plans, and then I didn't. I'd let her worry. Zahid had gone out of town that morning and she would have to realize that I was not there.

I couldn't bear the idea of eating dinner alone with my mother. This was sort of funny to me, since I couldn't bear the idea of eating one more meal with Zahid and my mother, either. She was flirting with him. There was nothing else to call it. It was disgusting. My mom might look okay, but she was old. There was no way of getting around that fact. It seemed like, if anything, Zahid wanted a mother.

For weeks now, he had been polite, almost indifferent to me. I had been telling myself that he had been hiding his feelings for me, but it occurred to me for the first time that maybe Zahid really and truly was indifferent.

But that wasn't possible. Was it?

It had been so good between us. I was young but I knew what good sex was. I had only had bad sex before that. And that had to be why he was there, in my house, in Connecticut, when he could be anywhere. He was waiting. Waiting for the right time. It would be soon. It would have to be soon or my head might explode.

I would go see my dad.

I would be his little girl.

There was something nice, comforting about that.

For the second day in a row, Ian Thornton came to the pickup line for Amelia. "You're coming swimming with us?" he said. "Right?"

I shook my head, glad to have a reason to say no.

"I'm having dinner with my dad in New York," I said.

"You have a dad," he said.

"Everyone has a dad!" Amelia screamed.

I shrugged. I did not want to see Ian again. Not after what happened the last time I saw him. I was not going to have sex with him, that was for sure.

"We'll walk you to the train," Ian said.

"You don't have to."

Ian and Amelia walked me to the train.

I was grateful they didn't wait with me. I couldn't think of a single thing to say to Ian, with his blond hair and his perfectly chiseled jaw. Or I thought of something but it seemed stupid and I did not say it. I wanted to ask Ian what was going on. Why was he messing with my head? Did he like me? More likely, he was bored. Like me, he probably had no friends in town. This, however, did not seem like a reason to mess with my head. My head, it felt like, had already been properly messed with.

It had been a long time since I had been to my dad's office. I always felt out of place there. Underdressed. Female. Young. Everything in his building was gleaming and fancy. His firm was on the eighty-sixth floor. There were gorgeous views of the Hudson River *and* the East River. I could see the Statue of Liberty from his office.

My dad used to work in the twin towers. He had been inside the second tower when the plane hit. He had walked down all of those stairs, with all of those people. He was one of the people who did not die. He walked straight to the train station and somehow caught the last train to Connecticut. I was just a kid then.

There was a good-looking woman standing with my father at his desk. She was wearing high heels, a short skirt, a creamy white silk tank top. She had short hair, big gold hoop earrings. She looked like a model or an actress hired to play a female employee in my dad's firm.

I stared. This must be the employee my dad had said reminded him of me, the woman who was black except she didn't look black. She was nothing like me. I felt upset that my dad had compared me to her. I felt shy coming into his office.

My dad waved me in. He looked pale, his skin chalky, almost flaky even. He looked thinner. He looked bad.

"Rachel," he said.

He came over and gave me a hug. He smelled different, too, like laundry detergent.

"This is such a nice surprise."

"You're still working," I said.

It came out sounding angry. I supposed that I was angry. It was over ninety degrees outside. I had taken the train and then I'd had to wait for the subway. I was late and still he was making me wait.

"Something came up. A client had some big issues. The issues. Jesus Christ. Clients are an awful lot like children. It turns out it's going to be a late night. I'm sorry, sweetheart. But give me a couple more minutes and we can grab a quick bite. I need a break."

I looked at my father blankly.

Did he not understand that I came into New York to eat dinner with him? I could have gone swimming with Ian and Amelia. I would have gone, I realized, if I did not have other plans.

At that moment, I didn't want to have dinner with my father anyway. What had I been thinking, after all? What a chore it would have been to have dinner with him. We would have to make conversation. He would ask me if I had given any more thought to my major. All my life, it had seemed like my mother was the only parent who mattered. But I had been the one who'd texted him. That had been my mistake.

"It's not going to take long. I promise." My father was back at his desk, frowning at the computer screen, next to his gorgeous employee.

I sat down in a chair across from his desk. I would go to the movies. It didn't matter. There was a movie playing in New York that I wanted to see. He had better give me some money. I pulled out my phone to look up show times.

"Wait a second. Jonathan, aren't you going to introduce me to your daughter?" the woman at his desk said.

"I didn't introduce you?" my dad said.

It was weird, actually. There was something seriously off about him. He looked *sick*.

"Forgive my bad manners. This day went to hell. This is Khloe," my father said. "My best junior analyst. I think I told you about her."

Khloe looked at me. She looked strangely familiar.

"Khloe," my father said, "this is my daughter, Rachel."

"Hi," I said.

"Hello, Rachel," Khloe said. "It's nice to meet you."

I felt like a dingbat.

I was always underdressed in my father's office, but before I had been a kid. It had never mattered.

"I'm sorry you have to wait a little bit. But we had a bit of a crisis," my father said.

"A financial crisis," I said.

Like a news headline.

But I was taking the summer off from the news. I was trying as hard as I could to stay off the Internet. I did not want to hear about the amazing summers my former friends were having. Their amazing jobs. Their amazing boyfriends, parties and vacations and internships. I didn't want to keep up to date with everything political and awful. I did not want to know. I did not have to feel guilty. I was taking care of kids. If anything, I realized, I should have been getting stoned.

"Is the market falling?" I asked.

I thought of Chicken Little.

Khloe laughed.

She was so gorgeous. It really was too much, all of these ridiculously beautiful people. Mandy. Ian. Zahid. Zahid swimming in my swimming pool in a pair of purple swim trunks.

I had started another short story. In it, Zahir meets Amanda, the airline attendant, on a flight to Los Angeles. She invites him to go with her to her hotel. She had tried to reform, to stop with the men and the sex, but there had been turbulence on the flight. She wanted a man. Zahir hesitates, unsure why. He wants a younger woman, not the older woman he was been dating, but he is resisting temptation. He wants to be a good person. The airline attendant was a hottie. What was the problem?

I had paused there. It felt wrong, somehow, giving him a sexual disease. I had hesitated at the keyboard, unsure. I had actually laughed out loud, at myself, as if I were God, as if what I wrote actually mattered. I could punish him if I wanted to. I wanted to.

"I shouldn't," Zahir says.

And then he does.

I ended it there. The reader would know what was coming.

"No," my dad said. "The markets aren't falling. Honestly, Trump has been good for business."

"Don't say that," I said.

"I didn't say I like him," my dad said. "My politics have not changed. Not to worry."

"You're a Democrat?" Khloe asked.

"Of course I am a Democrat. What did you think?" my dad said. "Jesus. What do you think of me?"

"I assume nothing," Khloe said.

"This firm gave a buttload of cash to Hillary Clinton and

she pissed it away," my dad said, as if it had happened yester-day. "The election was hers to lose and she lost it."

His face had turned red.

The subject always upset him.

I looked at Khloe and smiled.

"Honestly," Khloe said, "I could finish this up on my own. I can handle it. You go have dinner with your daughter."

"I can't let you do that," he said.

I didn't know why, but it occurred to me that my dad was lying. Maybe he had changed his mind about wanting to see me. It was fine. Dinner had clearly been a mistake. He could give me money, I thought for the second time that night. My movie started in half an hour. I could still make it.

"Forget it," he said. "The client can wait. We are going to take Khloe to dinner with us."

"We are?" Khloe said.

"Absolutely," my father said. "I want you and Rachel to spend some time together. You are a good role model for my daughter. This couldn't be better."

"Dad," I said.

The look on Khloe's face was apologetic.

"Are you interested in finance?" she asked me.

"This girl," my father said, "doesn't know what she wants to do."

"Dad," I repeated.

And then I hated myself, sounding the way I did. Like a pet-ulant child. Let him be sad and lonely. What did I care? He was an idiot, leaving my mother. She might not be there for him when he changed his mind.

"Forget it," I said. "You have work to do."

"I told you it's fine. Let's go get a burger."

"I'm a vegetarian," I said.

"Since when?" My dad looked up at me.

I'd had dinner with him and Mandy at the beginning of the summer. I had gotten the chicken tacos.

"Since last week," I said. Why not? "I saw a documentary on Netflix about meat production and I am done."

"I think I saw that one," Khloe said. There was always some kind of environmental documentary on Netflix. "It was disgusting, right?"

"Are you a vegetarian?" my father asked Khloe.

She nodded.

"Vegan," she said.

For some reason, I was sure that she was full of shit.

She winked at me. She was. And that was when I figured out who she looked like. A writer. Kristi Taylor. She looked just like her, only with short hair. It was weird, how much she looked like her.

"Whatever," my father said. "This is New York City. You can eat a veggie burger. There is salad."

I shook my head. The only thing I could do was tell him the truth. "I don't want to eat dinner with you. I changed my mind."

"Are you serious?" my father said.

And all of a sudden, he looked nervous. He looked frail. Jesus. The next thing I knew he was going to tell me he had cancer.

"You came all this way, Rachel," he said. "We can go to dinner."

I shrugged.

"Are you mad at me?"

I nodded.

"Why?"

I shrugged.

"You want to talk about it?" he said.

"Not really."

And there really was a movie I wanted to see. Greta Gerwig had directed her first film. Now, she was a role model to me, not some overdressed woman working in finance. Like I would ever dress like that. I would rather be shot than wear the kind of shoes she was wearing. It was fine. I would go see the movie. It was good that I'd said no to Ian Thornton. I was waiting for my professor. I would kiss him first. No big deal. I had done it before. I would do it again.

My father sighed.

"You are so inflexible," he said. "Just like your mother."

This, of course, was not fair. I was not like my mother.

We stared at each other.

"There is this movie I want to see," I said. "Do you want to see the movie with me?"

"No," my father said. "I don't want to see a movie."

"Well, then," I said. "I have to go. It starts soon."

"You'll still join me?" my father asked Khloe. "For dinner. We have to eat."

"I'm not sure," she said. "What movie are you going to see?"

"A Greta Gerwig movie."

"Who?" my father said.

Khloe nodded. "The woman I am seeing wants to see it," Khloe said. "I'll go. I gotta keep up."

"Woman?" my father said.

Khloe shrugged. She was a lesbian. Never, ever, would I have guessed that this woman was gay. Now I found myself blushing again.

"You are full of surprises," my dad said.

"I have a life," she said. "Outside of the office. I keep it private."

"As you should," my dad said.

"I'll go to the movie with you, Rachel," she said. She looked over to my dad. "If you think the situation is under control."

"Seriously?" my father said.

Khloe shrugged. "Jane loves Greta Gerwig."

"Who?" my father said. "Who the fuck is Greta Gerwig?"

The three of us stood there, in my father's office on the eighty-sixth floor, a work crisis that seemed to have been fabricated coming to an end.

"Let's go to the Greta Gerwig movie," my father said.

"You said you didn't want to go."

"I changed my mind."

"I'll get my bag," Khloe said.

"I never go to the movies," my father said. "This will be good for me."

It was true. He had no patience for movies. He only liked documentaries, because he felt like he was learning something. I felt a perverse sort of pleasure, taking him to see a film he wouldn't like.

We rode down the elevator together and then took a taxi to the movie theater. My father ordered a large popcorn and sodas for all of us. He got a bag of dark chocolate almonds with virgin sea salt. It was as if Khloe were my friend, not his employee, and he was taking us to the movies. We found three seats together in the middle of the theater.

"How is your mother?" my father asked.

I was surprised. Maybe he had wanted to ask me this all along. The trailers had just begun. He had waited until now. I shrugged. A movie about Tonya Harding, a figure skater. I had never heard of her.

"Tonya Harding," Khloe said, taking a handful of popcorn. "Seriously? She and her husband paid someone to smash Nancy Kerrigan's knees."

Khloe seemed into it. It was weird that she worked for my father. In a million years, I would not want to do what my father did, though I didn't know what he actually did. I just didn't want to do it. My father said that I did not care about money because I'd always had it.

"I was in town the other day," my dad said.

"You were?"

"I had a doctor's appointment."

A woman behind us *ssssh*ed us.

"It's a trailer," my father said. "Get a grip."

I had forgotten this. This was one of the things my father hated about the movies. He hated other people.

"I saw your mother on the beach. She was with a man," he said. "An Indian guy."

I nodded. I'd had no idea they went to the beach together. It was worse than I'd thought.

"Do you know who he could be?" My father looked nervous.

"My writing professor," I said. My mother was taking walks on the beach with my writing professor. He actually liked her. He had no idea that he was leading her on. "Zahid Azzam."

There. I'd said his name out loud.

Khloe burst out laughing. She spit up chewed-up popcorn. "Jesus," my dad said. "Get a grip."

Was that his new phrase? Was that something Mandy said?

"Zahid Azzam," she said, laughing, laughing too hard. "He is everywhere."

"Who the hell is Zahid Azzam?" my dad said.

I didn't know how to begin. Clearly he did not know we had a houseguest. The movie started. I wanted to see this movie. I really did.

"Who is he?" my dad repeated.

"The movie," I said.

"Shhh," the woman behind us said.

I would not talk to my father about my writing professor.

"Who is he?"

"The movie," I said.

"Are you okay?" he asked Khloe. She had cleaned up the popcorn from her lap. She had stopped laughing. She had reached for her soda.

Khloe nodded.

She was okay.

The beach.

They were taking walks together on the beach.

# *Becca*

Jonathan called in the middle of the night.

"Who is Zahid Azzam?" he wanted to know.

It was my mistake, of course, answering the phone. I had been fast asleep. I thought it was going to be Zahid, though he didn't have this phone number. Not to the landline. The only people who used the landline were Jonathan and telemarketers.

"Jonathan?" I said. "What time is it?"

"I saw you with him," he said.

"What do you mean?"

I sat up in bed. Saw me? Saw me when? How? Where? I felt caught, but I wasn't guilty of doing anything wrong. He had left me. He had seen me? Seen me? At the pool? My heart was racing.

Posey was looking at me, concern in her eyes. She knew this phone call was a disruption in our life, our routine. She was my dog now. I reached out and stroked her head.

What a strange day it had been. With Zahid gone, I had cried on and off all day long. I knew I was ridiculous but that was how I felt, and so I let myself cry. It was almost one hundred degrees out, but I made a tray of baked macaroni and cheese. It was one of Rachel's favorite meals, what she used to ask for on her birthday, three kinds of cheese and bread crumbs. But she had not come home from day camp. I had eaten more than half of the tray all by myself. It tasted so good. I opened a bottle of red wine and I drank too much of that, too.

I had waited for Rachel at the café, but she didn't walk by, and after an hour, I walked home by myself. I texted her and she did not respond. I wondered if I was supposed to worry. I had gotten used to having company for dinner, Rachel and Zahid, and suddenly I was alone again. Rachel was supposed to eat the macaroni and cheese with me. She let herself into the house around midnight, gently shutting the door behind herself, quietly going up the stairs. I knocked on her bedroom door.

"Are you okay?" I said. "I was worried about you."

"I'm fine," she said.

"You didn't answer my texts."

"I am fine," she said. "I'm home."

She did not invite me in and so I did not actually see my daughter. It did not feel good. Rachel was mad at me and I didn't know why. I had been careful. There was no way she could know. Zahid and I had only been together when she was at day camp.

But then again, I also did not know what she *did* see, what she observed when we were all together, what I was like during our dinners together. It took all the strength in me not to touch Zahid's hair, to touch his arm when I passed him a plate of food.

Now Jonathan was on the phone, asking me about Zahid.

"I saw you on the beach with him," Jonathan said.

I didn't know what he was talking about. He saw us? And then, I remembered, we had gone to the beach, just once, walking Posey. Weeks ago. That was before, before we had begun.

"Are you spying on me?"

"You did not answer the question."

"Jonathan. It is the middle of the night."

"Rachel says he is staying at the house. This writer."

"You saw Rachel?"

"You seem surprised. She is my daughter."

"I didn't know you saw her."

"Yes," Jonathan said. "Tonight. We went to the movies."

The movies. Jonathan never went to the movies. He hated the movies, he hated everything about going to a movie theater. He complained about the price of the popcorn. Whereas I had been home all alone. I would have gone to the movies with Rachel. I loved the movies. Why did I feel so betrayed? I wanted to ask what movie.

All day, I had had a bad feeling. Something would happen. To Zahid. To us. I didn't want to let him leave. It was only a job interview. But it was for a job far away. There was no reason for him to go, not if he didn't want the job. He'd told me he didn't want this job. So why did he go? Not only would this mean Zahid leaving me, he would take his dog with him.

I blamed Rachel for all of this.

She had brought this trouble into my life.

The standard poodle. Her writing professor.

I looked at the cordless phone I was holding in my hand, wondering why I was holding it. It was ugly. Jonathan had bought it at Costco, strangely pleased because it was so cheap. He had wanted this phone in the bedroom. I never talked on the phone. I should just cancel the line, there was no reason to pay for it anymore. I was about to hang up, but then I heard Jonathan, saying my name.

"Look, Becca," Jonathan said.

"What?"

"I did some research on him."

"What?"

"I Googled him," Jonathan said. "There is a strange man living in my house. I am going to find out what I can."

"This is crazy."

"Look, Becca. He is not a good guy. He has a reputation. He got dumped at the altar."

What? What was he saying? How was it that he knew more about my lover than I did? Zahid had almost gotten married? I had Googled him, too, but somehow missed this piece of information. I had reviews of his book. I wondered if Jonathan had read Zahid's book. What a funny book club we would make. The Klein family.

I did not know where to begin.

"Your house." That is what I landed on.

"My name is on the title, still," he said. "Yes, it is my house."

"Are you kidding me? You want to talk about this now? You seriously don't want to do this."

It was 2:06 in the morning; there was the time illuminated on the red lights of the digital clock. Jonathan was reminding me of all the shit that lay ahead of us. I had contacted my lawyer, of course, months ago, when Jonathan first told me about the pilot, but I had not acted on any of his suggestions. It did not seem as if there was any hurry. Rachel was at college. Jonathan had gone off to Tribeca. My lawyer had suggested mediation. As custody was not an issue, this lawyer had said, if we were willing to be amicable, a divorce would be simple enough.

"Half of the house is mine," Jonathan told me now. This had not been part of his leaving speech.

"No," I said. "It is my house. Every single part of this house is a reflection of me. My taste. It's my house."

"Legally, half of it is mine."

Now it seemed like I was going to have to go ahead and divorce him. He wouldn't just leave things be. He had everything he wanted and that wasn't enough. If he wanted a fight, I would give him a fight.

"It is the middle of the fucking night, Jonathan."

For some reason, I couldn't get past that.

I should have hung up right then, but I held off. Did I owe him something? Did I have to explain myself? We had never talked about it. About why. Why he was leaving. He'd told me he was leaving and he'd left. Just like that. I had cried for my dog.

"That man should not be in the house," Jonathan said. "Rachel is young. She is impressionable. He is a good-looking man. This has to be confusing for her. Hell, it must be confusing for you."

"Are you kidding me?" I said.

I was not confused about Zahid. I had made the first move. The first time, and then again, the next time. I had had to let Zahid know that it was okay. He was not going to get into trouble. We were almost there, I thought. Soon, it would be a month together. What we did not need was interference.

"Rachel seems moody and aloof," Jonathan said. "I am worried about her."

"That isn't why you are calling me in the middle of the night. Rachel is always moody and aloof."

"Why, Rebecca, are you spending time with him?"

"You saw us walking the dog," I said.

I did not know why I was defending myself.

"You were laughing."

"Do you hear yourself?" I said. "I am not supposed to laugh? You are living in Tribeca with your airline hostess."

"She is a pilot."

"A pilot. Whatever."

"Where is he sleeping, Becca?" Jonathan said. "Tell me."

"Are you kidding me?" I said. "Are you serious?"

"I am coming over tomorrow."

"No," I said. "You're not invited."

"I don't care."

"Don't come," I said. "You are not welcome here."

"Becca," Jonathan said. "I want to see you."

That, that surprised me.

"I want to see you," he repeated. His voice cracked.

"What about your pilot?" I asked him.

"This has nothing to do with Mandy," he said. "I just want to see you."

"I don't want to see you," I said.

This, I realized, was the truth.

"You're angry."

"That has nothing to do with it."

"You have every reason to be angry," Jonathan said.

"How is Mandy?" I asked him. "How is your pilot?"

"Did you hear me, Becca?"

"You didn't answer my question."

"Which question?"

"How is Mandy?"

"You didn't answer my question."

"Which question?"

This was getting ridiculous. There was no chance of my going back to sleep.

"Where does he sleep, Becca?"

"It's none of your business."

"Where does he sleep?"

It didn't matter. I wanted to get Jonathan off the phone. I told him the truth. "He sleeps in your office."

This was an acceptable answer, apparently. Jonathan did not explode. It did not tell the whole story, of course, but Jonathan had left me. My life was my own.

"Mandy is very young," Jonathan said. "There is a lot I didn't know about her, it turns out."

There it was. Of course. Trouble in paradise. What did he think would happen?

And then I wondered: How old exactly was Zahid? Was he older than Mandy? I was wide awake. My day tomorrow was ruined. I was angry. I was furious.

"How did this happen?" Jonathan asked.

"You are asking me this now? Shouldn't you find a therapist?"

I looked at Posey. Her tail thumped on the bed. I was so glad to have this poodle. Your husband could leave you for a younger pilot. Your lover could leave you for a job interview. But a poodle was loyal. This dog was my poodle.

"I wish you had gone to Paris with me," Jonathan said.

He always came back to that trip to Paris. That trip to Paris I'd never wanted to take. And if I had gone, would that have saved our marriage? Though I did not know it at the time, there was already a Mandy. If anything, I'd wanted to go to Iceland. There had been a picture of a swimming pool in front of a snow-covered mountain in *The New York Times* that I had never forgotten. I had told Jonathan I wanted to swim in that pool, but he hadn't taken me seriously.

"Do you know what I wish?" I said.

"What?"

"I wish that Posey hadn't died. I wish that you had been with me when I took her to the vet to have her put to sleep."

"She was just a dog, Becca," Jonathan said.

"Just a dog?"

I was out of bed. On my feet. I wanted to throw something. I almost threw the phone. Posey jumped off the bed, too, wagging her tail. She thought I was taking her out for a walk. Fine. I would take her on a walk.

"What if I wanted to come home?" Jonathan asked. "Becca? I am being serious. I want to come home."

And then I did throw the phone.

It smashed the TV, a big spiderweb crack along the black screen, but that was fine. It was just a TV and I had never watched the TV in the bedroom anyway. It was Jonathan's TV. I had been meaning to get rid of it. It was Jonathan who liked to watch the news before bed. It was the least healthy thing a person could do, especially during primary season, the debates, and then the goddamn election, and ever since. Poison on the television. For months, Jonathan ranted about

Hillary Clinton. And then Donald Trump. He ranted and he raved. Though I had not realized it until this moment, I was glad to get all of them out of my house.

"Good riddance," I said.

Posey was still wagging her tail.

It made me sad. She loved me, but she wasn't my dog. She wasn't the real Posey. Everything had been fine, I thought, until the election.

# *Zahid*

I understood why Kristi had made the choice she'd made: going back to school, the academic life. It was so bloody safe. She rented her cute little house. Her rent was ridiculously low. She used her fellowship money to pay for groceries and secondhand cardigan sweaters. She worked on her novel. She wrote papers about literature and she went to classes where people very much like her argued passionately about literature as if what they said and thought about books actually mattered. At night, they went to French movies and local bars. They also got plastered. Professors fucked their students. Grad students fucked other grad students. Some of this fucking led to marriage. There was accompanying heartbreak and scandal. There was a whole lot of fucking going on at writers' programs. Sometimes, there was writing. Strangely enough, I used to love this: the writer's life. Until I started to hate it.

I was as surprised as Kristi that I had started writing again. I was elated and exhilarated. I was not a has-been. I was not ready to be flushed down the toilet. Fame, I was beginning to understand, hadn't been good for me. I had liked it too much.

I had loved all of the attention and the interviews and the parties and the panels and being asked my opinion—about the best books, my favorite restaurants. I had a favorite pen to recommend, a favorite Moleskine journal. I had once been asked about the best bath products for writers and I had opinions about that, too.

I also loved the women who came with this life. It had come easy, starting with the story in *The Best American Short Stories*. My first published story. I was also lucky in my eyelashes, Kristi often said, as if that explained it.

In high school and college, too, the white girls wanted to fuck me. They wanted me to be their chem partners and debate partners, but they did not want to date me. I wasn't considered boyfriend material and I understood this was because of the color of my skin and I should have been profoundly upset, I recognized the inherent racism at play, but strangely, I didn't care. I did not want a girlfriend. I got what I wanted, sex and help with my homework, help that was invaluable, help that got me through my required courses. It was somehow assumed that I was good at math and science and I just wasn't. It was English where I excelled, writing that came easy.

"Because you are full of shit," Kristi liked to say.

I could wax poetic.

Suddenly, the girls had become women, and these women wanted real grown-up relationships. There was talk about the families they envisioned having. It seemed inevitable. I did not meet a single woman who did not want monogamy, kids, and so when I realized I had hit that turning point, I figured I would settle down with the most famous writer I fucked.

Emily was beautiful. Like me. She was rich, too. She came

from family money and I very much liked that. After getting engaged, I realized that I had the life I wanted. I was like that writer on the TV series people were so nuts about. Her parents had a big house in East Hampton, a gorgeous swimming pool, a trail through the dunes that led right to the ocean. My fiancée wanted only one child. I could do that.

Of course, the rules changed with a relationship. With the engagement, even more so. We had a fancy party and that was fun. Our picture appeared in the Sunday Styles section of *The New York Times*, with a little article, too. Emily loved that. She had it framed and hung it in the bathroom, which was supposed to be ironic, but it wasn't.

I was supposed to stop fucking other women. More important, I was supposed to care about someone other than myself. The truth was, I didn't love her. I thought I put on a good show of it. For instance, in the time we were together, I never got caught cheating on her.

In the end, I confessed. I had been forced to confess, because of the health issue, but I had confessed nonetheless. What if she had forgiven me? It seemed conceivable at the time. My fiancée knew who I was. It was not as if I hadn't come with a reputation, a user history.

"No one forgives a venereal disease," Kristi told me.

Was that true? Somewhere in the history of time, this transgression must have been forgiven. Maybe if we had been properly in love. I hadn't been the same since Emily called off the wedding. It was not that I lost the family beach house. Or that after she moved out, my rent doubled. It was not that she had been sending out my laundry for me and I had never appreciated that fact. Or the house cleaner that came once a week. Or the spot-on editing help.

It seemed that my ex had blacklisted me.

My bad behavior cost me speaking engagements. My bad behavior was the reason a short story was rejected from *The New Yorker* and *The Paris Review*. My ex, it turned out, was vengeful. She wanted to destroy me. She wrote angry posts about me on social media, leaving out my name, but people *knew*. She had fucked over my life, but I was the bad guy. I had no right to complain.

"She had every right to be angry," Kristi said.

Kristi also posited that it might be my attitude that had contributed to my undoing. My general lack of gratitude. My lack of modesty. My enormous ego. She thought I had work to do. She thought I had to earn my redemption.

"Most writers work really, really hard," she said.

My six-hundred-page novel had not been difficult to write. I was so stoned, in fact, that I barely remembered writing it. I was a complete unknown when it came out. No one expected anything from me. It felt impossible to get back to that place.

That working-really-hard bullshit. Fuck that, really. I was not a construction worker. I was not on an assembly line. I honestly believed that the rules could and should be different for me. Why not? Why was everyone required to work so hard? In the end, we all died. I had an advance from my publisher, and then a Whiting Award, a Guggenheim, and all of this allowed me to coast for quite some time.

"You became complacent," Kristi said. "That is what happened to you."

And so what? It was when I realized that I was out of money that I took that job at the college on the Hudson. It was an okay gig, a couple of years, and then that contract ended, and they didn't rehire me, they hired a new young superstar writer, and fuck. Now I was supposed to move to the Midwest? Was that really my fate? Had it come to that? How had it come to that? I was getting e-mail after e-mail from my new editor, some Jane So-and-so, asking me to lunch, asking about my ideas for the new book, inviting me to a party, asking again to meet her for lunch, asking if I would like to discuss my book, if I would like to brainstorm new ideas. They were friendly e-mails, growing possibly less friendly over time.

"You don't need a lawyer," Kristi assured me.

I was afraid the publisher would want the money back. But it would cost them more to get the money back, the lawyers and the bad publicity, than to let me rot. Better, Kristi said, would be to write the book. Everything Kristi said was maddening, but I felt like after losing my fiancée, I could not afford to cut her loose. I needed this annoying voice in my ear.

My beloved Amma was the only person in this world who had understood that I was different. That I was, in fact, truly special. Of all the grandchildren, and there were a lot us, twelve in fact, she had chosen me. I had been her favorite. She had told me that I wasn't suited for this world. I had always found this troubling. If not Earth, where? I was not a cat. I also didn't completely understand her. Her English was broken. My Urdu was broken. She called me her little kitty. I adored that. I adored her.

Becca seemed to understand me. She was eighteen years older than I was, and this felt right to me. Our bodies felt right. She had a terrific body. She swam laps. She did yoga in front of her large-screen television. Once, we did yoga in front of the television together and ended up with tangled limbs, making love on the living room floor. It was the only time we had sex inside the house. We had not made love in a bed. We did not talk about why. We did not have to. I understood. Her daughter. Rachel. Rachel was the biggest mistake I had ever made. I was afraid to look at her daughter. Becca was beautiful without her clothes, naked in the sun, unapologetic. I felt lucky.

I was afraid that I might tell Kristi everything. I could imagine how it would sound to my friend who did everything the way one was supposed to. She would think me ridiculous, falling in love with a fifty-four-year-old woman, not even divorced, with a big house and a swimming pool.

I would drink a few drinks with Kristi and she would inform me of the error of my ways. She would say that I had just been stroking my vanity but it was time to grow up, enter the real world. Up until now, that was what Kristi was for. Bringing me back to the real world.

But I had no interest in the real world. The real world was a miserable place. The real world was a shit show. America was a fucking laughingstock, worse than the third world, fascist, racist, classist. Home. My fellow writers, every day, were writing brilliant tweets and Facebook posts, protesting intolerance, sexual harassment, and every single thing that was important, that needed saying, and they were somehow also changing the literary landscape and gaining enormous numbers of followers. It was cool to be a person of color. Oppressed. This was not said, but understood. This, at least, I had going for me.

My new editor had begun following me on Instagram. I had an account but had never once posted on Instagram. I did not see the use of it. Kristi told me that it had been so many years since my book, that I needed to get more active on social media. Twitter was not enough.

"Your poodle," Kristi told me. "You post pictures of your dog. Easy. Everyone loves dog and cat pictures."

Instead, I reviewed my neglected Twitter account. I looked at all of my old posts, stunned at what I had revealed over time. I had laid my life bare. I went and deleted it all. Not my actual account, but two years' worth of tweets. I would return to Becca, cleansed, an open book.

From that day forward.

"Impossible." I could hear Kristi laughing. "Just Google yourself."


In Iowa, I was on my best behavior. I gave a reading on campus even though Kristi had not informed me there would be a reading. I read the first chapter of my new book and I was praised and patted on the back and it didn't even surprise me. I had been reborn. I was back, I was Zahid Azzam, once again.

I went to a party and I drank only four glasses of wine. I did not behave inappropriately. Tempted as I was, I did not touch Kristi's bare arm and shoulders, tantalizingly close. She could feel me pulling away and this was working. Had I made a move this time, she might have succumbed. I did not make a pass at my short-haired, tattooed driver, who had a strange kind of charm of her own.

Most important, I did not tell Kristi anything about Becca. Not a thing.

"Come on," she said. "You know you tell me everything. It's going to happen. Talk."

She tried to tickle me. This was a victory, of course. Kristi touching me. I did not respond. I told her nothing.

I taught my class. I made intelligent comments about the students' stories, stories I had quickly scanned on the airplane before falling asleep. I gave a short defense of adverbs, currently a part of speech non grata in the writing world. In the past, the one criticism of my work had been overwriting, which was ridiculous. Nothing was worse than those minimalist writers and their short, lean sentences. I was contradictory, I knew, rallying against *just* and *really* and *very* but fine with *leisurely*. I had an aesthetic. It had been called the Azzam factor.

"Use adverbs," I told a classroom full of earnest grad students, and I shook my fist, causing the students to laugh.

I went to lunch with the dean, a famous writer whose work I had never made the effort to read. I never saw the need to read everything out there. Basically, I was very pleasant. I wore nice clothes that I had made sure to iron and hang properly.

For once, Kristi was pleased with me. She thought I had gotten my shit together.

"You pulled it off, Z," she said.

She thought she was saving my life, that I was well on the road to being saved, and I was, but not in the way she thought.

"Tell me the truth," she said. "What is going on in Connecticut?"

"Kristi," I said. "I can't."

"You can't," she said. "Or you won't?"

"I won't."

She knew that I was staying with the lovestruck student and her mother. I had confessed, earlier, to a small crush on Becca, but that was all she knew. All I had told her. It was so hard not to tell her everything.

"Rich white people, Zahid," she said with a dramatic sigh. "You know how that goes."

My fiancée had been a rich white person but Kristi had liked her. Kristi was still friends with my former fiancée. Kristi's circle of friends were an exotic bunch, a literary Benetton commercial, but she exclusively dated white men. Kristi Taylor was full of shit. I had nominated her novel for the award she'd won and it was full of shit. She stole the life of her twin sister. I was surprised that Khloe had not killed her. I was afraid of Khloe. I realized that I should be grateful to her. She had sent me on my true path. Connecticut, she had said, is supposed to be beautiful. She had no idea.

"Do you know how racist you sound?" I told Kristi.

"I worry about you," she said.

"I know you do," I said. "You can stop already."

"Seriously," she said.

"Seriously," I said. "It's emasculating."

"What does this have to do with gender roles?"

"Not a thing," I said. "Your worrying about me just makes my penis shrink."

"I did not need to know that."

Kristi offered to drive me to the airport, but I had already arranged to have my tattooed writer take me. I had almost cracked, I had almost told Kristi about Becca, but instead, I'd pissed her off on a political level. That was better. I was getting better, as if I were recovering from a long illness. I thought about my grandmother. She had believed in me. I had achieved writer stardom beyond any writer's wildest dreams and she had not been surprised.

"I hope you get the job," Kristi said, walking me to the front door.

"Thank you," I said.

I knew that I would get the job. I was fairly sure that I would not take it. I was pleased with myself. I liked thinking this way. Envisioning my future. The house, the woman, the rocky beach, the swimming pool. The dog. The book. My destiny.

This time, my driver didn't charge me for the trip to the airport. I knew that she wouldn't.

Becca picked me up at the airport.

I wrapped my arms around her in a passionate embrace. I put my hands in her hair. She put her hands on my ass. I had left her, I had risked everything we had, and she was waiting for me.

We kissed until we were out of breath. I could feel people walking around us, making a safe circle for our love. We took a step apart and I beheld her beloved face.

"Zahid," Becca said, and I loved the way it sounded, hearing her say my name.

"I want to make love in a bed," I said.

Becca nodded, efficient and wise. She called her daughter, asking her to walk the dog. We would make love in a bed. It would not be her bed. This made sense to me; it also made me sad. I did not want for us to be a secret any longer, but I understood. I had not told Kristi about Becca. I was keeping our love safe. Becca was doing that, too. Every day, I was more and more impressed with my new lover.

"I'm having dinner with Shelley," she said on the phone to her daughter. I had never heard of this Shelley. Becca had a friend named Shelley. I listened to Becca lie. She was terrifically good at it. I would have believed her. For a moment, I began to worry that she had changed her mind about sleeping with me in a hotel bed and had made other plans.

"I have been drinking wine," she said. "Yep, windy roads, getting dark soon, so I decided to stay over. Mm-hmmm, I'll be back tomorrow. You're fine?" Becca nodded. "Are you sure?"

I listened to her, it was a different role, mother, and I almost felt jealous of Rachel, who had no idea how lucky she was. "The morning. Not too late. Just feed Posey and take her out before camp. I'll pick you up from work, okay? At the café."

There was silence.

"I have no idea," Becca said, and I knew she was talking about me. There was a new defensive quality to her voice, and I felt almost relieved; she was not the best liar. I watched Becca bite her lip, look away from me.

One day, Becca and I would have to tell Rachel about us, but I hoped we would be able to put this off for a very long time. Rachel, of course, had the power to destroy us. I was terrified of this young Rachel. Suddenly, I wanted to ask Kristi what she thought. I wanted to know how she thought I could fix this situation. But she had explicitly and repeatedly told me her opinion about rich white people and sleeping with students.

*You are a fucking moron.* That is exactly what Kristi would say to me. I had made the right choice, not talking to Kristi. I would stay strong. I realized I was probably done with Kristi. Our friendship had run its course. It had been a difficult time for me, being publicly dumped for the asshole that I was. After the humiliation, I was able to go out with Kristi on my arm. She had not taken sides. I had nominated her for the award she had won. We were even.

It made me feel sad.

We had broken up, Kristi and I, and she did not even know.

Becca drove us straight to a hotel in New Haven. She had only her left hand on the steering wheel so that we could hold hands. We did not talk.

At the front desk of the hotel, Becca asked for a room and she paid for it with her credit card, and then we fucked on a king-sized bed, and it was different, it was better, our bodies did not get stuck in the cracks of the plastic pool chairs. When we were done, we fell asleep spooned together, and when we woke in the morning, still spooned together, she turned over in the bed and kissed me and I felt happy.

I looked into Becca's blue eyes.

I looked at the lines around her eyes.

Her long brown hair.

"I love a good hotel," I said.

Did she know that this was my way of saying *I love you*? I did not want to scare her. I traced the creases around her eyes. I kissed her nose. I kissed her mouth. I liked kissing Becca in the morning. She tasted different, she tasted like sleep.

"Coffee?" she said.

I nodded.

"Breakfast?" she asked. "Are you hungry?"

I nodded again.

She ordered room service.

She kissed me, a real kiss, none of this butterfly-on-the-nose business. There we were, in our hotel bed. I was naked. Becca had put on a shirt to sleep in. I slid it over her head.

# *Khloe*

I didn't like the movie.

It was one of those art house films about a girl who was different, growing up, brave enough to be herself. It kind of made me nauseous how earnest and quirky and well done it was. I was supposed to love it, I knew. Jane and Winnie would have loved it. And this was why I had a job in finance. Why I was not in the arts. I was way too fucking cynical. I would rather have a chase scene in my movie. An actual movie star. I would have taken a black character, for fuck's sake. The sidekick best friend was overweight instead. She was cute actually.

Rachel Klein, of course, loved the movie. Jonathan Klein kept looking at his phone. He sent more than one text, which was very bad movie behavior. Something was going on with him, obviously. There had been no crisis at work. The woman in the row behind hissed at him every time.

"Cunt," my boss whispered under his breath.

It was a bad choice of words, not that I wasn't used to it. Guys at work, this language, it was all the time. I could give a shit. I felt bad for Rachel, because this was her father and she must have heard him. It was terrible to have to realize that your father was a shit. My father had died when I was in high school and maybe because he was dead, he had been become perfect in my mind. A saint. The very best dad. He had married a black woman before it was okay to marry out of your race. But our whole childhood, somehow, it had been okay. Life in a midwestern college town. A happy bubble. I had had a happy childhood. My father would never have called a woman a cunt.

I guess I did give a shit. It was at that moment, when my boss thoughtlessly cursed a woman under his breath, using a word that derogatorily described her genitalia, that I realized I didn't like him. I realized I might want to get another job. After I got my bonus.

In the taxi on the way to the theater, Jonathan had said how glad he was that his daughter had met me. He said that I was a good influence. This, of course, was after he learned that I was a lesbian. But I did not give him points for that. It was okay that I was a lesbian because I was the femme kind. It was the same way that I was black, the good kind, attractive and well educated. I wanted to say something to blow his mind. I wanted to channel some radical Kristi rhetoric and bust out some Angela Davis black feminist manifesto, but I didn't have the vocabulary.

"She doesn't know what she is majoring in," Jonathan had said, as if this were a real problem.

This clearly annoyed his daughter. A recurring conversation. Rachel glared at him. She was wearing a black T-shirt and tan Capri pants, her long brown hair pulled back in a loose ponytail, a style as boring and nondescript as clothes could be. Still, she was pretty. She was young and she was effortlessly pretty in a way that suggested she did not know how pretty she was.

She was not what I would have expected. I had always been suspicious of rich kids. Rachel Klein seemed all right. She was, I realized with a start, the student, the one Zahid had messed around with. I felt something catch in my throat. Poor kid, I wanted to say, then and there. I wanted to kiss the top of her head. Zahid should have known better.

I gave her my business card.

"Because I am, like, a mentor figure and all that," I said.

I didn't think she would ever call me.

On the way home, I stopped off at a bar in my neighborhood. I wanted a drink, two drinks, maybe possibly three. I felt loose and free, glad to be away from the Kleins, my boss and Rachel, with her sad kitten face. I had a feeling that anything that involved Zahid Azzam would turn to shit.

This made me want to protect Jane. She somehow believed she needed his next book. This was the dumbest thing I had ever heard. She was a great editor, the editor of many successful books. Jane did not need Zahid. I knew the real Zahid. I had seen him puke all over his own home.

I had not heard from Jane in a couple of days. I did not know what the rules were. Obviously, Jane wanted to maintain some distance, and I would respect that, stupid as it was. I was waiting for her to call me. That was why I'd gone to the movies.

I was not going to go home with anyone I met at the bar, no matter how cute she was, because I was with Jane. But I could always buy a woman a drink. I was making up rules in my head when I opened the door and saw Jane and Winnie, deep in conversation at a booth in the back of the bar, sitting next to each other instead of across the table. Jane's hand was stroking Winnie's hand, a hand that was on Winnie's knee. The intimacy of this told me everything, explained why Jane had not called, had not answered my texts.

Jesus fuck. Fucking hell. I had put an end to that. I had taken Jane home from the literary party and she was with me.

I was going to turn around, leave, but they saw me.

"Oh," I said.

Winnie waved me over. Jane removed her hand from Winnie's hand. Honestly, this kind of shit did not happen to me. I was tall and biracial and sexy. But then there was Winnie. Her blond hair fell straight like a pane of glass. This was who my Jewish babysitter wanted? I had planned on seducing Winnie, with the idea of making Jane jealous, but had gone home with Jane instead. No more games, I had thought, and now this. This. Motherfucking fuck.

I stood there, just inside the bar, where I had so desperately wanted a drink. The air-conditioning felt much too cold. Kristi had been so psyched for me. She had understood. The babysitter, she'd squealed, and I had squealed with her. I had told Kristi about Jane and I had fucking sabotaged myself. I knew better than to tell Kristi anything anymore and I'd told her anyway.

After all these years, Jane still didn't see me as a person. I was still that little kid. I remember giggling, reading books, snuggling under the covers, refusing to let her go, begging her to stay in my bed with me until I fell asleep. I remember Jane kissing my nose, kissing my ears, kissing my toes. *Go to sleep, sweet Khloe,* she said, and I would beg her to kiss me some more. Fuck, I was blinking away tears.

I wasn't sure what I was supposed to do.

Get a drink and bring it over to the booth in the back.

Get a drink and sit at the bar.

Turn the fuck around.

That seemed like the best option. Even though they had seen me. Even though I desperately wanted that drink.

"Khloe," Jane said. "Come here. Come sit with us. Let's talk. This is fine. This is okay. We are all friends. Come here."

Oh. So we were supposed to be mature. That was how we were supposed to play it.

"Please," Jane said. "Please. Come sit down."

I walked the fuck out of the bar.


I got a text message.

I thought it would be from Jane, apologizing.

It was from Rachel. Rachel Klein.

How the fuck did she get my number?

I had given her my card.

I was back in Zahid's apartment, drinking beer. I'd finished an entire beer in three sips and then opened another.

Rachel: I figured out who you look like.
Me: Who?
Rachel: This writer I love. Kristi Taylor.

I spit out my beer. First popcorn, then this. Fuck.

Me: I am her twin sister.
Rachel: Holy shit. Identical?
Me: I dress better.
Rachel: I didn't know she had a twin.

This had already happened to me a couple of times this summer. Kristi had always acted like she was famous, she talked about that literary prize as if it should mean something to me, but I had never believed her until I'd moved to Brooklyn.

Rachel: This may sound weird. But would you want to go
out for coffee?

I thought about Jane and Winnie at the bar, Jane's hand on Winnie's knee. I cracked open another beer. If I had to pick between beer and coffee, I would pick beer. I felt good about this. I nodded to myself, as if I had made an important decision. I would rather drink beer.

Me: Drink?
Rachel: Sure. If you're buying. I am ever so slightly under-
age.
Me: How old?
Rachel: 19

I could deal with that. I had no interest in drinking coffee as a social activity. Going out for coffee was a cultural activity I did not understand. A waste of time.

Me: Sure. I will buy you alcohol.
Rachel: I could get you in trouble at work. With my
father. Not worth it?

I stared at my beer. I was not the kind of person who got cheated on. I was also way the fuck hotter than Jane. I was just as hot as Winnie. Hotter. Fuck. I made more money than both of them. Still, she had not chosen me.

Now I had this little girl sending me texts. Leading me on and then cautioning me. What the fuck? I was not a child molester. I was better than that.

I was not going to fucking get into trouble.

I was not an asshole like Zahid.

The boss's daughter. Why was she writing me? I wouldn't fuck her. I could be like a mentor, couldn't I? Isn't that what I'd told her? I could steer her out of the arts before it was too late. I could steer her away from playboys like Zahid. I could help her, sure, but why would I do that? I didn't need to get involved with the boss's daughter, even if I wasn't going to fuck her, even if she had read the novel written by my twin sister, a book Kristi never should have fucking published, a book about the year I came out. It was *my* coming-out story, including flashbacks about me and my babysitter, tuck-ins and trips to the lake. Things I had told Kristi never realizing that she would one day write about me. I didn't know what Jane thought of this book, if she had recognized herself in any way. I had never asked her. My twin sister had stolen my fucking life for her career. She thought I wouldn't care, since I didn't read books or hang out with people who read books.

I cared.

Of course I'd read the book. I had read the reviews, too, critics pronouncing the main character, based on me, to be unsympathetic. Cold. Calculating. Amoral. Borderline sociopath. In the book, I had been molested by my babysitter, but that was not what had happened. Not exactly.

I wondered why I talked to either of them.

Jane.

Kristi.

I was done with them both.

We were over. I had decided, even if they had no idea. I stared at my phone. I was done waiting for Jane. My involvement with all of these literary people was starting to affect my judgment.

And then, Rachel? She was the student who'd taken in Zahid's dog. Was she sleeping with him, still? Zahid was taking walks with the girl's mother. Why the fuck was this something I was even thinking about? If I could change one thing in my life, I would not be a fucking identical twin.

My phone vibrated on the table.

I looked.

Again, not Jane with a forthcoming apology. Not that I would forgive her. It was Rachel. Again. I wanted it to be Jane.

Rachel: Forget drink. Want to go to the beach? Come to Ct? It's not far. You can take the train. It's pretty here?

The beach? With Rachel Klein. Not a chance.

But I had not been to the beach once this fucking summer. Not one single fucking time. I had been working and I had been drinking and trying to seduce my babysitter and working.

Me: Maybe. I might. Sure.

Why the fuck not? That is what I told myself. I got up and took another beer from the refrigerator. It was cold and good. I was getting drunk. I was still waiting for that text from Jane. Fuck, I was waiting for a knock on the fucking door. The bar was just around the corner. She should be here by now, begging me to forgive her. Begging to get into my bed.

The knock did not come.

My phone vibrated.

It was from Rachel Klein, again, a link to train schedules. I was not going to hear from Jane. So I opened Facebook. I went to Jane's FB page. There was a link to some article about one of her writers. Then a picture of her cat. She was a fucking lesbian posting pictures of her cat. I scrolled down and, yes, there was another fucking picture of her cat.

I scrolled farther down and someone had tagged Jane in a photo. It was a picture of Jane and Winnie at some book party, their arms around each other. This picture had been posted a week and a half ago. They were both wearing black dresses. I recognized the dresses. They were from the night I went home with Jane.

But they weren't a couple, they were co-workers. Winnie was experimenting. She had a boyfriend. The night we met, she had told me about her boyfriend. She had shown me a picture of him on her phone and he was as handsome as she was pretty. I was the one who was in love with Jane. I had been in love with Jane since I was five years old.

What the fuck?

Was I supposed to go to sleep?

How was I supposed to go to sleep?

I closed my eyes and I could see Jane's hand on Winnie's knee. I scanned my Facebook feed. I had three hundred-something friends; I didn't even know who the fuck they were. I was almost never on Facebook.

Somehow, all the posts were about guns.

*Not again.*

*I am praying for Texas.*

*26 people.*

Gun control. Blah blah blah. Something had happened. What else was new? So I went to *The New York Times*. There had, of course, been another mass shooting. The shooter had been another white man. Fuck white men. But I knew this already. I was a lesbian, for fuck's sake.

The news of the world would get you sick. I tried not to read it, except for the business section, which told me everything I needed to know, anyway.

I didn't click on the actual article. What the fuck did this shooting have to do with me? I drank more beer. Fucking guns. Fucking white men. I worked almost exclusively with fucking white men.

Why had I chosen this work? I wanted the money. I loved money. I loved a stack of fresh bills. I loved buying white silk shirts from French designers. Three-hundred-dollar shirts. They gave me a thrill.

Still.

Fuck.

I finished my beer. How many beers had it been?

I was drunk and I was heartsick.

She did not love me.

# *Rachel*

My mother had acted strangely while Zahid was away, and now he was back and she was just as strange. For the first time that I could remember, she did not go grocery shopping. She did not wake up early to help me get ready for camp. I had opened the door to her bedroom the night before, convinced that I would find them. I found Princess and my mother on the bed together. My mother was sleeping. Princess wagged her tail. I put my finger to my lips and closed the door.

Today I was up first. Made the coffee. I ground the last of the beans. Really, I wanted coffee waiting for me in the morning. I was angry at my mother for sleeping in. Gone were the days when my mother made me avocado toast. I wanted my avocado toast back. There were no avocados. We were out of bread. There was nothing for breakfast. I could not remember the last time this had happened.

To me, this was a sign.

Everything was wrong.

I wanted my mother back.

I heard a door creak open upstairs. Princess came running

down the steps and my mother followed behind her. She was wearing her pajamas, a soft pink V-neck T-shirt and matching short cotton shorts. She looked good. Slim. Fit. I did not want Zahid to see my mother like this. He had been at our house for more than a month. It was time for him to leave. Either I would sleep with him again or he would have to go. Enough was enough. I took a large sip of coffee. The coffee was much too hot, burned going down. I dropped the mug, the red ceramic cup shattering, coffee all over the clean floor.

My mother stared at the mess, confused. She did not make a move to clean it up.

"I love that cup," she said.

Somehow this made me mad. I had not meant to break the cup. I liked it, too. That was why I had chosen it for my coffee.

She did not ask if I was okay, if I had burned myself.

"Do we have paper towels?" I asked her.

The paper towels were on the paper towel rack under the cupboards over the sink, where they always were, but I wanted my mother to clean up the mess. She didn't move. I found the dustbin under the sink. I grabbed the paper towels and I cleaned up the coffee and the broken cup, and then, because my mother still had not moved in any way to help me, I poured myself another cup and one for my mother, too.

"Thank you, sweetie," she said.

My mother sat at the table. She took a sip of her coffee. I had given her the other red mug. At one point there had been six of them, all of them handmade, sold at a local store, but now we were down to one. "I didn't know you knew how to make coffee this good," she said. "What else don't I know?"

"I am nineteen years old, Mom," I said. "I can do a lot of things."

"Sometimes," she said, "I can't remember the time when you were a baby."

I looked at her. This was strange, too. Why was she talking about this?

"Sometimes, I look at babies," my mother said. "And I think, Did I do that? Did I change your diapers? Did I wake up in the middle of the night and feed you? I can't remember so much of that time."

"You don't remember? My being a baby? Really?"

"A lot of that time is lost," she said.

"Oh," I said.

I felt hurt. I was her only child. Her only baby.

"I know," my mother said.

"Do you have early Alzheimer's?" I asked. "Is that it? Why don't you remember?"

"That is a horrible thing to say."

"Well, it's sort of horrible you forgot my infancy," I said.

"I'm sorry." My mother looked at her red coffee mug. She did not look at all sorry. "I didn't know that would upset you. I was just thinking out loud."

"I saw Dad," I said.

"Jonathan?"

"Yes," I said. "Jonathan. That is my father's name. The man you are still officially married to. Did you forget him, too?"

My mother shrugged. "To tell you the truth, I don't like to think about that son of a bitch," she said.

I stared at my mother. My mother didn't curse.

"Well, you are old enough to make coffee. I can talk to you like a grown-up, can't I?"

Maybe, I realized, I would prefer if she didn't.

"I thought you weren't upset," I said. "Remember?"

That had been the party line. I remembered the weekend my mother drove up to see me, to tell me about Posey. My father was in Paris. We went for a long walk on campus. She looked at the people with dogs, her longing unmistakable.

"Am I upset that Jonathan left me for a younger woman? For a pilot named Mandy?" my mother said. "I'm not. Upset. What kind of name is Mandy anyway?"

"Okay," I said. "You sound upset."

"I'm not," my mother said. "I just don't much like to talk about him. Not on a beautiful day, with so much nice light coming into the room. Your father is not someone I want to think about."

"He misses you," I said. "A lot."

"What?" my mother asked. "He said that?"

"Not in those exact words, but I can tell."

"No," my mother said. "He doesn't."

I looked at my mother.

"He misses having a wife," she said. "He misses having a nice home. He didn't think about any of that when he left me. He didn't give it a second thought. He was just following his dick. I would say just like a dog, but he isn't as good as a dog. Right, Posey?"

Princess wagged her tail.

"Mom," I said. I didn't like her like this.

"Rachel," my mother said. "You're right. Why am I saying all of this to you?"

"I don't know. I wish you wouldn't."

I still felt hurt that she had forgotten my childhood.

"Can I make you breakfast?" my mother said.

I shook my head. There was no time. There was nothing in the house for breakfast anyway. I was going to buy a muffin at the café on the way to day camp. I would get a sandwich, too, for lunch. We were out of turkey and lettuce and bread and even mayonnaise. Everything. My mother was in outer space. I felt unsure about leaving the house. About leaving her.

"I have to go, Mom," I said. "I have work."

"Okay, good," my mother said. "Have a good day."

"Okay," I said, but my feelings had been hurt, again. Had she just said *good*, as in, *Good, you are leaving*? That was what it felt like.

I was on my way out when I passed Zahid on the stairs, wearing a pair of my father's striped pajama bottoms and a white T-shirt, sleep still in his eyes. I stopped in place, unnerved. It was not that I did not know that he was still here, in the house, but somehow, I never saw him in the morning. I could still remember what he looked like naked. Button by button, I had taken off his soft blue shirt.

"Good morning, Rachel," he said, and I felt my skin turn red.

"Rachel made coffee," my mother called from the kitchen, as if we were some kind of happy family.

I grabbed my backpack by the front door. I realized, as if for the first time, that I was leaving them alone, alone in their pajamas. I understood why my father was so upset.

"Where are you going, Rachel?" Zahid said. "It's so early."

"Day camp," I said. "One of us has a job."

It was a weird thing to say. It was as if my mother's anger had infected me. Was I angry, too?

I was.

I was angry at Zahid. He was living in my house, eating the food my mother shopped and paid for. Who did he think he was? Was it somehow okay to fuck a student and then pretend it hadn't happened? Was it okay to live in her house and flirt with her *mother*? It was not okay. It was definitely not okay. But nothing had actually happened. My father was just being paranoid.

"I was offered a job," Zahid said.

"Oh, yeah?" I said.

That was something. He needed a job. He could not keep living here for free, swimming in our swimming pool, drinking my parents' wine, taking advantage of my mother's kindness.

"Zahid," my mother called out. "You didn't tell me that. You got the job?"

Now we were both staring at him, still on the stairs. My mother had wandered in from the kitchen, holding her coffee, wearing her shortie pajamas.

"I just got the offer," he said. "There was a message on my phone. The call I didn't answer last night."

This, of course, implied that my mother had been with him when he had not answered the phone. What was going on? This was getting beyond ridiculous.

"I haven't responded," Zahid said.

"What job?" I asked him.

"Teaching," he said. "The University of Iowa."

"*Iowa* Iowa?" I said.

"Yes, that Iowa."

"That program is famous."

"I suppose it is," Zahid said.

"So that is amazing?" I said.

"I suppose it is," he repeated.

"No," I said. "It's amazing. Congratulations."

And then, because I had a reason, finally, a real reason to touch him, I hugged him, my writing professor, Zahid Azzam, who was living in my house. I wrapped my arms around him, my breasts pressing against his chest. He smelled good. I remembered his smell. He stood still like a statue. My mother was right there, in the hall, her mouth open.

Clearly, I was not supposed to hug him.

I was not supposed to touch him.

They were both appalled.

It was horrible.

"Day camp," my mother said. "Rachel. You are going to be late for work. You are going to have to hurry."

I stepped away from Zahid.

The look on his face was nothing less than fear.

# Three

———◆———

# *Jonathan*

I went to the house the next day. I had told Becca I would. I did not go to work. I wanted to see her.

Becca was not home.

I let myself in. There was a poodle, a dog I did not know, the one from the beach. I was afraid she might bite me, but I got down on my knees and let her come to me. "Here, girl," I said, and I petted her. This dog had apricot-colored fur. Posey had been white. Otherwise, they looked eerily alike. I found a biscuit in the kitchen, where Becca kept the dog biscuits, and I made a new friend. She was a beautiful dog. I blinked.

I had worried about Becca, alone in this house without a dog. She had gotten a new dog. She had found herself a lover. The pool was open, the water was turquoise blue, the filter was running. It looked good. It looked perfect. I was tempted to take a swim. She had hired someone. I was replaceable. I had not realized it until then. Just like that. Only this writer, this asshole she had shacked up with, he was not a keeper. I would see to that.

I walked through the hall, touching the walls, the books,

the art on the walls. This was my house, too. I walked up the stairs, listening for the front door, wondering how long before Becca came home. In my office, I found a comforter folded neatly on the end of the couch. A pillow in a white pillowcase. This man was sleeping here. Some of my clothes were still in the drawers. She had moved them out of the bedroom, but at least she had not thrown them away. There were also his clothes. Khaki shorts. Linen shirts hanging in the closet.

I waited for an hour or so. I was bored. She would have to come home. I found a purple J.Crew bathing suit in the drawer and I took a swim in the pool. I did not recognize this bathing suit. It looked like something Becca would buy me. I grew hungry. I opened the refrigerator to make a sandwich. There was no food. I looked at the clock. I did not want to be home when my daughter came home from her job at the day camp.

I sat at the kitchen table. I drank a glass of filtered water.

Where was she?

Eventually, I left.

I went back to Tribeca.

The small apartment had become even smaller.


For the second time that day, I waited.

Mandy came back from a flight, late, nine o'clock. We had not had sex in several weeks. I was reluctant to touch her. Of course, Mandy had noticed this. We had spent our first night together in a hotel, fucking our brains out. Sex was the basis for our relationship.

"Sex," Mandy had once joked, "and our passion for Hillary Clinton."

She did not like that I had stopped touching her and yet I felt reluctant to have that conversation. The reason why. It would be, I knew, the end of everything. I had been putting it off for as long as I could.

Mandy wheeled her travel bag into the bedroom and then came over to me on the couch. She kissed my neck. That should have been enough. That should have been enough to send shivers down my spine. I could have turned to her, begun to unbutton her black silk blouse and pull down her trousers. We had certainly made love on her tiny sofa before.

"Mandy," I said.

I patted the spot next to me on the couch. Mandy was pretty and trim. She had the haircut of a little girl. I loved her hair. I still felt affection for Mandy, of course. I wondered how I could appease her without sexual contact. There was a dystopian series on TV she wanted to watch. Up till now, I had been reluctant to watch it with her. But I had recently learned how easy it was to go out and see a movie that you did not want to see. You simply paid an exorbitant amount for the tickets and you went. It meant something to the person you were seeing it with. It was a way to spend time with a person you loved without having to talk.

"You want to watch that show?" I said. "The feminist one?"

"*The Handmaid's Tale?*" Mandy said. "You told me you wanted to watch that like a hole in the head."

She was sweet, Mandy. There was some depth to her, too. She flew an airplane. She was a female pilot, the only pilot I had ever had the privilege of knowing, and I knew her in the biblical sense. Her job, certainly, had been a turn-on for me. As I'd told Becca, I would have never left her for a mere stewardess. I always thought about the guy who landed his plane on the Hudson River. I had asked Mandy if she could do that and she'd said she didn't think so. Most of the flying now, she'd explained, was preprogrammed. I had found her answer disappointing. I was sorry that I would have to end things, but if we were to work it out, I would have to reinsert my penis into her vagina. I was not willing to do that.

"Let's go out," Mandy said. "I'm hungry."

The idea of this did not appeal to me.

"Order in?" I said.

I was getting the hang of living in the city. I had my favorite places. I was not against eating a bite or two of sushi. Most of the restaurants, however, that Mandy liked were too loud. The music, the people talking. I often had to ask her to repeat herself. The restaurants made me feel like an old man.

"Let's go out," she said again.

I put on a pair of shoes.

We went to the hamburger place in the lobby of our building. I bought Mandy a twenty-eight-dollar cheeseburger and shoestring fries and a twenty-six-dollar martini. It was more than a little bit silly in Manhattan these days. I was wealthy, of course, but I still cared about the prices of things. I raised my eyebrows at her. It was not just the prices.

"Cheeseburger, huh?" I said. "Since when did you start eating meat?"

I had lived with Mandy for three months. She was a vegan, which sometimes made life boring. Unlike my daughter, who told the occasional arbitrary lie, I knew this to be true. She would cheat from time to time, like when we were in Paris, but nothing like this.

"Somehow, I feel like tonight I need the protein."

I nodded. We were going to have that conversation. Right now.

"What's going on?" she asked me.

"What do you mean?" I asked.

"I kissed your neck, Jonathan," she said. "Your sweet spot. And nothing. Not nothing. You cringe when I touch you."

"You gave me herpes," I said.

"Oh, shit," Mandy said. "Shit."

She did not try to deny it.

She looked over her shoulder, searching for the waiter. "I hope the food comes soon," she said. "I'm starving. It's been a long day."

I nodded.

I waited.

"It's from a long, long time ago," she said. "I had an outbreak a few weeks back, when I was working a lot—you remember that big Texas, Los Angeles, Hawaii trip I took. I was away. I would have never . . ." Mandy's voice faded.

"Had sex with me," I said, finishing her sentence.

Mandy nodded.

"You should have told me."

"Of course," Mandy said. "I should have. I would have. I was away. I should have told you, but I was away. I thought you were safe."

"And you didn't."

I understood her reasoning, honestly. I would not have wanted to tell her, either. I also did not like the restaurant Mandy had chosen. The music, like always, was too loud. I did not like to eat after eight o'clock. I did not like living in

Tribeca. I was fifty-six years old. I had made a serious mistake. Rebecca did not even warn me. She did not try to stop me from leaving her. She should have stopped me. She could have. Even at the time, I knew that I wanted her to stop me. It was not that I no longer wanted to have sex with my wife. She had lost interest in me, turning me away, again and again, until it was too humiliating to even try.

"It may not feel this way right now," Mandy said, "but it's not a big deal. You got antiviral drugs, right?"

I nodded.

"It clears quickly. You might never even have another outbreak. Really."

"I had a fever."

"The fever," Mandy said, remembering. "When you couldn't find the thermometer. That was a while ago, Jonathan. I wish you had talked to me."

"I couldn't."

"This is nothing," Mandy said. "Really."

She reached for my hands across the table. I let her hold them. I wanted her to convince me. We had gone to Paris together. It had been the most romantic trip of my life. It had felt like a honeymoon. Becca and I had never taken one. I had married Becca and started my job the next week. Becca was already pregnant. She said she did not want the fuss.

Twenty years later, I had planned us a trip to Paris. She stayed home with our sick dog. I had already been cheating then. For a while even, almost six months. Whenever Mandy flew into New York.

And so, I took Mandy to Paris. We took long walks along the Seine, holding hands, walks that I had planned for me and Becca. We ate scrumptious four-course meals at five-star restaurants. We made love in a wonderful hotel bed. Mandy made love to me with such care and attention. She did things to me with her tongue.

What was supposed to be a simple affair changed in Paris. It had been a mistake to take her there. I knew it was wrong to take her on a trip that I had planned for Rebecca. It was the best trip of my life.

When I came home, Posey was dead.

Becca looked at me as if I were dead.

I told her about Mandy.

It was not a marriage that could be repaired. At least, that was what I thought at the time. Mandy was surprised but happy when I asked if I could stay with her in her apartment. It was too small for us, of course, but I liked it. It was like I was young again, we were playing house. She told me that she had talked to her friends. She said that there was consensus. I would never leave my wife. Husbands never left their wives. But there I was.

"Here I am," I said. "With you."

She was elated.

Mandy thought it was funny, too, playing house in her little apartment. She even tried to cook me a soufflé. We had eaten soufflés in Paris.

"Don't distract me," she said, laughing. "I don't want to mess this up."

I distracted her. She put the soufflé in the oven and I fucked her hard, her round butt cheeks facing out to me, holding on to the counter. This was nothing like married sex with Becca. This was like no other sex I had had before. The soufflé fell, but we ate it anyway. I never cared about the food.

It was the sex, that was her appeal. And maybe those girlish bangs. But at night, after sex, after a long day at the office, and getting expertly taken care of, her smooth soft hands on my member, I found myself thinking of Becca, alone in our bed, without her dog, her daughter away at college. Alone in our big, beautiful house. My sad and beautiful wife.

I thought about Becca.

I missed her, every day. I had been one selfish son of a bitch. I had never valued her, but she had never valued me. I knew that our marriage had problems. That was why I had planned that trip to Paris. That was me, trying. The affair itself made sense to me. Becca did not want to have sex. I found someone else to relieve her of that particular duty. The pressure had been removed.

"Jonathan?" Mandy said, reminding me that I was in a loud and trendy restaurant in Tribeca.

She was still holding my hands across the table.

I gave Mandy a pained smile. I knew what I had to say, but I did not have the words. I had seen my wife on a beach with that man. His name was Zahid Azzam, the name of either a superhero or terrorist. Both. My daughter said he was a famous writer.

The food came.

Mandy looked at me. She drank her martini in two large gulps. A single tear slowly made its way down her pretty face. I watched it fall. I watched as Mandy finished her cheeseburger, somehow she was still able to eat, and then we went back to her small apartment and I changed into my pajamas and Mandy took off her clothes. She had an incredible body. Small breasts. A minuscule patch of blond pubic hair. She got waxed down there, something that bewildered me at first, but I liked it, her almost hairless vagina. That haircut. She was exactly the kind of girl I used to masturbate to, only she was real. She was mine. I stared at her now, naked. My penis was flaccid.

"It's just a virus," Mandy said. "It goes away. I don't even think about it. It doesn't change a thing. It doesn't have to."

She slid her hand onto my dick. I could feel my penis respond. I disengaged her hand. I looked at Mandy's hairless pussy and I wondered how I would ever be able to put my lips there again.

I was old-fashioned, I guessed. I was a fool.

"This is not going to work," I said.

"Then you should go," Mandy said. "Right now. You should leave right now. Just get out."

She put on an oversized white T-shirt that she liked to sleep in.

"You don't want to talk about it?" I asked her.

"No," she said. "Why bother? You should leave."

She was right, of course. Mandy was as sharp as a pistol. Smart. Confident. Drop-dead gorgeous. If I did not want to sleep with her, we had nothing. I already had a daughter.

# *Becca*

Words. Sometimes they are unnecessary. I watched my daughter take a breath and then hug Zahid. I watched the bravery of this act, the conscious choice she seemed to be making, and I understood that what I had suspected the very first time she had started talking about her writing professor was correct.

I had known from the start that Rachel had feelings for him and I had known that this would be a problem. This was why I had been keeping our relationship a secret. This was why when Zahid said he wanted to make love in a bed, I took him to a hotel. And there was Jonathan, too. I did not particularly want him to know my business, but it was Rachel that I was worried about.

I also wanted to keep Zahid private for as long as I could. I didn't want to test our relationship with exposure to the world. I did not want to explain myself to the few friends I had left. I did not want for anyone to say, "You go, girl" or any other insipid comment of the like. I wanted Zahid just for me. I did not want Zahid to get a job. He could stay upstairs; he could write. We did not want for money. What we had was perfect.

I do not use that word lightly.

It was perfect.

I knew already, had known after Jonathan called in the middle of the night, that this sweet state of existence was over already. So fast. He might have come to the house, for all I knew. He still had a key. I had not changed the locks. I would have been in New Haven, making love in a king-sized bed. But I would hear from him again.

It was not enough for him to leave me for a pilot, to desert me when I was grieving for my dog, my sweet Posey. He wanted to come home. He wanted to talk. I wanted to kill him.

And now this.

Rachel had feelings for Zahid. This was bad enough, of course, but when I saw Zahid tense, I realized that there was more to it. Something else. Something wrong. Something way off. Zahid could have played it off as if it were nothing, a hug from my lovestruck, college-aged daughter. He could have returned the hug and said, "Thank you!"

And he didn't.

He stiffened like a board. His arms hung at his sides. Hug her back, I thought, do this for my daughter, don't embarrass her, but Zahid did not move. Rachel looked like she had been slapped. She looked like she had been rejected, which, of course, she had been. Just like that, she was out the door. I watched her from the front window. She was actually running from the house. My sweet girl.

My very first suspicion, before we had even met, had been that there was something going on between Rachel and the writing professor, and look what I had done. I had brought him into our home. I had not taken him into my bed, but that was semantics. Back at college, he might have been my daughter's lover for all I knew. It was the stuff of Lifetime movies, mother and daughter, sleeping with the same man. I did not know if Rachel would forgive me if she were ever to find out. She would have to, wouldn't she? I was her mother. Look at what I was risking. Was he worth it? Who was this man? I did not even like his novel, for Christ's sake.

"Zahid?" I said.

I wished he could have just stayed upstairs. One minute longer and we would have been alone in the house. I had not trained him properly. I had not set down the rules, because I'd thought they were understood. It was not as simple as stay away from my daughter, we ate meals together after all, but that was what I wanted. For Zahid Azzam to stay away from my daughter.

I was responsible for the hurt on my sweet girl's face.

I looked out the window again. Rachel was out of sight. I had a vision of Theo Thornton standing there, holding a gun. There was no one. It was a bright, clear summer day.

"Morning, Becca," Zahid said.

I thought one of us might make a move to kiss the other. A peck on the cheek, that would not be abnormal. We didn't. We did not move.

"Did you say there was coffee?" Zahid asked.

It was a smart move, bringing us back to normal. The ordinary. I nodded. "Rachel made a pot," I said, retreating back into the kitchen. I said her name as if there were nothing out of the ordinary about my having a daughter named Rachel. I poured Zahid a cup. I gave him the last of the milk. I would have to go to the grocery store. I was not sure how it had happened, but we were out of almost everything. That was not like me. I worried that I was not like me.

"What was that about?" I asked Zahid, offhand, as if his answer were of no importance to me.

Zahid shrugged.

"Kids today," he said. "Who knows what they are thinking?"

I laughed, a small fake laugh.

Zahid had dodged the question. He knew just what I meant. Would I let him get away with it? Would I? What was I supposed to do? I did not have to figure everything out now. I could leave everything left unsaid. I did not know what else to do. We had never had a conversation about our relationship. I had not set up boundaries. This was my fault. After our night in the hotel, I'd understood that things were starting to change and I wanted them to change. I liked having sex in a bed, waking up together. I liked taking a shower together, rubbing soap over his naked body. I wanted more and it seemed like Zahid did as well.

But I had not known that it would be today that we would have this conversation. I wanted more time. We had only had a few weeks. Not enough. Not fair. I was like a child. My relationship with my daughter was at stake. I was disgusted with myself. I just wanted more time. Me and Zahid, safe in our bubble, making love. I looked at Zahid, wondering how to begin.

Zahid held his fingers up to his lips, indicating that I should not speak. It was such a relief.

We would not talk.

But had he not just told Rachel that he had gotten a job in the middle of America? Was he leaving at the end of the summer? Was that it? No discussion required. It was just a summer fling. That made sense, that would be the most sensible path for this to take, but that was not what I wanted.

And had I not heard Rachel open the door to my room the night before? I had been sleeping, but I heard the door open. Did I imagine that or was she checking on me? Was she making sure that I was sleeping alone? Was that it? I reached over for Posey, lying beside me, and fell back asleep.

"I want to write," Zahid said. "If that is all right with you. And then, we can swim our laps? I want to practice my flip turn. Does that sound like a plan? We will go swimming in the afternoon?"

It was a question. It translated into: Will we make love in the afternoon after we go swimming? Is everything okay?

We would. It was. It was a good plan, fine with me. Here on in, I would be more careful. I would dead-bolt the door. I would call a locksmith and get the locks changed. We could pretend that the hug had never happened.

"That's fine. It sounds like a plan to me. I have to buy groceries," I said. "I'll be back soon."

"Do you want me to come with you?" Zahid asked.

I shook my head, without thinking. Of course I would not take Zahid with me to Whole Foods or to the local market. I might run into someone. I hated that about my small town, but there it was. I knew a lot of people. I had taught almost everyone's children.

But then, I thought, perhaps it would be nice. To have his company. To do something as ordinary as go to a supermarket together.

"You should write," I said. "It's fine."

Zahid shook his head. He put his coffee cup in the sink. He patted Posey on the head.

"I'll come," he said.

How did he know?

How did he know how much it would please me? Of course, it was not the words. It was the fact that he would rather go with me to the supermarket than work on his novel. He did not want to leave me, or be left alone. At the hotel in New Haven, turning in the key card, for a split second I worried that he might be using me. I was vulnerable. I realized that. I realized that if I had decided to return the calls of any of my friends who had reached out to me, they might not have encouraged this sexual escapade. They might have asked if I was charging Zahid rent.


Zahid pushed the cart at the Stop & Shop.

"This store is so big," he said. "And so empty. It's a little bit creepy. And cold. Are you cold?"

It was freezing cold.

I'd known to bring a sweater, but I had not warned Zahid. I was nervous. This was not the conversation we desperately needed to have, but it was something. An outing. I was well aware of the fact that I had taken him to a supermarket I normally avoided; the produce was bad and the fluorescent lights hurt my eyes. Still. The farmers' market was the next day and I could wait to get good produce and flowers. I was only going to get the basics. Milk and sliced turkey and paper towels and chocolate chip cookies, a pint of raspberries. Avocados. Things for Rachel. Food for dinner.

"Do you want anything?" I asked him.

Zahid's face was blank. It was as if he had never been in a supermarket before. He was shivering. We had made a mistake, I supposed, but this was a small one.

"Ice cream?" he said.

He seemed shy.

"Of course," I said.

We stood next to the freezer display. There was Häagen-Dazs and Ben & Jerry's and Breyers and Friendly's and an overpriced gelato from Brooklyn. There were ice cream bars. There was frozen yogurt. There was Tofutti. I was not sure what Zahid liked. Usually, in the summer, I did not keep ice cream in the house. If I wanted any, I would go out for it. Not once this summer, however, had I gone out for ice cream with Rachel.

"Ben & Jerry's?" Zahid said.

"Sure," I said. "Why not?"

I stood next to him, contemplating the flavors. I slid my fingers into his. His hand was cold. I would warm it up. This was okay, I told myself. We were okay. If a neighbor were to see us at the Stop & Shop, it would be okay. So what? I had taken a lover. Maybe this one was not the best choice, but there were crazier things. He made me happy. Jonathan had seen us on the beach. We had not been struck by lightning. Rachel was a big girl. She called herself an adult. She had a job. She was in college. She had started having sex in high school. I was not supposed to know this, but I did. She could handle this. She could be angry, she could be hurt. She would be okay.

Zahid looked down at my hand, at our fingers intertwined, pale and brown. He had the most beautiful fingers.

# *Zahid*

I was, of course, offered the job. The salary was not spectacular and the job was not spectacular. It was a four-class course load and it was only for one year. The pregnant professor would have her baby and she would return to work. I would be back in the position of looking for another job. It was bullshit, actually.

I wanted to write my book. I wanted to stay in Connecticut, beautiful white privileged Connecticut, I wanted to see the seasons change, I wanted to experience fall in Connecticut, take walks on the beach in winter, why not, I wanted to make love to Becca, and write my book. I wanted to eat meals with her and drink good wine. I had grand romantic gestures floating around in my head: a marriage proposal. I wanted Becca to know that I was serious. I was serious about her. That this was my life. I did not want this chance, almost a miracle, to slip away. I did not want Becca to go back to her husband. I did not want her to sacrifice me for the sake of her daughter. I could marry her. I lay awake at night and wondered about ways to propose.

I had the ring, the ring I'd used to propose to my fiancée. It was gorgeous. It was expensive. I had once considered returning it or reselling it, but I had taken too long. I found out that I could only get a fraction of what I'd originally paid for it, and so I held on to it.

"She is still married, fuckface," Kristi said, her patience for me completely used up. It was vexing to me that I had ceased to consult with Kristi about my private matters and I could still hear her voice in my head.

It was as if my life were a fiction workshop and she was my most annoying student, had an answer for anything. I had no idea why Kristi Taylor was so invested in my future. Nor did I know why I was afraid of Kristi. She would be so angry at me for not taking this job. So incredibly angry. She would say that she had put herself out for me. I would say that I'd never asked her to. She would say it was the last time. It was the last time she would ever stick out her neck for me. And that I was a fool to think Becca would ever marry me. You are a boy toy, that is what she would say. She did not believe I could be this stupid.

It was my writing time.

I was arguing with Kristi in my head.

I was staring at my Gmail, pondering what to do. Write to the university to tell them no. I could write Kristi to tell her that I did not accept the position but that I was grateful for her concern. I could write to my new editor. She had sent me a friend request on FB. I had ignored it. I could not be friends with her. I could not know about her daily life or have her know about mine. But I could write to her. I could tell her that I had one hundred new single-spaced pages. A new novel. That was an e-mail she would want to receive. I needed only to finish the book. There was a pot of gold waiting at the other end of this novel. I had spent the advance but that was only half.

Half a pot of gold. There were people out there, waiting for my next novel.

Kristi would think I was using Becca, but if I finished my book, if I finished it and turned it in, I would be solvent again. It had seemed impossible, but it was not impossible. I was one hundred pages away. My last book was long. I could write a short one. Genius. A short book. The idea filled me with glee. My book would be short. I was almost done.

Outside the window, I could see the blue sky. I could walk over to the window, look down and there would be the swimming pool, my reward after a morning of writing. The aqua-blue water. I had done a good job taking care of this pool. I felt a small measure of pride. I had proven, too, that I was useful to Becca. I had reminded myself that I was a competent adult. This would not impress my mother.

I did not send an e-mail.

Not to the university, not to Kristi, or to Jane, my new editor. My mother. Certainly, I owed my mother an e-mail. She had given birth to me.

I did not open my file.

My phone pinged, a sign of what I was supposed to do next. It was from Myra Alice Finley. It was not a text that I needed, not in this moment. Myra Alice was an old college friend. She was married to Sean, another old college friend, and Sean had cancer. This was not new. He had been in remission, and now, almost five years later, he was out of remission. He had something new, a fast-growing tumor that the doctors did not think was worth operating on, at least not until the cancer cells were stopped. That was how fast it was growing. His chances, honestly, did not sound good, but Myra Alice was one of those people. Who did yoga, believed in holistic medicine, didn't eat gluten, sprayed tea tree oil into the air, all of that woo-woo crap. She had put Sean on an anti-inflammatory diet and that had worked for a while. Now she was desperate. Back to Western medicine. But she was still Myra Alice, all about the healing energy. She sent a group text to her list. She wanted everyone who loved Sean to think, *Die, tumor, die* on the day his chemotherapy began. His second round would be starting soon and she wanted to enlist the power of their friends' love.

And now, when I had voluntarily sent myself back up to my room to write, I got this text. Now.

I'd known it was coming. I had agreed to be on this list. But, honestly, I didn't believe that the power of my thought would help Sean. I thought that this old friend of mine would die. His cancer was back. He had a fast-growing tumor. Jesus. I would be forty before long and my grandmother was dead and now my friends were starting to die, but right now, I was fine. I was healthy and young. I had one hundred single-spaced pages of a novel.

I realized how selfish this was.

I closed my eyes.

I tried to concentrate.

I turned off my phone.

I did not have to write an e-mail.

I would write my book. That was what I would do. I was alive. I had to live my life to the fullest. Here I was, thinking in clichés. If a student wrote that line in a short story, I would cross it out. Shut up. I actually said it out loud. I opened my file. I looked at the last sentence I had written and I deleted it. That was not useful.

Instead, I tried to think healing thoughts.

I did.

*Die, tumor, die.*

I put my hands on my knees, I closed my eyes, and wished for the death of the tumor killing my friend Sean. We had not seen each other in a very long time. He had been my freshman roommate. I had spent breaks with him in Vail, at his parents' winter house. The whole family skied, whereas I was a clown on the slopes. After a while, I stopped trying. I sat by the fireplace at the ski lodge, drinking whiskey toddies, reading novels and going to bed with girls who could not ski.

After graduation, Sean and I had gone in different directions. He lived in D.C. Myra Alice did something related to politics. Sean had not had a job for a while. He had been a rich kid and he had never gotten his shit together. He used to smoke an insane amount of pot, but apparently Myra Alice had made him stop. He arranged dinner parties and cooked Italian food. They took trips. It did not seem like a bad life. We did not have anything to talk about.

I did not know how long I would have to think this, about him, the tumor, sending the healing energy. I tried it again. Die, tumor, die. It was like meditation. I was bad at meditating. I always had been. My mind went everywhere. I was afraid that I was harming Sean. I found myself wishing that his chemotherapy had not coincided with my writing time. My file was open, but I hadn't written a thing. I had lost a sentence. I had not written anything since going to Iowa.

This was the wrong time to sabotage myself. I had just realized that I did not *need* Becca for her money, and this made me feel good. I would finish my book and then I would have money again. But I still needed Becca and this also made me feel better about myself. I did not want to use people. I wanted to be a good person.

Die, tumor, die, I thought.

I did not like the way the sentence sounded. There was nothing lyrical about it. Or powerful, even. It sounded foolish, inadequate, impossible. I wondered if I could write a better mantra and send it out to the group, but I did not know what it would be.

So, I repeated the sentence again, three times, because I had promised Myra Alice. It was like clicking my heels together, like Dorothy in *The Wizard of Oz*. I felt fortunate that I was young and healthy and not dying. I was lucky. I was not going to go to Iowa. I would not write a fucking word if I went there. I would be miserable there. Kristi wanted me with her. That was what it was. She wanted me to be her bitch. She knew that deep down, I wanted her, sexually, of course I did, everyone wanted Kristi, she was beautiful and talented and, for reasons I had never understood, completely off-limits. She had been living like a fucking nun since her last break up, Miss Fucking Perfect Writer Nun. Maybe she wasn't. Perfect. Maybe, secretly, she wanted to tank my career.

Paranoid thoughts. That was where I was going. I was not helping my friend. I hated that he was dying but I was not supposed to think that he was dying. His wife wanted me to send healing thoughts. I had had sex with his wife, Myra Alice, before they were married, before they were a couple even, my freshman year. She was one of those white girls. She had never considered me seriously as a romantic partner. With her, somehow, it hurt. Fucking Myra Alice. It had been painful to see them together. That was so long ago, another life.

I was sitting at my desk on a beautiful day in Connecticut and I was filled with rage. My *Die, tumor, die* wasn't heartfelt.

Maybe my friend wasn't my friend anymore, just someone I had hung out with when I was in college, and that didn't count for shit. He had come to one of my readings. I could not remember the last time we had talked on the phone.

I had wasted almost an hour, time I could have spent with Becca.

I had done nothing.

So I sent the e-mail to Iowa, turning down the job.

There. I felt better. I had done something. I did not have cancer and I wanted to live my life to its fullest.

I looked at my watch. Two more minutes had passed. I had done something definite, but I was not writing. I was going to admit defeat for the day. That happened sometimes. That was okay. It was just a day. I left Jonathan's office, unsettled, unsure of myself, glad to be out of his room. For the first time, I found myself thinking about Jonathan. There were no pictures of him in the house, but I knew that he must be handsome. I wondered if there had been photos of him, family pictures that Becca had taken down. Becca, of course, was beautiful. Rachel was plain and awkward and somehow much more good-looking than she knew. She had good genes. Standing in the hallway, I turned on my phone and looked up Becca's husband, and there was a picture of him in tennis clothes at a charity tennis match. I nodded my head. He was even better-looking than I'd thought he would be. A man who played tennis. A man who looked better older. Gray hair. He looked like money.

I was standing there in the hallway, staring at my phone, looking at a picture of Becca's husband, when Becca emerged from her bedroom. I had assumed she was downstairs.

"Is that a picture of Jonathan?" she asked me.

I had been caught. I clicked a button and I was back to my home screen, a picture of Princess and all of my apps, but it was too late.

Becca squinted at me.

"I'm sorry," I said.

"Don't be," she said, but she sounded annoyed.

She had never been annoyed with me before.

"I was curious," I said.

Becca did not say anything.

She did not talk a lot, I realized. We did not talk a lot. I thought of a faucet. It was as if her faucet was closed, and maybe, once I opened it, if I were able to, the water would gush out. I felt so much restraint in her, even when making love. She turned away when she had orgasms, as if she did not want me to know. It was the strangest thing. I was not sure she was even aware of it. It made me want her more. It made me want another chance to make her come, just to get her to look at me, to hold my gaze.

"I turned down the job," I told Becca.

"At the college?" she said. "You did?"

"Yes," I said. "I turned it down. I sent an e-mail. It's done."

*Die, tumor, die.* It came into my head unbidden. I realized that I wanted off that text list. Could I text Myra Alice and tell her this without somehow going to hell? As it was, I was going to hurt my friend. My thoughts were meaningless, powerless. Why did Myra think she was allowed to disturb my state of mind this way? All of the people on the list.

"Why?" Becca said.

"Why?"

"Why?" She sounded so angry. Only hours ago, we had been

holding hands in a supermarket. "Why did you turn down the job?"

"Because I want to stay here," I said. "With you."

I stared at Becca.

Becca stared at me.

"That's what I want, too," she said, still sounding angry.

She took my hand, the hand that was holding my cell phone, the cell phone that contained the picture of her husband, the fool who had left her.

We were stuck, standing there in the hallway. I was suddenly afraid of messing up, breaking a rule I had never been told. I could pull her into her bedroom and we could fuck away the ghost of her fool of a husband. It was probably five steps away. Or we could fuck in my room, her husband's office, and that would work, too. We could simply fuck inside the house. That would be meaningful, a sign of progress. We had done it once before, a yoga session in front of the TV that had gone wrong. Princess had stood in the hallway, wagging her tail, watching us, and when we were done, she came over and licked Becca's face. This was a good home for her. She had a yard, she had the beach. She had Becca, who she loved more than me. I understood that. We were lost, honestly, me and my dog, without her.

"Did you write?" Becca asked me.

I shook my head, ashamed.

She had just told me she wanted to be with me and then she'd changed the subject.

"Why not?"

I shrugged. I had so many different reasons why. I realized that I did not want to share any of them with Becca.

"Maybe you should."

I stood across from her, my arms at my sides. We had just

told each other that we wanted to be with each other. I did not want to write.

"Okay," I said.

"An hour," she said.

I did not respond. The idea of it seemed like torture. I was angry, angry at Becca for trying to control me like this.

"Half an hour," she said.

That was better. I agreed.

She opened the door to my room.

"It will be good," she said. "Really."

I felt like I was being punished.

I felt sympathy for Rachel, for having a mother who would not embrace joy but instead would send you back to your room to work. I sat back down at the desk, in front of my computer. *Die, tumor, die.* Fuck. It was stuck in my head like a bad song, and so what? I would put it into my novel. I would profit from the slow death of my old college friend. Myra Alice wanted me to think about him. That was what I would do. I blocked the Internet on my laptop. I turned my phone back off and I typed. Somewhere in Brooklyn, there was an editor, waiting for me.

I typed. One sentence and then the next.

Becca wanted me to stay with her. She wanted me. She had witnessed her daughter hugging me and had understood the significance of that moment. She was not stupid. I was what she wanted.

I typed some more.

I typed effortless, well-crafted sentences, I looked down at my brown fingers, fingers moving across the keyboard. My dying friend was now a character in my novel. I called him Shawn. I could change it later. Already, he was changing the story; he was alive, in my book at least; he was going to start skydiving, not dying. I might finish this book, and here I was, actually doing something to keep my friend alive, and maybe this meant that I actually cared.

And maybe, maybe I was not a son of a bitch. Which was an insult to my mother. It was a horrible phrase.

I finished the scene and triumphantly shut my computer. I opened the door and there was Becca, sitting on the steps, staring out a small triangular window above the front door. It was such a beautiful house. The way the light floated down the hallway. She was waiting for me. There was a book lying closed on her lap.

"That was more than half an hour," she said.

"You were waiting."

Becca nodded.

"I wrote a lot," I said.

"You see," Becca said, smiling. I loved her smile. "I am good for you."

I sat down next to her on the steps. I touched her cheek. She touched my face. We lay back on the steps, kissing.

"Ow," Becca said, laughing. I loved her laugh. "My back."

"A bed?" I asked. "Is that possible?"

"It's possible," Becca said.

We had done it before. In a hotel, of course, but it had been a bed. It had been a wonderful bed. We grinned at each other.

I removed my weight from her body. I looked down the stairs, to see if it was safe. We were alone. The front door was closed, presumably locked. Still, Becca did not move. She was lying flat on her back on the stairs. It looked uncomfortable. I did not want to ruin it. I did not want to push too hard. The beds would wait for us. That was fine.

"Do you want to swim?" I asked.

"Yes." Becca nodded, the relief flooding her face.

"So do I," I said.

I took Becca's hand, pulling her to her feet. We went down the stairs together, our bodies purposefully banging into each other. We walked down the hall, through the kitchen, and to the door through the living room that led to the swimming pool.

At the pool, I realized that I had left my purple bathing suit upstairs, but I had waited so long already, to be with Becca. I couldn't see myself turning around, going back up the stairs to get it. I had already gone to the supermarket. I had sent healing thoughts to my dying friend. I had written six single-spaced pages. I could not wait another second. I took off my clothes and dove into the pool naked. Underwater, I could hear the splash, and then another splash, the sound of Becca coming in after me, and she was pressed against me, also naked, our bodies pressed together, and then we came up for air. We were shiny wet seals, hands in each other's hair.

"I love you," I told Becca.

It was the first time I had spoken the words out loud. I would tell her this, again and again. She would believe me.

She kissed me, which was clearly not the same thing as saying, "I love you, too."

She was kissing my mouth shut. That's what it was. *Stop talking.* We climbed the steps out of the pool and made love on our pool chair, but this time, this time Becca looked at me as she came.

And watching her quiver and then catch her breath, before starting again, I had a moment of déjà vu, remembering her daughter, Rachel, beneath me, looking into my eyes as she came.

# Khloe

I went out for drinks with the guys.

First I drank a gin and tonic and then another. It had been a long day at the office. The team had reeled back in a big client that had been thinking of jumping ship. It represented tens of millions of dollars.

*Fuck you, Jane,* I thought, high-fiving Zach and Baxter and the other frat-guy analyst whose name I could never remember. Jonathan, my boss, grinned at me, because he knew that in the end, I'd sealed the deal. I had churned out a fluent recital of numbers, promises, paired with my cleavage and my legs. I had dressed for this meeting, the sleeveless silk blouse beneath my jacket. I had offered the idea of sex, sex the client would never have but could dream about. I was fine with that.

*Fuck you, Jane.* It was a refrain, going on in my head, over and over again, every time I checked my phone, still waiting for an apology that did not come.

As a rule, I never went out for drinks with the guys, but today I went and I immediately remembered why. My co-workers were grade A assholes. I watched them grope women in the bar as if they had a free pass. I watched the women they groped, the waitresses and the women who actually went there, clearly on the lookout for guys in finance, and it seemed to be okay with everyone. Danny Tang, I noticed, did not come out with the guys.

The asshats I worked with wore suits. They oozed money. They were good-looking and they were repulsive. I felt lucky, at least, to sit back and observe. There was so much need in this bar, almost too much humanity on display. I looked at my cell phone and finally, there it was. A message. The message.

So sorry, K. We need to talk.
We never said we were exclusive.
Let's have coffee.

Fucking coffee. It was as good as being dumped.

"Heard you were a dyke," Zach said, joining me, placing four shots of tequila on the table, a bowl full of limes. He was talented. He did not spill a drop.

We did a shot together.

He had heard I was a dyke, huh? Was he making this shit up or had he actually heard this? Was Jonathan Klein spreading gossip about me? Terrific. I didn't know why, but I didn't expect it from him. It was not like I liked the man, but I sort of liked him, despite myself. Or I respected him. I thought he was decent. No one, if you thought about it, was truly decent. My twin sister, for instance: Kristi was also a cunt when it came down to it. She had betrayed me—for art had been her bullshit explanation. Even still, I expected things from people.

Meet for coffee.

It would make me stop drinking coffee.

"You got something to say?" I said.

"Nah. Not me," Zach said. "I love dykes. My little sister is a total bull dyke. Looks like a boy. Whereas you, Khloe, you are hot. I would totally fuck you."

"Gee, thanks," I said.

I was being sarcastic but I was not sure that Zach was aware of this.

I did the other shot.

"You're welcome," he said. "What are you doing out here in this meat market anyway?"

"Leaving," I said, standing up.

He seemed relieved.

"Don't get raped on your way out."

"What?"

Zach winked. I shook my head. His sister was a lesbian, but that didn't make him decent. I was without words. Nights like this made me think I had made a wrong turn in my life. The MBA, the job, the entire course of my life. I also hated thoughts like this. I hated introspection. I wanted the money, I told myself, I wanted the money, that had always been my goal, but it seemed like maybe I was going to want more than that. I wanted Jane. It would all be bearable if I had Jane.

I read my message from Jane again.

Not exclusive. Coffee. There was an apology, at least. Was I supposed to write back? What could I possibly say in a fucking text. I wanted to show up at Jane's brownstone and shake her. She had made a mistake. The biggest fucking mistake. She was not admitting her feelings for me because of things that had happened when I was a child. I could convince her, only I was so angry, I worried I might want to choke her instead.

My phone dinged.

Only this time, it wasn't Jane. It was from Rachel. For a moment, I didn't remember who she was. I had slept with so many women in Brooklyn that summer, before Jane, and I tried to remember which one was Rachel. Only it was my boss's teenage daughter, asking me if I liked turkey sandwiches, if I wanted to have a picnic. Did I still want to go to the beach? She would understand if I was too busy.

I had forgotten.

Of course, I wouldn't go. I was not going to mess around with this child. Because deep down, unlike every other single fucking person I knew, I was decent.

Jane did not let me into her apartment.

She was wearing oversized shorts and a tattered T-shirt, smeared with chocolate. She came out onto the steps of the brownstone.

"Can I come in?" I asked.

I had never been inside her apartment. It was always at my place. Zahid's place. And every time Jane came over, she was opening drawers and closets, clearly looking for something. I don't know what she thought she might find. Zahid, himself, under the bed, writing in longhand. A novel in a drawer. It was idiotic.

"It's late," she said. "It's too late for this. Didn't you get my text?"

"You want to have coffee," I said.

"Yes," Jane said. "Can we do that? Tomorrow."

"You're serious," I said.

Jane sighed. "Like I said, it's late. I'm watching TV. I'm too tired for this."

"You are a mess," I said. "Did you know that?"

I touched the smear of chocolate on her T-shirt. There was a small tear in the armpit and another one beneath the V-neck. I hadn't known this about Jane, that she wore rags when she was alone, but somehow I wasn't surprised. I had seen the state of her underwear.

"Are you drunk?" Jane asked me.

I might have been a little bit drunk. Gin and tonics. Tequila. Maybe I was drunk. I sat down on the steps. I took off my shoes. These ridiculous high-heeled shoes. They were necessary for work and I was used to them. I liked them even, liked the way they made my legs look, liked the power they gave me, but my feet were tired after a long fucking day. I looked up at Jane, still standing in the doorway. I wasn't going anywhere. I had a bad feeling about where this was going. It was already backfiring on me, showing up the way I had, but she had to talk to me.

Finally, Jane sat down next to me.

"Khloe," she said.

I put my head on her shoulder. Jane stroked my head. "I like your short hair," she said. "Did you know that?"

I nodded.

I let her touch my hair.

She liked my hair. She was attracted to me. I knew this. The air felt good. I had spent the whole day inside, freezing in air-conditioned rooms, feeling numb, feeling nothing. It had been so hot outside, but now it had cooled down. I felt a breeze. Jane's hand was on my head. It felt so good.

"You are such a baby," Jane said.

I shook my head. This was the problem, that Jane had met me when I was a child and she would not let this go. There were tears streaming down my cheeks.

"You only think that you love me," Jane said. "It is just an idea that you have been clinging to. It's flattering, of course. And it's not as if I don't have feelings for you."

"You do," I said. "I know you do."

Jane was still stroking my head.

"It's complicated," Jane said. "There is Winnie."

I hiccupped.

"I was already seeing her," Jane said. "Before you showed up."

Technically, Jane had been cheating on Winnie when she slept with me, except Winnie had a boyfriend. And Winnie was not gay. Winnie was experimenting and she would come out straight and squeaky clean. Any lesbian could see that.

"Winnie isn't gay," Jane said, as if she were reading my thoughts.

I nodded, glad that Jane knew this, too.

"This isn't the first time I have fallen for a straight girl. You'd think I would learn."

"I'm gay," I said. "One hundred percent."

"But I don't feel that way about you," Jane said.

This was stupid. We had had sex, more than once. It had been amazing. She did, she did feel that way. She just felt like it was necessary to deny it. She did not want me because I wanted her. She was going to get fat, spend her life alone with her cat. Her cat would die. They always did. Her cat would die and she would be alone and she would get another cat and twenty years later that cat would die, too. It was no way to live a life. I lay my head back down on her shoulder. My head was spinning.

We belonged together. This was how it should be.

"You scare me a little," Jane said.

"Why?"

It came out muffled, my lips on her shoulder.

"Because you want me so much."

I sat up. "No, I don't," I said.

Clearly I was lying. We both laughed. This felt better.

"What's wrong with that?" I said. "Wanting you?"

"I was your babysitter," Jane said.

"I am thirty," I said. "I am not a baby. I am not even a little girl."

"You're thirty?" Jane said. "Really?"

I nodded.

"I used to kiss you," Jane said, looking straight ahead, out onto the street. "Too much. When you were little. When I tucked you in. Sometimes when you were sleeping. I might have touched you. Nothing bad. Nothing gross. But maybe a little bit. I still feel ashamed of myself. You were so pretty. Like a doll. I have talked about this with my therapist. I don't think you know this. I don't think you remember."

"Of course I remember," I said.

"You do?" she said.

"I was only pretending to be asleep. I liked it. I always did. And you were the only person, the only person who liked me more than Kristi."

"Khloe," Jane said. "This is all wrong. You should hate me. You should be in therapy because of me."

"No," I said. "It's not wrong and I don't. I love you. You are denying what is right in front of you."

"You are drunk," Jane said.

"I don't see what that has to do with anything," I said.

I turned to Jane. I put my hand on her breast and I kissed her, dry lips on dry lips, but Jane did not return my kiss. She also did not remove my hand from her breast. She had put her hand back on my hair. It was possible. I only had to push. I could sense people walking by us. This was not safe, even in Brooklyn. We should go inside. Jane needed to let me inside. Inside, I could convince her.

Jane pulled away.

"I know that I have confused you," Jane said. "Right now, I am only making it worse, and for that I'm sorry. I'm truly sorry. But you are not what I want."

"You're wrong," I said.

My hand was still on her breast. I kissed Jane again and she returned my kiss.

"I don't want to break your heart," she said, pulling away again.

"So fix it," I said. "Fix my heart."

"That's so corny."

"Fix it," I said.

Jane kissed me again. I slid my hand under her dirty T-shirt. I fingered her nipple. I knew I could do this. I knew that I could change Jane's mind. And then, she pulled away again.

On the street, there was an older woman with a small dog watching us from outside the iron fence.

"Don't mind me," she said. "I'm just watching the show."

"This is stupid," I told Jane. "Let's go inside."

Jane shook her head.

She handed me my shoes.

"You're asking me to leave?" I said. "Now?"

I was drunk, sure, but I had fixed everything. She had kissed me back, I could feel her heart beating, her body responding. But faster than I could react, Jane went inside the brownstone without me. She closed the door behind herself. I heard the door firmly lock.

"Jane!" I screamed. I stood up. I pounded on the door. "Let me in. What the fuck? Let me inside. Jane!"

"Oh, honey," the woman with the dog said. "It's going to be okay."

"Fuck you," I said.

I started to pound on the door again.

"Go home, honey," she said.

"Fuck you," I told her.

The woman with her little dog left.

And I sat back down on the steps, drunk, waiting for Jane.

"Come back," I said. "Come back."

I lay down, looking up at the sky.

Sometimes, I missed the stars.

I woke up there in the early morning, the sun rising, the sky a crazy pink I did not know was possible in Brooklyn. I had fallen asleep on the steps. My head was resting on my purse. Someone had stolen my shoes.

# *Rachel*

I saw Ian on the pickup line at day camp and I knew I would go with him. "I have no plans today," I said.

"So you're gonna join us, huh?" Ian said.

"If that's okay," I said.

I had not considered this.

"Doing us a favor."

"What?"

"All right," Ian said, scratching his chin as if he were considering it. "We'll let Rachel come over. Right, Amelia?"

"Fuck you," I said.

"Whatever," Ian said.

I did not understand this. Why couldn't Ian say, *Great. Hooray.* Be pleased like his little sister. I must have hurt his feelings, but I wasn't sure he even had feelings. I went with them anyway. I was not going to go home. I was not going to meet my mother at the café and drink lemonade and pretend that everything was fine. What I wanted, really, was never to go home again.

So instead, I set off with two members of the most notoriously disturbed family in town.

"Let's go back to the house today," Ian said. "Swim at home."

I shrugged. Their beach was rocky, there was no sand, but it was fine. It was too late at this point anyway, after practically begging to be invited, to change my mind. What I needed to do, really, was pack my bags and go back to college.

Amelia slid her fingers into my hand on the walk back to their house. Like a reflex, I thought about Zahid, his fingers. The way I had taken his hand. I did not understand what Amelia's gorgeous older brother was doing, hanging around, hanging out with his little sister in the afternoon. I had asked him, the other day, what he was doing home, but he had ignored me. Something had gone wrong for him this summer, obviously. He had a story, but I didn't know it. Had he been fired from a job? Had he graduated from college? What was he doing in the fall? Why did I not know this? I only knew about the brother with the gun.

I was in the downstairs bathroom, peeing, when Ian came in without knocking. I thought I had locked the door, but apparently I hadn't.

"Jesus," I said. "Get out of here."

My underwear and shorts were on the floor between my feet. I was planning on changing right into my bathing suit. Ian watched as I wiped myself. Was this his way of flirting? It was beyond creepy. It made me think of the brother again, the one who brought the gun into my mother's classroom. My mother had told me he had a penetrating gaze. The word *penetrating* made me think of sex. Ian seemed like he wanted to fuck me, but I did not think he actually liked me. He seemed bored. Still, he wanted to fuck me and because he was so crazy good-looking, I could not ignore it. Zahid had rejected me.

"You don't have your period, do you?" he said.

"What? That's gross," I said. "What business is it of yours?"

"I hate having sex with women when they're bloody."

There, he'd confirmed it.

And he was disgusting.

"What?" I said. I walked over to the sink to wash my hands. "What are you talking about. We aren't having sex."

"Why not?"

I had to come up with a reason.

"We haven't even kissed."

"Is that what your problem is?"

Ian turned me around from the bathroom sink and kissed me. It was a forceful kiss, forceful in the way that he had once pushed me underwater, this time pushing my back into the white ceramic sink, forcing his tongue into my mouth. It was not a nice kiss. It felt like a violation. The last person I had kissed was Zahid. He had been hesitant; I'd had to let him know that it was all right

"There you go," Ian said. "We've kissed."

I frowned.

"That was sort of rough," I said.

"Fine." Ian sighed. "I know what you are looking for. All of you little girls."

I was going to object and then Ian kissed me again and it was better. Much better. It was not gentle. It was not tentative. But it was intense. It made me want him. I had not anticipated this. I did not understand any of this. I had never had a proper boyfriend, a normal guy to watch Netflix with, to text and go out to dinner with. Ian was in another league, too good-looking for me. He was also an asshole. It was completely in my power to step away. I could leave the bathroom, I could go home. I knew that was what I should do. But Zahid would be there. Zahid and my mother. She had texted me a picture of all the groceries she'd bought.

Ian's hands were on my ass, his erection pressed against me. I did not know what to think. I was afraid Ian was going to rape me. I was also worried that I wanted to have sex with a guy who wanted to rape me. Ian put my thumb in his mouth and sucked it and I gasped.

"Your sister," I said. "She's in the living room."

"She is playing Animal Jam," he said.

"This isn't romantic," I said. "The bathroom."

I was lost and I knew it.

"No," Ian said, still pressed against me. "But it's hot."

"We haven't gone on a date."

"You wanna go on a date?"

"Maybe," I said. I felt my mouth open into a moan that I held back. "Yes."

"I'll take you on a date," Ian said. "Later, tonight. I'll take you to the shooting range."

"Okay," I said.

I could hear the music from Amelia's computer game in the living room.

"Could we go into a bedroom?" I asked Ian.

"No," Ian said. "I want you right now."

He slid his finger inside me. My underwear was still on the floor. I was not objecting. I leaned back against the sink, grounding my feet on the ceramic tiles.

"Birth control," I said.

Ian had a condom in his bathing suit pocket. He ripped it open, pulled down his bathing suit, put it on. No awkward fumbling. My breathing was shallow. He pushed himself into me. The angle seemed impossible and it worked, like he was good at this, like he had something to teach me. I had never had sex standing up. My hips were pressed into the ceramic sink, my knees bent.

"Oh my God," I said.

Ian shifted, pushed in deeper.

"That feels good," I said.

"Of course it does," he said.

I was fucking Ian Thornton in the family bathroom on a Friday afternoon.

"Oh my God," I said. "Oh."

I had always thought it was dumb, in movies, when people said this. Oh my God. Those were the words that came out of my mouth. Ian's eyes were open, his gaze penetrating me, like his penis, almost as if he could go straight through me.

"Ian, Rachel," Amelia called out from the other side of the bathroom door. "Where are you? I'm bored. I want to go swimming."

"Shut up," Ian yelled, still looking into my eyes. He kept on fucking me. I prayed for Amelia to go away. I had my hands on Ian's ass now, pressing him in deeper. Again and again. My legs started slipping and I was going to fall but Ian pushed me back up. "Not yet," he said. "Stay with me."

Amelia was knocking on the bathroom door, banging on it with her fists. Ian was thrusting again. Somehow, it seemed even sexier, heightened, wrong, Amelia just outside, about to discover us. This was all so wrong. The door wasn't locked. She could burst in and catch us.

"Now," Ian said.

He came. I came with him. We came together. His hands were caught in my hair. He tugged through a knot to get his fingers loose. "Ow," I said. Was this all I had ever wanted? Sex in a small bathroom with a guy I barely knew. No. This wasn't it. I was confused. Ian pulled out of me and I sank down to the floor. I felt clammy all over, covered in sweat and out of breath. I reached out for Ian, wanting him to sit with me, hold me even.

But Amelia was still there, pounding on the bathroom door. Somehow, I had tuned her out. Either that or she had stopped knocking. Probably she had heard us. How could she have not? Maybe she wouldn't know what it was. She was just a kid. I wondered how I would be able to look her in the eye, be her counselor after this. Ian pulled up his swimsuit, calm, unruffled even. Blond. Perfect. He was not someone I would ordinarily talk to.

"I'll meet you outside."

I blinked.

"You could use a swim."

Ian blinked. He had thrown the used condom in the trash, there for anyone to see. Amelia. His mother. His father. I reached for the toilet paper and wiped myself again. I got more and covered the condom. I stood up and splashed cold water on my face and then I looked at myself in the mirror. I looked different. Was that even possible? But I did. I looked like I'd had sex. And I was grinning. I really was. My God. Even if I did not exactly like him. Ian Thornton.

"Look at you," I said to the mirror.

My heart had stopped racing. Slowly, I was coming down. I reached for my bathing suit. My mother had bought it for me.

It was purple. It was plain, unflattering, a bathing suit perfect for my mother, nothing that I would ever pick for myself, but I needed bathing suits and I hated shopping so I wore it.

"Come on, Rachel!" Ian yelled. "What is taking you so long? Hurry up."

I blinked. Ian wanted me. I had to hurry up. I put on my suit and rushed outside to join Amelia and Ian. They were already walking down the rocky beach.

"There she is," Ian said. "Rachel."

I smiled.

He knew my name.

I watched Ian dive underwater. For the longest time he did not come back up. The surface of the water was flat.

"Ian!" Amelia screamed. "What if he drowned? What if he drowned?"

"He didn't drown," I said.

He was underwater for a long time, though. I reached for Amelia's hand. What if he had drowned? What could I do? Swim until I found his body? Would I call the police? What would I do?

"Where is he?" Amelia whispered.

I did not know.

And then Ian emerged, far out in the water.

"Ian!" Amelia screamed, happy, but not letting go of my hand.

I did not understand what had happened. I stared out at Ian, a small blond head, bobbing in the water. Did I just have sex with him in the bathroom? A terrible thought came into my head. I wished that Zahid had cancer.

I led Amelia into the water.

"Let's go swimming," I said.

Later that night, Ian took me to a shooting range.

"I thought you were kidding," I said.

"I don't kid," Ian said.

"I've never held a gun before," I said.

I did, in fact, want to go to dinner, a movie, that whole traditional thing. Somehow, instead, I had been left alone with Amelia, responsible for making her dinner. We had macaroni and cheese and sliced cucumbers. Ian had to go somewhere, he did not say where. I didn't know where the parents were. Clearly, I was doing him a favor, filling in for a babysitter, except that I wasn't being paid. I was being taken for granted, already. His leaving had seemed so strange. My mother had texted, wanting to know where I was. *Come home,* she wrote.

*On a date,* I responded.

It was not completely inaccurate.

Ian came back from wherever he'd gone.

"Let's go," he said.

The mother, Amy Thornton, had returned, too. She looked at me curiously. She poured herself a glass of white wine. She poured me one, too. "You look like your mother," she said, squinting. "I can never thank her enough. Tell her that."

The shooting range was half an hour away. Ian drove the gold Lamborghini. I had seen this car before, seen his father driving it around town. It was the kind of car you noticed, too ridiculous to be real. I got in the car, and then I was a person who had driven in a gold Lamborghini, out with Ian Thornton. It was weird, surreal even.

"I don't want to do this," I told Ian at the range.

My legs were shaking. My arms were shaking. I was holding a loaded weapon. I knew that accidents could happen with guns. I had read so many stories about small children shooting their siblings. I did not want, for instance, to accidentally kill Ian. I did not want him to kill me.

"I can't," I said.

I tried to hand the gun back to Ian.

"First of all, chill out," Ian said. "You are freaking out. Right now, the gun is locked."

I looked at Ian.

"You're safe," he said.

"I'm safe?"

Ian nodded. His eyes were too blue.

I knew what my mother would think. She would be livid. Guns. Shooting with Ian Thornton. They were Republicans. Which made them Trump supporters. There was nothing worse in her book and I did not disagree with this. But Ian was not really one of them. He was a cute guy, a really, really cute guy. He was not a professor. He was not abusing his power. He could not get fired for having sex with me. Probably, rich as he was, he didn't even have a job. Anyway, I did not care what my mother thought.

I hated that I took my mother's thoughts into consideration. I didn't want to think about my mother. My mother in her pink pajamas this morning, home alone with Zahid. Her distracted gaze. Jesus. Just the thought of them made me hold my arms out straight, aim the gun toward the target.

"I don't believe in guns," I told Ian.

I was starting to understand why, imagining myself shooting Zahid in the chest. Which would be a lot quicker than cancer.

Ian laughed. "You're holding one in your hands," he said. "What don't you believe?"

"That's not what I mean," I said.

"I know what you mean," he said.

"Especially after what your brother did."

Ian shook his head.

"Poor sick fuck," Ian said. "Little baby brother Theo. Honestly, Rachel, he didn't do anything."

"Seriously?" I said.

"Seriously," Ian said. "No one got hurt. He's the one locked up in an institution."

He looked pissed now, which was unnerving. I didn't know what the rules were in the Thornton family. One of them probably was *Don't talk about the sociopath brother at boarding school,* but Ian had taken me shooting. How could I not think about this brother? Ian could have taken me to a bar, a restaurant. A motel, even.

"You wanted to go on a date," Ian said, as if he were reading my mind. "We are on a date. I can take you home if you want."

"I don't want to go home," I said.

But he didn't understand that I did not ever want to go back home. It was not that I actually wanted to be on a shooting range with him.

"So don't be a whiny baby," Ian said. "Try this. This is it. This is your chance. Right now. You might never have it again."

I looked at Ian.

"Just try it. It's better than sex."

I blushed.

I also felt insulted. Because we had had sex.

"And I know you like sex."

I could feel my face turn red, my stupid face giving everything away. If Ian said, *Jump off a cliff,* would I jump off a cliff? Part of me was afraid that I probably would. I had fucked him in a bathroom. I thought about the rules, the games women were supposed to play. I could not sink any lower. All of a sudden, I wanted to go home. It didn't even matter about what I would find there.

I lowered my arms back down.

"You shoot this gun, Rachel, and I will take you back to my house and fuck you."

Almost involuntarily, I licked my lips.

"That is what I thought," he said.

"You scare me a little," I said.

Ian laughed as if he already knew.

"You like it," he said. "Come on. Concentrate."

He came closer to me, moving right behind me. He put his arms around me, hands on my hands, and lifted my arms. I let his hands guide me. With his hands on my hands, I pointed the gun.

"Okay," he said. "Here we go."

Ian unlocked the gun. He took a step away. "Just hold on tight and shoot. It's as easy as that."

I nodded. I bit my lip. I pulled the trigger. The gun reverberated in my hands, and I took a step back. The bullet had hit the target, right in the middle. My ears were ringing.

"Very nice," Ian said.

And Ian was right. It did feel sexual to me.

I wanted to do it again.

———

Ian did not take me back to his house to fuck me. "It's getting late," he said, breaking his promise to me, driving right past the road to his house and not stopping.

"Oh," I said. "Okay."

What else was I going to say? *I wanted you to fuck me.* We drove in silence until he pulled up in front of my house.

"I'm going back to L.A. tomorrow," he said. "I have to pack."

"Los Angeles?" I said.

"Yeah," he said. "I gotta get back to work. What did you think I was? A fucking loser living with his parents?"

"Work?"

"The entertainment industry," he said. "Duh?"

I looked at him.

"I'm an actor," he said. "You don't know?"

"You are?"

"You seriously don't know."

Ian told me the name of the TV show. I had heard of it. It was on the CW network. One of my housemates once asked me to watch his show. It was her favorite show, even. I started watching, but left during a commercial break because I had a paper to write. My short story, actually. About the flight attendant with a venereal disease. It was one of those slick, impossible shows, sexy adults playing teenagers, wearing amazing clothes, delivering unbelievable lines of dialogue. Ian was on that show. He was famous.

"You're serious?" I asked again.

How could I not know?

Ian smirked. It was like charity, then, the time he had spent with me. He'd been killing time. I was nothing, nobody.

"I thought you were just another groupie," Ian said.

I couldn't tell if he was serious.

"I am not," I managed to say, "a groupie."

"I was kidding," he said. "Kidding."

"You said you didn't kid."

Ian shrugged.

We were in front of my house.

Ian leaned over, which was tricky in the Lamborghini, there was a stick shift, and he kissed me good-bye. It was a new kind of kiss, sweet, tender even. A real and proper, lingering kiss. What I had been hoping for. This felt almost normal, what the end of a date should be. But he was going back to his life in California, where he was a TV star. I basically did not exist.

"You shouldn't have slept with me," I said, "if you knew you were leaving."

"Honestly?" Ian said. "You seemed plenty into it."

And then, out of nowhere, I was crying.

"This is not about you," I said. It was mortifying. I would have done anything to make it stop. "Don't think it is. This has nothing to do with you."

"Of course it is," he said. "Don't worry. I have this effect on women. All the time."

I actually laughed. It was perfect. He had said that. There was something wrong with him. There was comfort to that. It wasn't me. It was him.

I was lucky to be getting out early, unharmed. I could already feel a sore spot on my hip bone from getting slammed back into the bathroom sink.

Ian kissed me again, and once again, I returned his kiss. He was such a good kisser. It was so stupid. I was so stupid. It didn't matter anyway, how stupid I was, because he was leaving. He was not going to be my boyfriend. None of this actually counted. My phone started to vibrate in my pocket. I did not have to look. It was my mother, again. The fourth time that day.

The kiss ended when the phone started to buzz. I looked at my house, the lights on in the living room. She would be awake, waiting for me. Ian wiped away a tear on my cheek.

"I'm coming home for Christmas," he said.

"So," I said.

"So," he said. "I'll call you. You're sweet."

That seemed nice, actually nicer than anything I could have expected from him. It was a good moment to leave, my dignity almost intact. I opened the door to the car, slung my backpack, somehow heavier than it had been that morning, over my shoulder. It was a gorgeous car, almost too nice to be a car. I wondered how much it cost. How many immigrant families it could save.


I stood there, on the driveway of my mother's house, outside, looking in. I dropped my backpack at my feet. I sighed audibly. I was so tired. I wanted to go inside, but I also could not fathom the idea. I had grown up in this house, only it didn't feel like my home anymore. The dog was dead. My father was gone. Zahid was sleeping in his office, swimming in our pool. His poodle was eating from Posey's dog food bowls. It was like we had both been replaced. My mother was a stranger.

I opened my backpack to confirm what somehow I already knew.

There was the gun, in between a library book and a plastic

bag holding my wet bathing suit. I looked down the street. Ian was gone. He was fucking with me, still. I did not want this gun. I did not know what I was supposed to do with it. I was not going to use it. A gun could not make me happy. Could not get me what I wanted.

I wanted Zahid to love me.

I wanted Ian to love me.

I wanted the stupid dog to love me.

The front door to the house opened and there she was.

"Rachel," my mother called out. "Sweetie? What are you doing out there? Where have you been? I have been so worried about you. Come inside. Please? What's wrong?"

I zipped my backpack shut.

A gun. I had a gun. It felt incredibly dangerous to have a gun in my possession. I had hit that target on my first try. It had felt so good.

"Rachel?" my mother said. "Honey?"

She walked down the front path, coming toward me. She was barefoot.

"What's wrong?" she said. "Who was that with you? Was that the Thorntons' car?"

I did not say anything. She knew whose car it was. I did not have to say. I was having very bad luck with men. Was this to be my fate? I bit my lip so hard that it started to bleed.

My mother hugged me, but I did not return her embrace. It seemed unkind on my part, but what else could I do? I had done nothing to suggest that I might want comfort from her. I stood straight and tall, like a tree. The moment felt familiar, like déjà vu, and then I remembered. That very morning, I had hugged Zahid and he'd recoiled from my touch.

Zahid's face appeared in the living room window. My writing professor, his swoopy hair in his eyes, his beautiful eyes, his brown skin. I could see the concern on his face and I understood that it was not for me. I had thought I loved him. It was a secret love, a love I had never thought would be returned, but I had not expected it to be thrown in my face.

# *Becca*

I knew that car. It was Richard Thornton's ridiculous car, and of course, if there was one person in this town that I disliked, that I loathed, because *loathed* would be a more accurate word, if there was any one person that I recoiled from if forced to share the same space in the same room, it was him.

Fucking Richard Thornton. Republican. Card-carrying member of the NRA. This was the man who'd made it possible for his son to show up in my elementary school classroom with an assault weapon. Who smoked cigars in public places. His alcoholic wife continued to send me gifts. Once a month, I received a bottle of wine from a wine-of-the-month club.

They had invited me to dinner once, for family lobster night, and I had almost said yes, curious about their house, which had been featured in *Architectural Digest,* curious about the dynamics of their family, even, but that had been a moment of folly. I had saved their son's life. This did not mean that I had to like them.

The Thorntons were dysfunctional. They were toxic. They were bad rich people, Jonathan had once said, during the run-up to the election, and we, he'd insisted, were the good ones.

He had said it like it was black and white.

I wasn't sure I agreed. Supporting Hillary Clinton, for instance, was not evidence of our good character. She was just the better choice. I had once brought up the horrific and perhaps even criminal mismanagement of the Clinton Foundation and Jonathan had inexplicably yelled at me. He had become furious, as if I had flipped a switch. I had never seen him so angry. Maybe that was the moment everything started to change. Was he with the pilot then, already?

Now my daughter was being dropped off late at night, tears streaming down her face, in Richard Thornton's gold Lamborghini. Was that old son of a bitch fucking my daughter? That was absurd. Impossible. And then I remembered. Their eldest son was in town. This was the kid who had been expelled from boarding school for drinking and drugs, and then expelled from the public high school, too, for drinking and drugs, and then, he took off for California. I'd thought he would end up dead, but instead he was starring on some TV show.

This very son had participated in a fund-raiser in town. A local girl had been born with a rare disease, born without a nose, and he had helped raise money for her medical treatment. He appeared at a charity dinner, which of course I did not go to. I'd wondered what the Thorntons were pulling. As if their family could possibly restore their reputation in our tiny hamlet. It wasn't possible. Did Richard Thornton publicly renounce guns? Make a donation to the families of children senselessly gunned down in schools? He did not. Instead, he sent his kid away, out of sight, out of mind, and he carried on.

I knew for a fact that not a single family wanted to have little Amelia Thornton to their home for a playdate. The girl seemed odd. Seven years old, she still peed in her pants. She played imaginary games by herself on the playground, flying on a dragon named Firebolt and defeating her enemies. Rachel had mentioned that the girl was in her group at camp. She had made Rachel a bracelet with wooden beads spelling her name.

"She's like a sad puppy," Rachel had told me.

Of course, I had not told my daughter to stay away from the little girl. I had held my tongue, proud of my restraint.

It was not enough that Theo had tried to kill me, had terrorized my students. Now it was the older son. This family was fucking with my child.

"Did he hurt you?" I asked Rachel.

"Who?" she said. "Ian?"

Ian. That was his name. His picture had been on the cover of the local paper, smug, just like his father.

"No," she said. "Of course not."

"Then why are you crying?"

Rachel did not answer the question, looking into the house, and there was Zahid, looking out at us.

"What is going on here?" Rachel asked me. "You tell me that."

"Nothing," I said. "We were waiting up for you."

Zahid and I had been in the living room, watching a movie on Netflix, waiting for Rachel. She had done this the other night, too, when Zahid was away, stayed out late without explanation. Yes, it was true, when she was away at college, I knew none of her daily whereabouts. But this was different. Rachel was home and I had no idea where she was and I didn't like it.

Zahid and I had been eating bowls of the ice cream we had bought at the Stop & Shop. I had started a film, one of the recommended movies on the menu, some independent thing that was popular. It was so innocent, of course, the two of us watching a movie together, that it occurred to me that it was strange that he had lived in this house with us all this time and we had not watched a movie together. Rachel could come home and find us watching a movie. It would be a good thing.

Tonight, for the first time, I seriously considered telling Rachel about us. She was, of course, an observant child. I had no idea what she knew, what clues might have given us away. I had gone so far as to wander into her bedroom, looking for a journal. I'd even turned on her computer, to see what she was writing. There was a password.

"We could tell her," I said to Zahid. "About us."

I methodically ate my ice cream, waiting for him to respond. Zahid was uncomfortable with the idea, talking to Rachel. I understood this was a warning sign, his reluctance, that there had to be something more behind his reticence. I could just ask him straight out if he had messed around with my daughter. And so what if he had? I could take it. I could take this information and process it and continue to love him.

Or could I?

If it had happened, it had happened before. Before me. Before us. It was an abuse of power, sure, but I was not that old. I remembered college, all of the coeds falling for their professors. How hard it would be to resist a pretty nineteen-year-old girl.

This was also rationalization, I thought. I did not like the idea of Zahid having sex with my daughter, taking advantage of her youth, of her innocence, while criticizing her short stories. Maybe that part was the most bothersome to me. He was supposed to be building her confidence. I would have told Zahid this, except that we did not talk about my daughter.

"I don't want to tell you not to tell her."

That is what he said.

"But you don't want me to?" I said. "Is that correct?"

Zahid agreed. I turned on the movie.

And now, Rachel and I stood outside the house, together, looking in. It seemed symbolic, as if Zahid were an intruder. I could call the police and have him removed, arrested.

"Something is going on," Rachel said. "I know you are lying to me. It just makes it worse when you deny it."

I hesitated.

"You spend every day with him," she said.

She did not know. She was guessing.

"We do our own thing," I said. "He sits in your father's office and he writes. He makes pleasant dinner conversation, I grant you that, but I have been missing you. We were watching a movie, just now, waiting for you to come home."

"You are a terrible liar," Rachel said.

She looked down at her backpack, like there might be something in it she wanted to show me.

"What is it, honey?" I said. Because Rachel had started crying again. "What's wrong? Tell me."

I remembered what it was like, to be her age, to feel everything that intensely. It also did not seem that different from right now. I was also feeling things intensely. My heart flip-flopped. Maybe it was me, hurting my daughter, and how could I explain that away?

"I want you to stay away from the Thorntons," I said.

"Seriously?"

"You haven't forgotten, have you, what happened? At the school?"

"No," Rachel said. "Of course not."

"You were at college."

"So?"

"That entire family is seriously disturbed, honey. Not just Theo Thornton. All of them. Even the little girl."

"I am not talking to you about this."

"But that was Ian, wasn't it? Dropping you off just now?"

"I just said that I'm not talking to you about this."

"That doesn't work for me."

"You're lying to me, about him," Rachel said, pointing to the house. "That doesn't work for me, either."

"Your father left me for a pilot," I said. "Do you remember that?"

"The pilot. Mandy," Rachel said. "Like the Barry Manilow song. How could I forget?"

I did not like the way this conversation was going. I had told Rachel, back when Jonathan and I split, that I was okay with it. Only it wasn't okay. I don't know why it had taken me so long to realize this.

"And so that makes it all right?" Rachel said. "Whatever it is you are doing now. Because of Mandy."

"Yes," I said. "It does."

Shit, I thought, shit shit shit. I wasn't sure what I had done, what I'd just admitted to. I had admitted to nothing, it was more like in principle. In principle, there was absolutely nothing wrong with what I was doing with Zahid. Except, of course, that there was. It was wrong. I knew that.

She was my daughter.

"Seriously, Rachel. I am being very serious," I said, trying to regain control. "Everything about that family is toxic. Richard Thornton collects guns. He has had his picture taken with Trump. Did you hear me? Amelia is in counseling at school."

"You aren't supposed to tell me that, Mom. That's a violation of her privacy. I like Amelia. What is wrong with you?"

"And that boy," I continued. "The older one. Ian." I had actually watched an episode of his TV show. He had taken off his shirt, displaying a hairless, almost disturbingly perfect chest. He had proceeded to take off the actress's shirt, she was wearing a pink underwire bra, and they had continued to talk, half-undressed, as if they were one hundred years old, plotting a murder, and then a commercial came on and I turned off the TV. "What do we know about him?"

"Exactly. You don't know anything about him. So suspend judgment."

"I don't think so," I said. "I don't trust him. There is something about his expression. He is ice-cold. Even his character on the show was plotting a murder."

"You've watched it?" Rachel seemed surprised. "You knew he was on TV?"

"I would not trust him alone with any young woman," I said. "Especially you. You're my daughter. I love you. Don't you see? That is why I worry."

"And you trust *him*?" Rachel asked.

She pivoted back toward the house. Zahid. She wanted to know if I trusted Zahid.

"It's two different things," I said.

Rachel looked at me like I was full of shit.

"I trust him," I said.

"I don't," Rachel said. "I think he is just as toxic. I don't just think this. I know it."

She knew it.

How? How did she know?

What did she know?

And her father, he said he knew.

He had seen us walking, walking on the beach.

They did not know, but they knew.

What was the problem? Zahid and I were both adults. I had done nothing wrong, nothing. I wanted to scream. I wanted to shake her. This daughter of mine would go back to college and lead her own life, and what about me? Wasn't I allowed to be happy? Why couldn't I have him?

"You are like a child, Mom," Rachel said. "You don't know anything."

"That's not true."

"When was the last time you went on a date?"

"That is irrelevant."

Zahid had not left the window. He was standing there, watching us as we watched him. He should have walked away.

"He is like a big man-child!" Rachel screamed at me. "He is using you, Mom, it is so incredibly obvious, I don't know how you don't see it."

"No," I said. "That isn't true."

"Oh my God. He is using you for this house. For the swimming pool. For the room to write in. For the meals you make for him. He is using you for the fucking grilled chicken with tarragon. He eats all of the strawberries."

"No," I said. "That's not true. I am nobody's wife."

"Exactly!" Rachel screamed. "That is what I am saying. He wants a mother."

"That's disgusting," I said.

"Your words," Rachel said. "Not mine."

I was stunned. I felt my mouth hanging open. Rachel stormed inside, carrying her backpack with her, and I followed behind her. She slammed the door in my face. I opened it. She was already halfway up the stairs.

"Rachel," I called out to her. "Let's sit down and talk about everything. I don't think you understand. You have the wrong idea," I said. She did. She did. She did have the wrong idea. Zahid was still standing in the living room. Frozen. Useless. "Let's all of us talk about this," I said. "We can talk about it."

"Fuck you," Rachel said. She was talking to both of us.

Her bedroom door slammed behind her. Posey started barking. I went over to the poodle to calm her down. Poodles, they don't like violence. This wasn't violence, I reminded myself. This was a fight. It was okay, sometimes people fight. Mothers and daughters. Rachel had had an uneventful adolescence.

"It's okay," I told Posey. I sat down on the floor, petting the dog, Zahid watching us. I had royally fucked up, but I wasn't even sure how. I could have picked a better boyfriend? But how? Tinder? He was right for me. It was only that Rachel wanted him, too.

"That didn't go well," I said to Zahid.

"Becca," he said.

I should have asked him then. Did you have sexual relations with my daughter? But it would be better not to know. I did not want to know. Why did everything have to be spelled out? I was okay with plausible deniability. I continued to pet the dog. My sweet Posey.

"It's going to be okay," Zahid said, which was such a cliché, I was surprised. I thought he might have something better than that, award-winning writer that he was.

"I think you should go," I said, surprising myself. I didn't want Zahid to leave. I did not want to lose my daughter. I did not see why I should have to choose.

"Becca?" he said. "No," he said. "I don't want to leave."

I was glad. I was glad that he did not do what I'd told him to.

"She is so angry," I said. "So angry. I don't know what to do. I have to do something."

"Let her be angry," Zahid said. "She is young. That is their natural state."

Somehow Zahid was on the floor, too, on the other side of Posey. He leaned over the dog and kissed me. It was incredibly risky, this kiss, we were out in the open, my daughter upstairs, but this was the right thing for him to do. Zahid was not a coward after all.

"I don't want to go," he said. "I want to be with you."

I returned Zahid's kiss. My daughter already knew. I had not told her, I had taken pains to hide it, but she knew anyway. The way she'd just looked at me, the hate, the contempt, it was as bad as anything could be. I understood that I was making the wrong choice. She was my child. My little girl. My baby. The only child I would ever have. I needed to lead Zahid and his standard poodle to the door. It was the only thing for me to do and I did not do it.

In the morning, I found a new short story slipped under my door. It was well written, like the first one. And mean-spirited. Cruel, even. I certainly no longer felt that Rachel was rooting for me.

She had moved on from her fictional father and now there

was a new character, Zahir, the writer, who has been infected by the very same Amanda. He had also been a passenger on one of her flights, on the way to a job interview.

This Zahir is never treated for his venereal disease.

*I will get better,* he thinks, because basically, he is an idiot. He runs a high fever, but he ignores it. He works on his novel, desperate to finish, getting sicker and sicker. He gives up coffee. He gives up alcohol. He even gives up women. Still, he does not get better. He starts to see spots dancing before his eyes, but he is sure that will get better if he finishes the book. He wakes up one morning and he cannot see.

He is blind.

Meanwhile, Amanda, the flight attendant, has changed her ways. She is done with men and she is done with flying. She has quit her job and moved to Morocco, inspired by the Kate Hudson character in *Almost Famous*. Unlike Zahir, Amanda has received proper medical attention. She has taken her second round of antibiotics.

Amanda goes to a nightclub wearing a short sequined dress and high-heeled sandals. She catches the eye of a beautiful princess. They dance until the sun comes up.

Amanda moves into her new girlfriend's castle, overlooking the sea.

"You are like no one I have ever met before," the princess tells her. "I love you. I adore you. I love your bangs."

Amanda shrugs, unsurprised.

# *Zahid*

Rachel was going to ruin everything for me.

I knew it and I did not know how to stop it.

I could beg her.

I could sneak into her room and beg her not to tell Becca.

I could offer to read her fiction. To write her a letter of recommendation. I could offer her money, except that I did not have any money and also, that would offend her. I could talk to her like an adult, that's what I could do, except the thing about these kids in college, all of them, they were treated with these kid gloves and not as the adults that they actually were also expected to be. My God, were these students coddled. Rachel could not even accept a constructive comment on a short story. She retreated as if she had been wounded. She stopped turning in work. I had not even told her that her writing was bad. I was just trying to make it better. That was my job.

Poor, wounded Rachel Klein, who grew up in this house, a house that was like a dream, and she took it all, everything, for granted. She had wanted a sexual experience with me. She had wanted it and she had made this abundantly clear to me.

She had held my hand. We had walked slowly up the stairs together. There had been at least fifteen stairs on which she could have changed her mind.

She had unbuttoned the buttons of my shirt. There must have been eight buttons and she had been painstakingly slow, careful, deliberate. Nothing about our experience had been hasty or tacky or crude. It was erotic. It was tender. I remembered. It was not as if I had forgotten. It was not as if I did not think of her in Pakistan, after my grandmother died, wishing that she were there to comfort me. It was not as if I did not think about it almost every time that I saw her. Even now.

It had been mutually satisfying. That was all it was ever going to be.

Could we not be friends?

This, this was what it was to be an adult.

I could try to explain all of this to her. I could explain to her that we did not have fast-growing tumors inside our bodies. That we were lucky. I could explain to her that I had not been taking advantage of her and that I was not taking advantage of her mother, either. That I was not that kind of person.

I had never wanted to hurt Rachel. It had never occurred to me. It was just that she was young. She was young and impressionable, so of course she was going to get hurt. That was just part of life. That was part of being alive. We did not have to regret what we had done. It had been nice. Very nice.

But now, it was different. It was altogether different with Becca. With her mother. It was unexpected and wonderful. I could explain to Rachel that this was love. That I was in love with her mother. I understood that she would have difficulty processing this. She would think that she was perfect, with her perfect body, as if that was everything, all that mattered.

I heard Becca open the door, taking Princess out for a pee, and I decided I would try. I could try to talk to Rachel, quickly, and assess her state of mind. I hadn't talked to her once that entire summer, not once, properly, one-on-one. Of course, I realized, that must have hurt her feelings. Why had I not thought of that before? I did not need to be afraid. I knocked on Rachel's door.

"Come in," she said, and I opened the door.

Rachel was naked. She was standing twisted in front of a full-length mirror. "Do I have a bruise?" she asked me. "On my ass? Can you see anything?"

I slammed the door shut.

I could see her still, on the other side of the door, not wearing any clothes. She did have a bruise, or what looked like the beginning of a bruise, a rather large one, the size of a baseball. The skin a strange yellow.

"Why did you say 'Come in'?" I said.

"To fuck with you," she said. "That's why."

"That wasn't nice."

"No," Rachel said, from behind the closed door. "I suppose it wasn't."

I stood there.

I had a very real reason why I wanted to talk to Rachel. I wanted to assess the situation. It was bad. And yes, yes, she was going to ruin it for me if she had her way. I should pack my bags right now and get out while I was still unscathed. I could write to Iowa and see if I could still have the job. Why had I sent that e-mail already? I could write to Kristi and beg for forgiveness. She would love that, me begging her.

"Did you have something to say to me?" Rachel said.

"I did," I said. "But I forgot."

"You forgot."

"Yes," I said. "I forgot."

I stood there on the other side of her door, still frozen. I would not go back into her room. I would not risk being alone with her ever again. I could hear the front door open and close. Becca was back with the dog.

"Good night, Rachel," I said to the closed door.

There was an update from Myra Alice on Facebook about my dying friend. His hair had started falling out from the chemo and so he had shaved his head. Now he was bald. She had posted a picture. In no way did Sean look handsome bald. He looked like he had cancer.

A tumor, I wanted to tell Rachel. She could have a tumor. She had everything. She even had a story she could tell her little friends. I wanted to shake her.

There was a stream of positive comments from friends, saying how good Sean looked when obviously he looked awful. Shit, he looked like he was dying. We were the same age. I remembered watching him on the slopes at Vail. With a pair of skis on his feet, he was like a different person. Fast, sleek, confident. On campus, he was tentative and careful, unwilling to talk in class. I think it was not until after she had seen him ski that Myra Alice was able to view him as a romantic partner.

I bet he was not skiing now.

It was hard, looking at this picture of a skinny bald man, to remember what Sean looked like when he had hair. He had red hair. He was not a particularly masculine-looking guy. He was pasty and pale. Whereas I was swarthy and my hair was dark, but otherwise we had the same haircut. We were the same height. We dressed the same, signed up for the same classes. Myra Alice had joked once that we were twins, Kermit and Fozzie Bear. I had pretended for months after they had gotten together that we could still be friends. But I was not big enough a man to watch them together, happy in love.

My hands hovered over the keyboard, wondering what it was that I could possibly write. My head was all over the place. I was thinking about Rachel, naked, her breasts, that bruise on her backside. I wrote a comment and deleted it.

I started another comment, and again, I didn't post it. There was nothing I could say that could change the situation. Nothing I could say that would make him feel better. There was nothing to say that would make me feel better. What could I do? Nothing. I could get on a plane and visit him and that wouldn't make him feel better. That would just be awkward. Where would I stay? A hotel in D.C. would cost a fortune. I could not stay with them. It was not like when we were in college.

Hopefully, Myra Alice was taking good care of him. He would be loved and cared for until the end. I wanted that for Sean. I had been dumped by my fiancée. He had gotten married. He had been married for ten years already, and I had been the reluctant best man. I had always, only been jealous. The truth was, I had thought that I was in love with her. She was the first girl I had slept with at college, but by the next day, I already knew the score. I would watch her hook up with Sean and then fall in love and I would pretend that I did not care. At a certain point, I stopped caring.

But I also never told him, about me and Myra Alice. She didn't, either.

Die, tumor, die.

I thought the words, but I didn't believe them. He had an inoperable tumor. My old friend, the one who had gotten the girl, he was fucked, pure and simple. It was as if the dice had been rolled and he got terminal cancer. This time, I was the lucky one. Our friendship had been over a long time ago.

It felt unfair that I was burdened with this now. I sat on my bed, staring at my phone. I was trapped in this stupid room, the least realized room of the house, wanting desperately to be with Becca, unable to go to her. This was her house. Rachel was a smoking gun. I had to wait. I had to wait. Follow Becca's lead.

The phone vibrated in my hand. I was so nervous that I dropped it, and the screen cracked. Of course it did. It was a text from Kristi. Fucking Kristi Taylor. I wanted it to be Becca. I was afraid to read Kristi's text. But I had nothing better to do and I was trapped and so I read it.

It said everything I already knew.

You are a fucking moron.


And those were the words that I told myself, over and over, as I struggled to fall asleep. I hoped against hope for a knock on the door, a knock that did not come. I wanted it to be Becca, of course, Becca wanting me as much as I wanted her. I wanted her to choose me as I had chosen her.

It was three in the morning.

I was lying in bed, but I wasn't any closer to sleep. My phone vibrated again. I had no self-control. I would not wait until the morning. I grabbed for my phone, saw the cracked screen. I had a warranty but I was sure it had expired.

My message. It was not a text but an e-mail. Probably just a political e-mail, another Democrat asking for money, or maybe PEN asking me to stand up for oppressed voices in literature, some stupid shit like that that had slipped into my important mail. Or it could be real, a real e-mail. Something good. My mother might have written me. She might finally be done being mad with me. It was time. Becca was not mad at Rachel, after all. She would forgive her anything. She was threatening to end our relationship to keep her daughter. My mother would forgive me. Or Kristi might have written again, compelled to tell me off one more time and needing her full keyboard to express her vitriol.

I reached for my phone, illuminating the screen, knowing that the chance of sleep would be even more remote.

The e-mail was from my new editor.

I had sent her the pages of my novel before dinner. Becca had been monosyllabic with worry and I'd thought, *Why not? Why not take this chance?* Because I wasn't dying. I did not have cancer. I had everything ahead of me.

I read my editor's e-mail quickly, and then I read it again.

The pages I'd sent were wonderful, WONDERFUL, more than she could have hoped for, so different from my previous book. Fresh and to the point and entertaining, and she was SO EXCITED.

"Fuck," I said, my hands clenched into fists. "Fuck, yeah."

# *Khloe*

The first time I texted Rachel Klein to tell her that I would go to the beach with her in Connecticut, I didn't mean it. I was just texting shit, the way people do. And then, it was the actual weekend and I didn't have any plans. Jane had literally shut the door in my face. So I would go to the beach in Connecticut. Fuck it. Maybe I would see Zahid Azzam and I would fuck with him. So hard. I would tell him that his editor was busy counting his shoes, opening his underwear drawer.

I woke up early, packed a bag, took the subway to Grand Central, looked at the board, figured out the train I would have to catch, bought my tickets, bought a coffee and a croissant. I bought a straw hat. It was like a fucking mall down there. I texted Rachel and told her I was on my way. And if she couldn't meet me, if she had made other plans, whatever. I would be in Connecticut. I would find a beach. I had never been to Connecticut before.

But Rachel was there at the station, waiting for me.

"I didn't think you would come," she said. "You surprised

me." She smiled. She seemed happy to see me. This was the first proper vacation day I had taken all summer.

"I love your hat," she said.

But the beach was nothing much. Disappointing.

It was small. There weren't real waves. The sand was sort of gray and muddy. There was a playground next to the parking lot and there was a mother there with a little girl and a baby and she looked sad and tired.

"This is really it?" I asked Rachel. "This is all there is?"

I knew what I'd been expecting. I'd been expecting Fire Island. The Hamptons. I'd been expecting a big long stretch of sandy beach, tons of people, beautiful people, beach umbrellas, breaking waves. I'd been expecting a few other people, at least. This, according to Rachel, was the Sound. It was not the actual ocean. This was the only public beach in town, she informed me. She had not told me this before. Apparently there were nicer beaches, located in people's backyards. Rachel, however, did not have her own private beach. There was a lifeguard stand and two teenagers, a guy and a girl wearing red bathing suits, looking out onto the empty water. Jesus fuck.

"I thought there would be more people than this," Rachel said.

She kept talking: "I went swimming here last week, with this guy and his little sister, who goes to my day camp. He held me under the water. For a long time. I could have drowned and no one would have known."

I did not know what she wanted me to make of that. It still

seemed odd that she had invited me out here in the first place. We barely knew each other, had nothing to talk about.

"Except for the guy and his little sister," I said.

"Eventually my mother would have missed me," Rachel said.

"Your father, too," I remarked.

Rachel agreed.

"I wouldn't hang out with guys who try to drown me," I said, because I felt like something was required. I was older and therefore wiser. Why had she invited me? Why had I come?

"He's in California now."

I was relieved. Story over. I was definitely not the right person to share your sexual abuse story with. I had made a choice, though I would also argue it was not a choice, but I was with women. I did not date men who systematically tried to shove their dicks down my throat. I had spared myself that particular kind of abuse. But then I thought about that door, closing in my face. Right now, that didn't seem that much better. It felt to me that as human beings we were fucked all around.

The beach, at least, was starting to grow on me. It was quiet. The air smelled like salt. The sun was strong. There were a couple of seagulls. Rachel was fine. It was nice enough here. I had to lower my expectations.

"There is a good place nearby to collect shells," Rachel told me. "We can go there next if you want if you don't like it here."

"I don't want to collect shells," I said.

"Okay," she said.

"Let's swim," I said.

There was a faraway look in Rachel's eyes, like she didn't actually care if I had a good day or a bad day, which was annoying. We waded out into the water. The sand felt good under my feet. I walked out until it was too deep to stand and then I swam out deep into the warm, calm water. As a rule, I never swam out this far. I was usually worried about drowning, but not here, there were no waves, and I was enjoying the sensation of my arm slicing through the surface of the water like a knife, and then, out of nowhere, a motorboat flew past me, and all of a sudden, the placid water was filled with choppy waves, and I was swallowing water. I went beneath the surface and came back up. I wanted to put my feet on the bottom but the water was too deep. Fuck. Motherfucking fuck. I just had to stay calm. Not panic. I thought about Rachel's story, the asshole who held her under. I could die out here. Today could be the day that I die. I had swum out too far. It was like I had entered a highway of sorts, there were more boats coming, and I had become a deer in the headlights. This was insane. I was not going to drown, not here, in Connecticut.

"Fuck you," I called out to the motorboat, already long gone. I looked back at the beach, the teenage lifeguards still in their tall chair, still talking to each other, oblivious. What the fuck?

I kept on treading water, waiting for the waves to go away before I started to swim back, and then I saw her, Rachel Klein. For a moment, it seemed like a coincidence.

"Are you okay?" she called out. "I saw that boat. I was scared. Wow, you swam out far. I can't believe how far you swam. Are you okay? Are you tired? The lifeguards aren't even paying attention."

Rachel Klein was swimming out to me, doing a crawl but keeping her head out of the water, talking as she swam. She would have noticed if I'd drowned. It was a small comfort.

———

Rachel took me to lunch, leading us to a small restaurant, more like a deli, down the street. She bought us turkey sandwiches and lemonades. I offered her money. She shrugged. "They know me here. It goes on our tab."

A tab. I had never heard of a restaurant that kept a tab. "So you mean, your father pays?"

"I'm not sure," she said, seriously considering the question. "I suppose he did before he left my mother. So he probably still does. I hadn't thought about it. It seems unfair now that he is gone. My mother comes here all the time."

"But you don't pay?" I said.

"No," Rachel said. "I suppose not. Not in the immediate sense, at least."

We sat at an outdoor picnic table on a deck that looked out onto the small street. Main Street. Just down the road was the small beach where we'd just been swimming. So this was Connecticut. It felt small. It felt weird. I felt like I'd stepped into an old J.Crew catalog. I watched the cars drive by. A BMW SUV. A Mercedes. A Mini Cooper, a Prius. A Porsche. An old silver Jaguar, my kind of car. I felt sandy and hot. I was tired. Irritable. Hungover. Somehow it was only one o'clock in the afternoon. The sun was relentless. There wasn't even an umbrella over this picnic table. It was a horrible place to have lunch, but I didn't say this to Rachel. This seemed to be what she liked to do. What happened now? I would take the train back to Brooklyn and drink more beer? Drink and drink until I passed out and then went back to work on Monday? Fuck.

"It's hot here," Rachel said. "Do you want to come to my house? We have a swimming pool."

Perfect. That, of course, was precisely what I was going to do. That was what we should have done all along. A swimming pool. I drank my lemonade down in two long sips. It was good. Tart.

"Sure," I said.

Rachel smiled shyly. It was cute, adorable even. She seemed straight, but she was still young. She might not know. Maybe that was why she texted me. I watched as she went back into the deli and came out with two Ben & Jerry's ice cream bars. It was a good move after how the day had gone down so far. She was okay, Rachel Klein. She'd picked me up from the train station. She'd made sure that I did not drown. She'd bought me lunch.

"I should warn you," Rachel said. "Things are a little bit messed up at my house."

I nodded.

"Zahid," I said.

"You know him?" Rachel asked me, licking her ice cream bar, looking away from me as if she did not care.

"Not well," I said.

"I think my mother has a thing for him," Rachel said. "My dad is right to be worried."

I could tell Rachel about Jane, the way she had stared at Zahid's shoes, but I certainly was not going to talk about Jane. And I knew about Zahid and Rachel, but I was not going to tell Rachel that, either. I could see no real reason to pursue a friendship with this girl. I wondered if maybe I should not want to go back to her house, swim in her pool. But I would. I had the day to get through.

"That is troubling," I agreed.

"It is completely unacceptable," Rachel said. She had chocolate smeared on her lips. Her cheeks were red from the sun. I took a napkin and cleaned her face.

"Can I tell you something else?" she asked me.

I put the napkin down and finished my ice cream bar. I did not answer. I wondered why I had cleaned her face. I did not want to know Rachel Klein's secrets.

"I have a gun," she said.

She looked down at her backpack as if to say, The gun is there. She was full of shit, of course, but I didn't particularly like the joke.


Zahid Azzam was in the swimming pool.

He was wearing a pair of purple bathing trunks, the same purple as Rachel's one-piece bathing suit. He was swimming laps. He did a flip turn at the deep end of the pool. I was surprised. For some reason, he had struck me as unathletic.

Rachel's mother was lying on a lounge chair wearing a purple bikini, again with the purple, reading a book. Zahid's dog, the standard poodle, was lying on the deck next to Rachel's mother. Rachel's mother was a gorgeous woman. She was what I wanted to look like when I got older. I did not entirely understand the situation, but I recognized it for what it was. Fucked up.

It was a very nice swimming pool.

This, I realized, was why I worked in finance.

# Rachel

I ended up taking Khloe back to the house. We were both hot, tired, burnt out from the sun. The summer guests were still there, of course, out by the pool. My professor and his apricot-colored standard poodle. They were squatters, really.

Zahid was swimming laps. Posey was lying in the shade, her paws stretched out in front of her, one crossed on top of the other. I loved when she did that. At some point, I realized, she had become Posey to me. Princess was a terrible name. My writing professor was a terrible writer. He was the big joke. Not me.

There was my mother, too, leaning forward on a pool chair, a book open on her lap, watching Zahid swim. She was wearing a purple bikini.

We were all wearing purple bathing suits.

I'd had no idea my mother had done that.

Humiliation on top of humiliation.

I, of course, should have been wearing the bikini. The feeling of fury—rage, even—that I had been holding back rose in the back of my throat. I could taste the bile.

Khloe took her clothes off right away and dove straight into the water. No hellos. No introductions. She came back up, wet and gleaming, like an Amazon goddess. I still had no idea why she was here, why she even agreed to come. We were not friends. Soon, I would go back to college. I might even take a psychology class. Try to understand the human psyche.

"Oooh, that feels good," Khloe said.

Khloe was wearing a white off-the-shoulder bathing suit, incredible against her creamy skin. Somehow I had not properly noticed it, or her, really, at the beach. I had watched her almost drown, curious to see how long she stayed under.

"Hey, stranger," she said to Zahid.

Zahid's mouth dropped open. He stopped in the middle of the pool, mid lap, noticing our arrival.

"Khloe?" he said. "What are you doing here?"

"Crazy, right?" she said. "It's me. Here in Connecticut."

My mother got up from her pool chair and walked over to me. I watched her from the corner of my eye. She tried to hug me, but she had come at me from the wrong angle. My shoulder pressed into her chest. I certainly wasn't going to make it easy for her. She was brave to try. Stupid, even.

I waited until she was done and then I sat down at the edge of the pool, my legs cradled around my backpack. I put my feet into the water. Khloe was right. The water did feel good.

"We are all wearing purple bathing suits," I said.

There were so many things I could have said at that moment. I settled on this.

"That's really weird, Mom."

My mother nodded.

I had hurt her feelings, I understood that, but it was noth-

ing, nothing compared to what they had done to me. My feelings. If this was a contest, I was going to win.

"They were on sale," my mother said, as if that explained
everything. "Who is your friend?" she asked.

"Khloe," Khloe said, without missing a beat. "With a *K*."

"Like Anne of Green Gables," my mother said.

"Exactly," Khloe said. "One of my few literary references."

I splashed my feet in the water.

*Splish splash.*

We could be on our own TV show. It was all starting to seem
silly to me, all of this drama. Emotion.

"She works for Dad," I said.

"Really?" My mother looked confused. "Your friend works
for Jonathan? And how do you know Zahid?"

"Khloe," Zahid repeated, like he was stuck back in time,
thirty seconds ago. It was rude the way he did not let Khloe
answer my mother's question. "What the fuck are you doing
here?"

Khloe had begun to grin. She seemed to like the pool, to
like the situation, even.

"Zahid," she said. "Dude. What the fuck are *you* still doing
here?"

"I came for my dog," he said. "You know that."

"Yeah," Khloe said, laughing. "That was more than a month
ago."

"I never left," Zahid said to Khloe.

"That works for me," Khloe said.

I looked at Zahid's chest. His brown skin. His small dark
nipples. His swoopy hair was wet, slicked back. I used to go to
his class and stare and stare at him. I barely listened to his lec-

tures or the other students in workshop, always kissing up to him. It felt almost like a miracle, that he was here, half naked in my swimming pool, and then I remembered, as if for the first time, that he did not want me. It was like a slap in the face, every time, every single night that he did not come into my room. And I wanted him still.

There was something wrong with me.

"Kristi told me you're moving to Iowa," Khloe said.

"She told you that?" Zahid said.

Zahid looked at my mother. I did not exist for him anymore, that much was clear. And clearly, he had been lying to her. It seemed like she actually wanted him to stay, to keep living here, in my house. She had chosen him.

"Uh-huh," Khloe said. "Kristi told me that you got a job at her college and that I could keep your apartment."

Zahid shook his head. "She shouldn't have told you that. I can't believe her. Sometimes, I swear, I want to kill her."

"You're going?" my mother said. Her eyes were wide. "You told me you turned down the job. You told me you were going to stay. With me."

"I turned down the job, Becca," Zahid said. "I turned it down. I told you. I wouldn't lie to you."

This made me want to laugh. He had been lying to her all summer. Every day, from day one, when he neglected to tell her what we had done together.

"You aren't going?" my mother said.

Her relief was palpable. It was totally nuts. It was as if she actually *loved* him. My poor mother had fallen in love with my writing professor.

"Not until you kick me out," Zahid said to my mother.

They stared at each other, as if they were the only two people at the pool. Only yesterday, I would have done anything to have him look at me like that.

It was as if they had forgotten all about me.

"He can't stay here," I said.

"Rachel," my mother said.

"This is my house," I said. "He can't stay here."

"Honey," my mother said. "This is my house."

"No." A new voice entered the conversation. I turned to look. My father had appeared, as if out of nowhere. He had a suitcase, his travel bag. Maybe that was it, then, no more pilot, no more Mandy, with her little-girl haircut, but he appeared to be too late. "This is my house."

Khloe laughed.

Thank God for Khloe.

"Whose house is it?" she said.

"This is my house," my father repeated. "And I want that man out."

"Yes," I said, relieved. Game over. It was simple. It was not too late. "Out. Now. He has to leave."

My mother looked like she was going to turn the same shade of purple as her bikini.

"Wait a second," she said. "Wait. Stop this."

Posey emitted a low growl. She was still lying down, but her tail wagged, slow and steady, thumping on the ground.

"You need to leave," my mother said to my father. "And take this woman with you, too. She works for you, apparently. You can go together."

"Khloe?" my father said. "Now, this is a surprise. How did you come to be here?"

"Rachel invited me."

"I did," I said. "Khloe is my guest. She doesn't have to leave."

"Fine." My mother closed her eyes and then she opened them. "Of course, Khloe with a *K* is welcome."

Khloe nodded.

Nobody moved. Nobody left.

"He has to leave," my father said, pointing at Zahid. "The writer."

"I haven't done anything," Zahid said.

It was unbelievable. He said that.

"You are fucking my wife," Jonathan said. "I think that's enough, don't you?"

Khloe gasped. My mother's hands balled up into fists. She did not deny it.

"No, Dad," I said. "That doesn't even begin to cover it."

He looked at me.

"Rachel," my mother said.

"Zahid is fucking *me*," I said.

There. I'd said it. I stood up. I looked at my mother, ridiculous in her purple bikini. It was almost sad. Did she believe that Zahid actually wanted her? For herself?

"Is this true?" my mother said to Zahid. "Zahid? Are you fucking my daughter?"

Posey got up and started to bark.

"No," Zahid said. "That isn't true. It's not true. Let me explain."

"Seriously?" I said.

My professor had lied.

About me. In front of me.

He had lied about making love to me. Denied it. I was supposed to be okay with this? It was not okay. I had already asked him to go. I pulled the gun from my backpack and I pointed it at my writing professor.

My mother screamed. Khloe put her hand over her mouth.

My father was standing to my other side. I couldn't see his expression. Zahid had started to shake.

"Rachel," my father said. "Honey. Put that gun down. Put the gun down. Where on earth did you get a gun? Put the gun down, sweetheart."

I did not put the gun down.

I was done being ignored, denied, treated like dog shit on the bottom of someone's shoe.

"Tell them, Zahid," I said. "Tell the truth. Don't deny it. Don't you dare. I thought you were better than that."

I looked down at the gun, metallic gray. Funny. I had been furious with Ian for giving it to me, and here I was, brandishing it like a crazy person.

"It was only once," Zahid said. He crossed his arms over his chest. This was not a declaration of love. "It was only that one time. Before I knew you, Becca. Just once."

I was pointing a gun at him, a loaded gun, and he was looking at my mother. I waited. I had the gun. I could shoot Zahid Azzam's brains out, they would splatter into the swimming pool, chunks of his flesh. I was not going to do that. I loved this swimming pool. I would not go to jail for him. I would not ruin my life for this man. It felt good, knowing that. Already, I felt better.

"It was only once," Zahid repeated. "It was nice, Rachel. Very nice. I really like you, Rachel. I like and respect you. Just please, please don't shoot me."

He had said *please*. And *very*. And *really*. And *just*. If I wanted to, I could give him shit about his poorly chosen use of language. I knew that it was wrong, but I was actually starting to enjoy myself.

"It's okay, everyone," my father said. "You can put the gun down, Rachel, because I'm going to kill him for you. I promise you. Put the gun down and everything is going to be all right."

Posey was still barking.

"Shhh," my mother said. "Good girl."

She looked at the dog, as if she wanted to go to her but was afraid to move.

"Forget about the dog," I said.

There was something so incredibly wrong with her, my mother, worrying about the dog instead of me. She was constantly making the wrong choice. Zahid, at least, was still shaking.

"Hey, Rachel," Khloe said. "Put the gun down. Honestly, none of these clowns are worth it."

"Rachel, honey," my mother said.

Tears were streaming down her cheeks. I felt bad for her. She had gone through this before, after all. Those fucking Thorntons, that's what she had said.

"Please," my mother begged me.

I kept the gun fixed on Zahid. I was tempted to put the gun down, but it felt wrong to stop now.

"Zahid will leave," my mother said.

An announcement.

I nodded. Finally.

"Okay?" my mother said, wiping the tears off of her face. "Zahid," she said. "You have to leave. Right now. This second.

Don't stop to get dressed or get your things. You just have to go."

"Becca," Zahid said.

"Now," my mother said.

"Get this joker out of our house," my father said, his voice triumphant. "Time to go, asshole."

"You, too." My mother turned to my father. "This is not the right time for your opinion. This is about Rachel. You are not welcome here. You left me. You left us. You can't come and go whenever you please."

I shook my head.

I was making the decisions.

I kept the gun trained on Zahid.

"He's my dad," I said. "You don't get to decide. This is his house, too."

"He left us," my mother said.

I wished she could have told me, from the start, how upset she was. I could have helped her. I don't know how, but I could have tried.

"Only him," I said. "Zahid."

"I'm sorry, Rachel," he said. "I'm so sorry. I didn't want to hurt you."

"You didn't hurt me," I said.

I sighed.

He was being so dramatic.

I was pointing a gun at him, which I understood might make me seem off-balance, but I did not feel worried about myself. I was making things happen. I would have called Ian to thank him, to thank him for the gun, for the sex in the bathroom, for everything, but I didn't have his phone number.

"I'm fine," I said. "I don't know why you thought it was okay to move into my house and fuck my mother. You sick motherfucker."

Khloe let out a loud laugh. Then she covered her mouth.

"I'm sorry," she said. "I'm really sorry. That was funny, though. You have to admit."

I smiled.

It was. Funny. I could see the humor in the situation. But it wasn't over yet. He was still here. It was as if he was daring me to shoot him.

"Zahid," my mother said. "It's okay. We'll figure it out. Right now, you have to leave. Get out of the swimming pool. Go."

"Leave," my father said.

Now Zahid was crying. He was blinking away tears.

"Please," my mother said.

"I don't want to go," Zahid said, like a little boy, but at last he had started to move, making his way to the end of the pool, taking the steps at the shallow end. At this point, I think we all wanted to cheer.

Zahid reached for a folded towel on the bottom of a chair and wrapped it over his scrawny shoulders. I had agonized over him? It was hard to believe. He was going much too slowly, as if he thought somehow that if he moved slowly enough, I would change my mind.

"I'm serious," I said, rotating my body, my arms tired but still steady, the gun cocked. "I know how to shoot."

"Since when?" my dad said.

"Since Ian Thornton," my mother said to my father.

"Jesus," my father said. "Those fucking Thorntons. Haven't they done enough?"

I liked this, my parents together again, thinking the same thoughts. The fucking Thorntons. They had no idea.

Zahid called to his dog.

"Princess," he said. "Come here, girl," he said. "It's time to go."

Zahid's dog wagged her tail, but she did not budge. I was glad. Posey had made her choice. My mother would keep the dog.

"That's my dog," Zahid said.

"Not anymore," I said.

My mother did not disagree.

"Leave this house," my father said to Zahid.

"I want her to put the gun down," Zahid said. "She is making me nervous."

I did not lower the gun. It would have been nice if Zahid could have called me by my name.

"Will you come with me?" Zahid asked Khloe. "Khloe? We can take the train together."

"Khloe stays."

My arm had begun to waver. I was hot and I was thirsty. I wanted Zahid gone already so that I could go into the kitchen and get a glass of seltzer filled with ice. A slice of lime. There were so many things I wanted in life.

Not him. I was done with him.

"Sorry, Zahid," Khloe said.

"Okay," Zahid said. "Okay. I am leaving. I am going."

It was as if he expected someone to stop him.

And finally, he left.

Zahid walked through the living room and then the kitchen and then he was out the front door. He was wearing only his purple bathing suit. He did not have his clothes. He did not have his wallet. His dog. He did not have his laptop computer.

Poor, pathetic motherfucker. He would figure it out.

My mother took a deep breath.

"Oh, Rachel, honey," she said. "Thank God," she said. She looked like she wanted to hug me again, but did not dare. "Thank God. I love you. I love you so much. Do you know how much I love you?"

I nodded.

Finally, she had said the right thing.

I looked back down at the gun. Somehow, I was still holding it. My fingers were slick with sweat.

"I love you, too," I said.

Everything was fine. My mother still loved me. Suddenly, I wanted only her. I wanted to crawl into her arms, have her stroke my hair, hold me close, only I was not sure about what to do with the stupid gun.

"Don't worry, everyone," I said. "I would never shoot anyone. Did you think I would? Did I scare you?" I smiled. I even waved the gun a little bit. "I scared you."

I had scared them.

I liked that.

I lowered my arms.

It had been a long day. It was hot. My finger slipped.

The blood came right away, thick and red, gushing into the water. I had shot myself in the foot. Somehow, I did not feel a thing. I dropped the gun, finally, watching it sink to the bottom of the pool and I started to laugh.

# Acknowledgments

Thank you, Alex Glass, you gave me deadlines and suggestions and almost gleeful encouragement and I wrote this book.

Jennifer Jackson, for being my editor, Zakiya Harris, Paul Bogaards, Robin Desser, Rachel Fershleiser, Nicholas Latimer, Danielle Plasky, Katie Shoder, and every one at Knopf for giving *Very Nice* such a splendid home.

Shelley Salemensky for being a perfect first reader, nearly stepping out into traffic while reading the opening chapters. Ellis Avery for being inspiration. Sara Levine for taking me to the beach in Connecticut and the long distance writing dates. Jillian Medoff for a summer of poolside coaching.

Lenny Letter and *Joyland* magazine for publishing short stories that would become part of the novel.

And my family, always. My mother, Ann, and my sister, Julie, and my brother, Michael. My daughter, Nina, who sat down with me to write upon occasion, even though she often interrupted me to read aloud what she had written. And thank you, Dad, Ira Sidney Dermansky, who was so proud of me and excited about this book.

A NOTE ABOUT THE AUTHOR


Marcy Dermansky is the author of the critically acclaimed novels *The Red Car, Bad Marie,* and *Twins.* She has received fellowships from the MacDowell Colony and the Edward F. Albee Foundation. She lives with her daughter in Montclair, New Jersey.

A NOTE ON THE TYPE

This book was set in Legacy Serif. Ronald Arnholm
designed the Legacy family after being inspired by the
1470 edition of *Eusebius* set in the roman type of Nicolas
Jenson. Its serifs, stroke weights, and varying curves give
Legacy Serif its distinct appearance.

*Composed by North Market Street Graphics,*
*Lancaster, Pennsylvania*

*Printed and bound by Berryville Graphics,*
*Berryville, Virginia*

*Designed by M. Kristen Bearse*